ERICA LAINÉ has been an ac
office manager for an arts f
a reader liaison officer, a spec
of TEFL textbooks for Chi
educational project manager
Kong. She was awarded an .... work there. She
summed up that work with the quote, 'He jumped on his
horse and rode off wildly in all directions.'

She lived in London in the late 50s as a drama student
and then as a young wife and mother until 1977. After her life
in Hong Kong she came to south west France in 1997 with
her architect husband to the glorious house he had designed,
a conversion from a cottage and barn. She lives here with him,
a cat and a dog and rooms filled with a lifetime collection of
books. She is president of An Aquitaine Historical Society
and through that organisation came to know about Isabella
of Angoulême, the subject of her trilogy. She continues to be
fascinated and intrigued by 13th century France and England
and their tangled connections.

Also by Erica Lainé

The Tangled Queen part 1
The Tangled Queen part 2

Isabella
OF
Angoulême

THE TANGLED QUEEN PART 3

ERICA LAINÉ

Erica Lainé

SilverWood

Published in 2018 by SilverWood Books

SilverWood Books Ltd
14 Small Street, Bristol, BS1 1DE, United Kingdom
www.silverwoodbooks.co.uk

ISBN 978-1-78132-734-0 (paperback)
ISBN 978-1-78132-736-4 (ebook)

British Library Cataloguing in Publication Data
A CIP catalogue record for this book is available from the British Library

Page design and typesetting by SilverWood Books
Printed on responsibly sourced paper

For Charlie, Isobel, Eleanor and Harper Alice
It is important to be an ancestor...

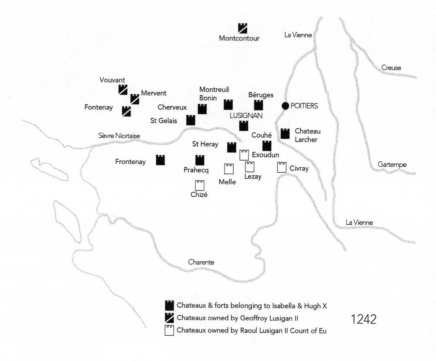

Montcontour

La Vienne

Creuse

Vouvant
Mervent
Fontenay
Cherveux
St Gelais
Montreuil Bonin
Béruges
LUSIGNAN
POITIERS

Sèvre Niortaise

Couhé
Chateau Larcher

St Heray
Exoudun
Gartempe

Frontenay
Prahecq
Melle
Lezay
Civray

Chizé

La Vienne

Charente

■ Chateaux & forts belonging to Isabella & Hugh X
◪ Chateaux owned by Geoffroy Lusigan II
☐ Chateaux owned by Raoul Lusigan II Count of Eu

1242

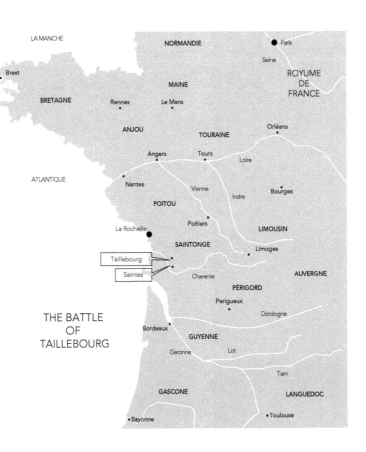

LA MANCHE

NORMANDIE

Paris

Seine

ROYUME
DE
FRANCE

Brest

BRETAGNE

Rennes

MAINE

Le Mans

ANJOU

TOURAINE

Orléans

Angers

Tours

Loire

ATLANTIQUE

Nantes

Vienne

Indre

Bourges

POITOU

Poitiers

La Rochelle

SAINTONGE

LIMOUSIN

Taillebourg

Limoges

Saintes

Charente

AUVERGNE

PÉRIGORD

Perigueux

Dordogne

THE BATTLE
OF
TAILLEBOURG

Bordeaux

GUYENNE

Garonne

Lot

Tarn

GASCONE

LANGUEDOC

Bayonne

Toulouse

ELEANOR OF AQUITAINE

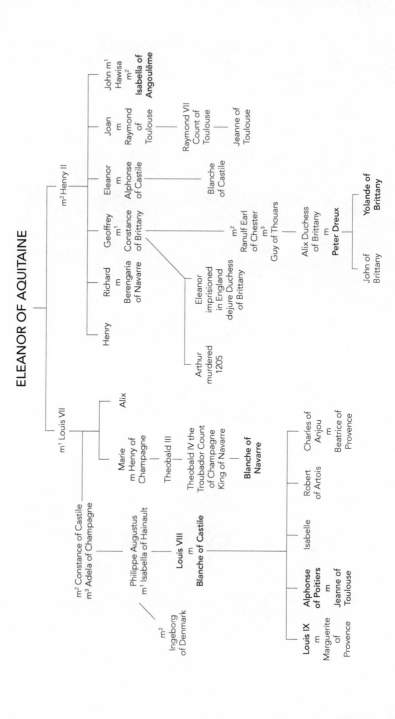

ISABELLA'S CHILDREN

JOHN m ISABELLA OF ANGOULÊME

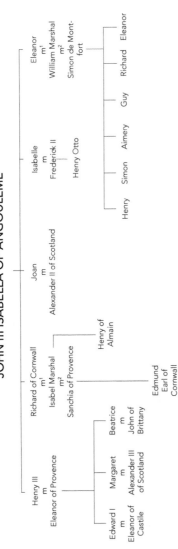

HUGH LUSIGNAN X m ISABELLA OF ANGOULÊME

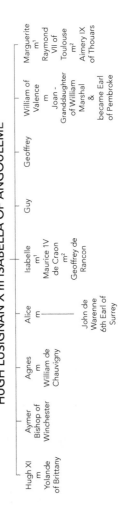

Characters

The House of Brittany

Peter Dreux, Count of Brittany, known as 'Mauclerc', married to Alix, Duchess of Brittany half-sister of Arthur of Brittany. Peter had to relinquish the title when his son John came of age

Their children:

John Duke of Brittany, married to Blanche of Champagne and Navarre

Yolande, married to Hugh Lusignan XI

Seneschals of Poitou/Gascony

Bartholomew du Puy

De Neville

Philip Oldcoates

Savary de Mauléon

Poitevin and Saintonge Counts

William, 'Archevêque' of Parthenay

Viscount of Thouars

Viscount of Limoges

Seigneur Renaud of Pons

Geoffrey IV of Rançon

The House of Capet

Philippe II Augustus, died 1223

Philip, known as 'Hurepel', Count of Boulogne, half-brother to Louis VIII

Louis VIII, died 1226, married to Blanche of Castile, a granddaughter of Eleanor of Aquitaine and Henry II

Children of Louis and Blanche:

Louis IX, St Louis, canonised in 1297, married to Marguerite of Provence

Alphonse, Count of Poitiers, married to Jeanne of Toulouse

Isabelle of France, honoured as a saint

Robert of Artois

John, Count of Anjou and Maine; betrothed to Yolande of Brittany, he died 1232

Charles of Anjou, born posthumously, married to Beatrice of Provence

The House of Blois

Thibault IV Count of Champagne and King of Navarre, a grandson of Eleanor of Aquitaine and Louis VII

Blanche of Navarre, married to John of Brittany

The House of Plantagenet: the Anglo-Angevins

Henry III, married to Eleanor of Provence

Richard of Cornwall, married first Isabel Marshal, daughter of the First Earl of Pembroke and widow of the Earl of Gloucester. Married second, Sanchia of Provence

Joan of England, married Alexander II of Scotland

Isabelle, married Frederick II, the Holy Roman Emperor, as his third wife

Eleanor, married first William Marshal, Earl of Pembroke, and second

Simon de Montfort, Earl of Leicester

William Longespée, Earl of Salisbury, half-brother to King John

The Marshal Family

William Marshal, the First Earl of Pembroke, and protector to King Henry

William Marshal, the Second Earl of Pembroke, married to Eleanor, Henry's sister

Richard Marshal, the Third Earl of Pembroke

There were two more Marshal sons and they all died without male heirs. The title passed to William of Valence, Isabella's fifth son, when he married Joan, William Marshal's granddaughter

The Circle of Advisors and others around King Henry in his Minority

William Marshal, 'the greatest knight', protector and regent to Henry, 1216–1219

Peter des Roches, the Bishop of Winchester, and Henry's guardian

Hubert de Burgh, chief Justiciar, 1215–1232/4

Peter de Maulay, custodian of Corfe Castle and of Eleanor of Brittany. Guardian to Richard of Cornwall

Stephen Langton, the Archbishop of Canterbury, 1207–1228

Edmund of Abingdon, Archbishop of Canterbury 1234–1240

Pandulf, the Papal Legate, 1213–1216 and 1218–1221

Guala, the Papal Legate, 1216–1218

Popes

Honorius III, 1216–1227

Gregory IX, 1227–1241

Innocent IV, 1243–1254

Frederick II: the Holy Roman Emperor in dispute with the Vatican. He modelled himself on Ancient Roman emperors

I

1226 Lusignan

The sky was full of the poignant cries of a flock of cranes. Stragglers, very late to leave the north and fly across the Aquitaine to the south, to warmth. Isabella watched them circling above Lusignan, gathering the wind to help them beat on. Three or four family groups joined together, the parents guiding the young to the marshlands beyond Bordeaux, and down to the coasts of Navarre and Castile. She glanced up at the stone-carved Melusine coiled under the eaves of the church and wondered if she would like to fly with them. Take her family from this rocky promontory in the middle of the Poitou and go somewhere warmer where she could bask in the sun and feel the heat on her serpent coils.

A smile for Agnes and Mathilde close behind her, and walking behind them the midwives Ellen and Alys; behind them the dairymaids, the weavers and embroiders, all the women of the castle coming to the church with her to give thanks for the birth of a son, Guy. Born in early December on Advent Sunday, born as candles flickered and shadows grew and shrank on the walls of Isabella's chamber, born with speed, just a few hours after the pains began, a few fierce contractions and he slid into the world, his face screwed tight and his fists clenched.

'I have hope for this boy,' said Isabella as she cuddled him when he was washed and swaddled, 'See how he holds tight to everything, he will be another son who will help us keep fast all that we have gained.'

Guy had been baptised at three days old, now he was safe and warm with his nurse. But Isabella and the women continued their procession to the church porch. She waited there, kneeling, a candle lit and glowing in her hand, until the priest arrived with two servers, who carried candles to match her own and containers of holy water for the service.

Father Robert began the blessing, thanking God for delivering this woman from the perils of childbirth. Psalms were sung, thy wife will be like a fruitful vine, your children will be like olive shoots around your table. He sprinkled Isabella with the holy water, saying, 'Purge this thy servant with hyssop,' and then led her by the right hand into the church, asking God for eternal life and rest under the wings of mercy.

Mathilde was standing in devout worship praying hard for her cousin and thinking how good it was to see Isabella as a wife and mother, such a celebration of her survival after something so dangerous. Even if this birth had been easy, it was a time of worry and stress. And Mathilde had given Isabella a charm for the safe delivery; she was secretly a little ashamed of this now. Help and prayer were always needed; perhaps the charm had been a nonsense. She prayed even harder that the welcome back into the church and the community would make Isabella see how important it was to be blessed by the priest. That it was not just a time for gossip and feasting after being confined. But everyone was thronging together, beaming and holding hands. The mass had begun. And Isabella was solemn and making the responses with decorum.

She watched with care as the priest took the wafers from the pyx, a small enamelled box, chosen from several made in Limoges. Now consecrated and her lasting gift to the church for this healthy birth. A blue-black enamel background, scrolling gilt and green ivy, glowing white medallions with their angel heads – for was not the bread, the bread of angels?

The procession back to the castle was noisy and happy,

chattering and snatches of song. Two kitchen maids held hands and swung their arms high, their voices joined together, singing about a man who had a quiver full and then collapsing into giggles. 'Not very reverent,' sniffed Mathilde as she hurried past them. She caught up with Isabella who looked magnificent, walking strongly, walking tall and free. Her hair coiled tight around her head, the jewelled crespinette just visible under her hood and her face framed by the dark grey fur that lined it. A face that still had that perfect clear complexion, her eyes bright with a certain mischief. Although, Mathilde noticed with a degree of satisfaction, there were now fine lines etched about them, and two deeper lines at the corners of her mouth. Even the woman once considered to be the Helen of Troy of the Aquitaine had to age.

She said, 'You were always so beautiful, but wilful I think, and spoilt by those who should have known better.' Her tone was testy as it so often was when she spoke to Isabella. Resentment under the surface threatened to bubble up.

Isabella regarded Mathilde, her cousin. Mathilde, always so suspicious and ready to find fault. A cousin seen as second best. Married to the man that Isabella had once been betrothed to. Married to Hugh Lusignan after King John had swept through the Poitou and plotted with Isabella's father to take Isabella for his queen. Something to secure an alliance. Perhaps riches and prestige for the Taillefers but it put everything into jeopardy, for this was a most unjust move by John. Hugh owed fidelity but would not give it to a man who treated him with such arrogant disdain. And he turned to his king, his overlord to seek help.

Mathilde and Isabella looked at each other and both remembered. That time of distrust, old alliances breaking, John seizing whatever he wanted, ignoring a summons from the French king, humiliating the Lusignans, capturing them, releasing them, and then later giving them his eldest daughter

Joan as a sign of peace. Expecting their loyalty and being betrayed by them. Losing Normandy because the Lusignans rode away from his army and took the Poitevin knights with them.

Isabella stood still in the cold air and remembered more. Aged twelve, riding north with John to visit Eleanor of Aquitaine en route for England, London, and Westminster, to be crowned Queen of England. Kneeling at Fontevraud in front of that formidable old woman who had seen clearly what the stakes were, who had patted her head, approved of her looks and murmured words about pawns and possessions. And Isabella – a widow seventeen years later after John died – helping to make sure that her son Henry was crowned but pushed away from the close group around him. The nine-year old king enclosed by councillors, a regent and a guardian. No place for his widowed mother. So she had taken a long cool look at her position in England and decided to return to her domain and county of Angoulême. A second marriage to the son of the man she had once been betrothed to, another Hugh. A marriage that was considered very ill in some places, frowned on by the Pope. For this younger Hugh had been the Lusignan betrothed to Joan, her eldest daughter. True, Joan was only a child and Isabella a grown woman, known to be fertile, and it was true the Lusignans needed heirs and as quickly as possible to guard their interests. But she had not only married Hugh but held onto Joan too. That had been another difficult business, arguing about dowries and domains until eventually agreements were reached. And Isabella remembered the ring she had given to Joan, as she said goodbye, the black star sapphire with its hidden light. She always thought that gentle girl had hidden light. Now Joan was as far away as she could be as the wife of the King of the Scots. Isabella bit her lip; there was no more wrangling with Henry – that was all over. For she and

Hugh had sworn fealty to Louis, they had paid homage to the French king. And he rewarded them magnificently. Far more money than any that could come from Henry and his penniless court. A fierce but fleeting pang for the children she had left behind and not seen for so long. Her son, the King of England. Richard of Cornwall, Isabelle and Eleanor. She turned her gaze on Mathilde and tried not to be sharp-tongued.

'I might have been spoilt as you say, Mathilde, and perhaps I was when young. But now I have to be a mother to my five children here, I do not spoil them, so perhaps I have learnt something? In all these years perhaps I have learnt something,' she repeated under her breath.

Mathilde in a spurt of anger thought of Isabella's two sons, Angevin sons. Henry sitting in England and sending his brother Richard to make a nuisance of himself in Gascony, and to look north to the Poitou with an appraising eye. Well, Louis had mopped up the Poitou and taken La Rochelle and that was that. He had given knights and men to Hugh, Count of La Marche and Lord of Lusignan and now Count of Angoulême, and encouraged him to strike south. Mathilde thought it all very foolhardy and she burst out, 'But Hugh did not take Bordeaux!' and then clapped her hand over her mouth. Isabella raised her eyebrows and said very slowly, 'We will not think about that or talk about that today, for now we have the feast for my recovery and we will celebrate together.' And she turned away from Mathilde and walked with Agnes, her childhood friend who could comfort her and calm her when her dreams were troubling. They had been restless and worrying when she lay in her chamber waiting for the birth, waiting for Hugh to come home. News had been sparse and when it came there was no rejoicing, Bordeaux was too well defended by the river and by solid walls and gates, and people who were determined to keep the prosperous place for themselves.

Hugh had dragged himself into Lusignan, limping, bruised and angry. His knights were downhearted and sullen as they made their way home, no rich pickings this time. Hugh's chief ally, William 'Archveque', was back in Parthenay, saying as they parted, 'No need to feel defeated, we can try again in the spring.' They both knew it was not only Bordeaux that rankled but the ambush when they had turned to break La Réole.

Isabella had sat in bed, watching the door; she watched and listened for Hugh to come home. He could not burst into her chamber as she waited for the birth, he would have to shout and bluster about outside. She listened with a heavy heart to the tumult and longed for the baby to be born so she could speak to him and see him again. He had sent messages that he was riding out to see his cousin in Vouvant. That Lusignan was cold without her to warm his bed. That he would be back when there was news of the birth. And that he would bring her a present. And so she had to be content, but it was hard waiting. The children squabbled and cried outside the door and were hurried away with promises of games in the new covered walkway.

And as her pains began one pale moonlit night when the owls called to their mates across the woods, messengers were sent to fetch him. And in the morning as she half dreamt and half woke while the new baby snuffled in his cradle she heard someone say, the Count of La Marche will arrive tomorrow. And another voice adding, the roads are like bogs – very wet, it is not an easy ride with streams spilling over and washing away the route. Isabella pulled her covers high and slept. And the next morning she sat up in bed, spooning a broth of onion and parsley thickened with bread, looking well and strong.

He would rush in soon enough she thought, ready to greet this new child. Agnes sat close by embroidering a length of green linen and silk for a belt, a fine new girdle. She was stitching small spring flowers, pale primroses and purple violets.

'This will be good to wear with any of your skirts when you are ready to walk to church.'

Isabella took one end of the silky material and said, 'Such fine stitches, so tiny. Will you not make something for yourself Agnes?'

'I will mend my cloak and perhaps find some new lining for the New Year – and I have a new purse to hang from my belt, I made tassels for it and all is ready now.'

'Beautiful and practical, Agnes I would not have you be anything but that!'

And then door opened and there stood Hugh, in need of a long bath and fresh clothes to restore his temper but in truth he did not rage for over long. He opened his arms wide and roared, 'Isabella by all that is good, another son! You watched her well Agnes, and the wise women are skilled are they not? No troublesome birth for my wife. Her lying-in has been a happy one.'

And he pulled back the bedclothes and said, 'Look at you; you are not some weak whimpering wife. I think your strength is your beauty,' and he stroked the length of her body, seizing her feet and fondled them, tickling her. 'See my present?' Hugh picked up the bundle he had dropped on the end of the bed. Isabella unwrapped it as he beamed at her.

A pair of tapestry slippers lined in silk and with deerskin soles. 'For dancing. Dancing at your feast after the churching. They were made by the women in Vouvant, some very old tapestries, beginning to fray and the moth had eaten away the threads. So those clever women cut up the material and have made slippers. I thought of you and your love of the dance.'

'I will wear them for that with the greatest pleasure.'

And she turned them over looking at the colours, red and gold, deep blue and the dull brown silk that lined the insides. 'And Agnes has made me a new girdle; I am to be well dressed when I leave this chamber.'

Hugh cupped her face in his hands kissing her closed eyes and open mouth.

'I wait. I must wait for you. Perhaps the churching could be advanced?' Isabella agreed it might well be possible and Hugh strode out calling that he would speak to Father Robert this very day. Isabella looked at Agnes who raised her eyebrows and packed away the slippers.

'You may bring the churching forward a few days but if you do not rest now there will be little dancing then.'

The women flocked into the castle, like the cranes thought Isabella, seeking warmth and food – and it was said that the cranes danced too. Hugh was waiting for her and as she sat down to take off her heavy leather shoes, he knelt carefully, helping her into the tapestry slippers.

'First something warm to eat and drink.' And he poured water for her to wash her hands, using the enamelled basins, the gemellions he had given her for the birth of Aymer. Turtle heads for spouts and gilded dragonflies around the edges of the midsummer-sky blue, red and turquoise champlevé of Limoges. And in the centre of each basin a seated queen.

The company of women bustled to the trestles and men from all quarters of the castle joined in. Food was being carried to the tables. Isabella ate carefully, the dishes were well chosen. Two large pies sat in the middle of a huge platter surrounded by smaller pies. Each one full of a mix of venison and pigeon and hard boiled eggs – all seasoned with salt and black pepper, cloves and dried herbs. Six dishes of fish covered in a sharp sauce and sprinkled with ginger. A loin of veal and baked onions. Cream cheese covered in small pungent fennel seeds. Dried plums stewed in rose-water and honey. Crisp fried pastry stuffed with preserved apples and walnuts. Rounds of dark bread and pitchers of red wine.

'I am pleased to eat again with enjoyment, my belly has been grumbling since the birth.' And she still felt the heaviness in her breasts, bound a little tighter today for leaving her chamber, for the walk to the church and for the dancing. Already the minstrels were playing a prelude on their pipes and someone beat at a tambour, deep and slow. There was an air of excitement in the hall, as the tempo began to quicken and then the line of a song clear and bright. *Fair one who holds my heart.*

Hugh took her hand and they moved into the space by the doors, a group joining them, the lines of dancers facing each other. Isabella could see Agnes, round faced and jolly opposite Geoffroy who, despite his limp, was determined to dance at least once. They all stepped to the left, once, twice, then to the right and left again, the men strutted and jumped to cries of admiration from the women, the women twirled and turned and hopped. Their partners grinned and took their hands once more. Again steps right and left, three little jumps each, faster now and yet more steps and more music. The fiddle, the drum and the pipes were joyful together. Laughter filled the hall as couples left the lines, declaring they were tired and hot and needed to sit, that they needed refreshment.

Hugh held her hand tightly and said, 'Hear the words of the song. I am lost completely.'

Isabella was singing the verses to herself, she knew the words so well, the insistent refrain that sang of love, forsake me not, forsake me not. She whispered to Hugh, 'Borne on the wings of love, remember how we danced here once before, and I was the swallow and you the hawk that hunted and caught me?'

Hugh drew her closer to him, the music was slowing, the circle grew smaller, soon it would end. He whispered back, 'I have wandered but I am wholly yours.'

She lifted her face for Hugh to kiss; she would bind him to her like never before.

II

Lusignan and England, 1226

Isabella and Hugh lay entwined in bed in the chamber at the top of the new stone staircase. Away from the noisy morning courtyard, away from the stables and kitchens, away from the snow that lay in drifts around the walls, the east wind blowing along the ice-fringed river. They were in a world of their own.

'I have an illusion that there is a woman in my bed.' Hugh stirred and stretched out his arms.

Isabella murmured, 'Where are you? What do you touch here?'

'You will not escape me; play your part, my queen, for I am truly your man.'

He knelt over her and brushed his lips across her breasts. Isabella opened her eyes and smiled as she pulled him closer.

'Come, my love, to this my centre. I dreamt of you when you were away. I woke and thought to find you in my bed.'

'I am in your bed and in you; we have found each other again.' He groaned. 'I no longer belong to myself.'

And they closed out the clamour of the day to make their own music.

Later, sitting side by side in the small room that led from the Great Hall, the door firmly closed on the chilly garden, they were busy with accounts, many rolls of parchment laid out before them. A fire burnt in the hearth, logs stacked ready to throw on for a great blaze, and the candles had been lit early. Hugh was reading through the scrolling list of numbers, making tallies and checking sums. There was an abundance of money for every plan: the new rooms and covered walkways now completed here, fine places for cold rainy days or fierce sunshine; a beautiful tower for Melusine, standing to menace all who might try to attack from the river; a splendid set of rooms for Isabella, facing south, sheltered by the walls: the queen's lodgings. For miles around were towns and castles, all sworn in fealty to Lusignan and Taillefer: Niort and St Maxient, Melle, Chizé – more and more connections with important local families. The Lusignan cousins that kept close to Hugh also offered places of strength and safety.

Isabella looked up at Hugh, a scroll in her hand.

'It seems we have much that we dreamt of. I worried they were dangerous dreams, but how we dominate! The castellans make no trouble, they protect the land, and they are effective, independent, but they stay with us.'

'Who would not stay with us? Our land stretches from the edge of the Massif to Cognac on the Charente. The block is in place. No one can march from the north to Bordeaux unless they cross here. No one can march from the east to the west without crossing our domaines.'

Road and river tolls, taxes, forest revenues, the salt trade, the corn mills and the bread ovens, the wine harvest – all paid their dues.

Isabella handed Hugh a package, wrapped in linen.

'For you. For your seals.'

He opened it with care and placed the engraved enamel box on the table between them. The shades of copper, dark blue, translucent green glowed in the firelight. Hugh smiled at her and said, 'Chosen with great thought.' For in the centre was a confident rider on a horse. 'An emblem that chimes with all Lusignans. Thank you my lady.'

Isabella held out both her hands and Hugh kissed them and then leant across and kissed her mouth, a sweet affectionate embrace.

They worked on in a companionable silence for a few minutes, Hugh was pensive.

'Tell me more about Peter Dreux; he rode away to his Breton lands at some speed. Had he hated being here with you?' Hugh teased Isabella, who glanced at him with amusement.

'He was full of talk. He has problems with inheritance, both in Brittany and some lands and a title in England. He has revenue, good revenue from that. And he will continue as the Breton Seigneur for another ten years or more. But after that?'

'So he wants to marry a wealthy heiress, I suppose?' Hugh continued to tease and Isabella stood her face grave.

'He had a great deal in common with you,' she said, steady and calm, 'but he will not find a wife to match the one you have. I am a queen.'

Hugh caught her to him as she swept out of the room. 'Isabella, I have done well. We have both done well. Do not quarrel with me now. I am waiting to see what moves Louis will make. That son of yours, the young knight Richard, who even now borrows money so that he can advance on the Poitou. . . the English want it back again, Isabella!'

Isabella relaxed into his arms. Hugh kissed the nape of her neck and held her around the waist. His thoughts ran on the campaign.

'Your Richard has been far too clever and bold. He besieged La Réole. I went with Poitevin and French mercenary knights. We paid them double! Money sent by Louis. But Richard of Cornwall, Count of Poitou...'

Hugh let go of Isabella and turned her to face him. 'Your son knows how to lay an ambush. He forced me back, fought hard. And then La Réole's outer defences fell to Richard; the inner ones surrendered.'

He moved away from her, flashes of angry memory. At least he had gone on to secure Bergerac; that was something he had thought he could offer to Louis. He spat into the fire.

'The Lord of Bergerac was so keen for silver he switched to Richard's service as soon as we left for the Poitou.'

Isabella felt a certain pride; one son was proving a soldier with strategy and tactics, well taught by his uncle Longespée, she thought. His father, on the other hand... She made a face. John was not to be remembered.

'It was hard, to have my son fighting against us. No doubt the pope will complain about us and issue mandates to make us swear another allegiance. He sends Henry much sympathy and advice but little else, it seems.'

'This is the way of men. Shifty allies. The pope expects loyalty at all times, but at a price. His tithe is great for some.' Hugh stretched and yawned. 'Enough talk of the campaign. Let us be content until the snow melts and I have to wear armour once more.'

'I prefer you without armour, it is true.' She wrapped herself tight in her cloak and looked at him so seriously he thought she was in a bad temper, but the mischief was in her voice as she continued. 'I wonder who will melt first: you, me or the snow?' And she ran for the staircase, daring him to catch her.

Peter Dreux rode out of Brittany, skirting the coast and picking his way across country to meet Hugh and Isabella in Lusignan.

'I have plans to talk with your son, Richard. To make offers there to weld us closer together.'

Hugh looked sharp and wary. Isabella raised her brows and said pointedly, 'Why? After being so close to the king and his family. Why? Were you not brought up together? You told me many tales of how Philippe knighted you alongside his son, how benevolent the Capets were to you.'

Dreux shifted from one foot to the other.

'I have some inheritance in England, and the kings of France' – he paused and drained his beaker of wine – 'would cut me off from those. Perhaps my natural lord is the king of England?'

Isabella and Hugh exchanged a look. Hugh muttered something about the most profitable way to proceed and Isabella said with a silky voice, 'Of course you must strive as we all do to increase our power, our authority. We wish you well on your journey to Gascony. There will be more to discuss after your time there. Come, let us show you the new walkway and you can see how those dogs you saw as pups have become such faithful companions.'

In the spring Richard was still in Gascony, still borrowing money from wealthy wine merchants and their families, eying the Poitou. Wondering if he would be needed in the Languedoc to support the Count of Toulouse, but making no move. But others made moves. An unlikely visitor: the Duke of Brittany, intent on visiting the English king's brother. Making offers.

'My daughter, Yolande, twin sister to my son John, who will inherit Brittany. She will be promised fiefs of her own. She is now ten, and a girl who can fulfil duties soon. A bride for the King of England.'

Salisbury looked at him coldly. Richard, irritated, pushed back his sleeves and folded his arms. A threatening air.

'You are ambitious and arrogant.'

'That can be said of many. Your family wants to recover the Poitou, Anjou, even Normandy. You need alliances in France; you need every friend you can find.'

Richard stepped away. This stung. Bordeaux wine merchants and Gascon lords, but he could boast no ties north of the Dordogne.

Dreux carried on. 'I have spoken with La Marche, your

mother's husband. He would support the English again if favourable terms were offered.'

Richard gave an exasperated snort of derision. But Peter continued. 'I have an ally in Thibault, the Count of Champagne. He is young, fond of the troubadour way, some sighs, some songs.' A dismissive gesture. 'He has a temperament that dips and soars. But two things are steady with him: he deeply dislikes Louis and deeply admires Blanche.'

'Go on.' Richard was listening now. Peter did not hesitate.

'He was slighted for the command of a crusade against Albi, passed over by Phillippe. Louis rode at the head of that expedition. Thibault wants honour, glory, something to sing about. If he and I were to link together, if England were to join us, well...' He spread his hands. 'This would rattle the king.'

'What else do you know?'

'I know that Louis plans a crusade this summer against Toulouse. He will not be watching the Gascon stew pot. I will ride with him. Thibault will ride with him. We obey our feudal duties for now.' A slippery tone, such an obvious mock sincerity, thought Salisbury, who was sitting, listening with his eyes closed.

'You most recently guarded Lusignan for Louis. You have been friends with him since birth. Why do you turn to his enemies now?'

Dreux's face was baleful. He chose his words with care; behind them was a story of checked ambition, a plan to make the most profitable of marriages. The heiress to Flanders no less. Louis, looking at the maps of royal domaines saw threats in the union and made sure that it was impossible. Peter Dreux, great boyhood friend of Louis, now turned his face away from his companion of more than thirty years and planned to humble him.

'He has overturned plans of mine for an alliance that he knew very well would have provided great security. I have lost all chances there. I seek some compensation for myself, my family.'

Richard considered. Salisbury considered.

'We will take counsel, but it is possible some agreement can be reached.'

Peter rode back north to his Brittany, where he was the master until his son came of age. Now he must ready himself for the crusade against the Cathars. He had no doubt he would hear from Henry.

The harsh March winds had blown all month but finally they stopped. The Lusignan gardeners shook their heads over the battered blossoms in the orchard and warned of a poor picking in the autumn. The rain that had been driving hard at the castle walls ceased. The meadows by the river had flooded. The April sun shone weak and watery, very welcome for all who had been mewed up in the castle for weeks on end.

'The covered walkway was finished at the right time. We could amble and look at the sky like caged birds, but we were not drenched.'

'The children ran many races. It was a good way to relieve the tedium and rid them of such restlessness,' said their governess. Isabella had chosen her because she reminded her of Agnes. Good, firm, wise and fair. The children had need of more than wet nurses and someone to tend the cradle now, and Emilde Bisset came from a well thought of family in Aubeterre. She was fastening cloaks and shoes for Agnes and Alice, and pleased to see them looking so fresh and clean.

Hugh had been to the stables and now with grooms at the ready, ponies patiently waiting, he was shouting for Young Hugh and Aymer.

'Hurry up! I want to see you sit straight and hold the reins. Lusignans are horsemen like no others. See, we have the best ponies for you.'

He lifted his eldest son into the saddle and took the halter rope. An attendant groom led Aymer. It had been months since the boys could take their riding lessons: snow, rain, cold wind – a dreadful wet winter. But the boys had forgotten nothing. Five and four years old, they sat tall instinctively. Their hands were light and relaxed and they watched the ponies' heads at all times.

Isabella was proud and loving as she observed them walking and trotting around the yard. These sons were true heirs to the Lords of Lusignan.

Agnes and Alice stood on either side of her. Agnes had her thumb in her mouth as usual and Isabella reproved her gently. The nursemaid was carrying Guy swaddled and wrapped in a shawl, three months old, another dark haired sturdy Lusignan boy. Hugh had greeted his third son with a cry: 'By St Martin and all the saints, you are a fighter, the spit of my father!'

Agnes was tugging at her mother's skirt. 'Mother, I want to ride too. Tell Father to find me a pony.'

Isabella bent down and whispered, 'In the summer, my little lady, and I will help you, for I love to be on horseback.'

'Me too, me too!' Alice stomped her feet on the cobbles.

'You too. Do not be unhappy. All will learn, and what fine riders you will be.'

'And baby Guy, he will learn?'

'He will. All Lusignans can ride and hunt, and the Taillefers can match everything they do.'

'That is more than true,' called Hugh across the yard, pleased with the progress that his sons were making.

'I'm hungry, Mother.' Agnes was tugging at Isabella again. She picked her up, kissed her cheeks, and set her down, taking both daughters by the hand and walking back to the Great Hall.

An hour until noon and the tables were being set with jugs, pewter plates, boards heaped with round white loaves. A dish of pork mixed with eggs, cloves, currants and sugar cooked up in a bladder was being cut into thick slices. Under a huge domed pastry crust, coney with onions, peas and parsley. Two large bowls full of a white bean, leek and herb pottage. Preserved quinces baked in wine. Little cheeses rolled in ash and wrapped in young nettle leaves.

The children queued to wash their hands, Hugh and Aymer jostling their sisters, but Isabella gave them both a sharp word and held out towels. She inspected fingers and nails, kissing each child in turn before they sat at the table. Emilde made sure they sat straight and helped them settle. Guy was being fed by his wet nurse who sat close to the hearth, turned away from the throng. The gardeners, stable lads, grooms and maids came in at a rush, and then the priest, more slowly but just as eager to eat. After grace was said, serving began. Hugh cut the bread and passed slices to his family. Isabella looked around her. Such honour, such wealth on display. Five children, healthy and strong. She sighed her contentment.

Mathilde looked up from the bowl of potage she was spooning slowly, one sip at a time. 'It is good,' she acknowledged in a thin tone as she crumbled the bread. Isabella was not sure if she meant the food or the company. With Mathilde there was usually a complaint, so this was unexpected.

'It is good to see the sun too,' she continued. Isabella agreed.

'Will you walk outside today?' Mathilde had hardly left her chamber all winter.

'I may take some air in the arcade. That will suffice.'

She looked around at the table, at the children.

'So many; so noisy. Your brood grows.' She raised her voice, 'Hugh, how will you manage to give them all they need? Oh, I forget, you are to be Lord of Bordeaux.'

A silence. Hugh struggling to hold his temper.

'Another attempt in the spring will be more successful.'

'Against the second son of your wife, who chased you away I hear? Against the seasoned warrior, half-brother to her first husband? Well, divisions are easy to make among family. I know that very well.'

She crumbled more bread and dabbed at the crumbs.

'Who will have what? An eternal question. The good book says that the meek shall inherit the earth.'

Isabella wanted to slap her. Did Mathilde think she was truly meek? Pious maybe, but never meek; too knowing, too sly. Hugh was roaring at the steward to bring more wine, and he glared at Mathilde.

'Have a beaker of this, it will put colour in your cheeks.' But Mathilde was leaving the table, ordering some cheese and fruit to be carried to her chamber and shuddering as she walked behind the boys.

'Close your mouths when you eat,' she hissed at them.

The busy spring day came to an end, and now Isabella sat with her family as the nursemaids plumped the beds and settled them in for the night.

Nightgowns were pulled on, prayers were said, Guy in his cradle blowing milky bubbles as he slept.

'Sing to us, Mother.'

She sang, they all listened, Hugh leaning against the wall by the door. He had never seen her so still and quiet and gentle.

I saw a sweet and seemly sight,
A blissful bird, a blossom bright,

That morning made with mirth and song.
Lullay lullow, lullay lully,
Lullay lullow,
Lullay Lully,
Do not cry my child sleep softly now.

'Sleep softly now.'

Isabella and Hugh sat together again, comfortable by the fire in their chamber, sharing a bowl of walnut meats rolled in sugar and drinking deep red wine from the engraved silver beakers; a present from Hugh when Guy was born.

'It was in this room that we first spoke of marrying.' Isabella gazed into the fire. The past years had brought such comfort to her. She never wanted to be spurned or denied anything again. Her resolution was to have everything she wanted and give everything she could to her family: Hugh's children and hers.

'You want Bordeaux. I want Bordeaux too.'

She continued. 'A great city. A Bordeaux that is difficult to take.'

'And do you see it in the fire?' Hugh was leaning forward, intent on the curve of her cheek, her long neck, the beauty that was his wife. 'I could possess it,' he said. 'I would take it and it could be ours. Louis has not helped me enough. He looks to the war against Toulouse and the heretics once more. But it is Henry's to give.'

A long silence, and then a careful sentence from Isabella.

'Richard is there still, with his uncle Salisbury.'

'What would Henry pay to have Lusignan and La Marche and Angoulême on his side again? The pope has written to us all saying we should return our allegiance to England. He tells Henry not to interfere and not to make plans against Louis in the Languedoc. I read and I listen, but I sniff the air to find out where the game goes.'

Isabella smiled at him. 'My lord, you are looking for more? You will need allies from further afield.'

Hugh stood and walked behind her chair, sliding his hands down her bodice and cupping her breasts. He whispered in her hair, 'I am working towards that, madame. Thibault, and Peter Dreux – you were right to think him ambitious. There will be a strong union. Strong treaties.'

'Tell me more when we have come together.' Isabella stood and walked towards the bed. Hugh followed, tugging at his leather belt, reaching out to catch her to him. Undressed they moved slowly and seriously, open mouth to open mouth, bodies turning over, a cry from Isabella and then they curled to sleep against each other.

Finally a hint of deeper warmth. An early summer morning, swallows swooping in and out of the barns and swifts screaming over the cliffy outcrops. Hugh paused in the Great Hall to speak to the children who tumbled in from the garden, their mouths stained red with strawberries.

'Father, we have been finding the little berries. Mother said we could and then Mathilde made a fuss about them being green and sour, but they were ripe!' Agnes was indignant as Emilde helped her wash and dry her hands.

'All of you get clean, please.' Emilde beckoned to Aymer. 'And then we are all going to learn some letters. You must try too.' Aymer began to bawl and Hugh reached out and cuffed him. 'Stop that! You can play with your brother later. Letters first.'

'Did you speak to the messengers, Father? They had fine horses. I walked with them to the stables.' Young Hugh was as anxious as Aymer to be off out into the bright sunshine again. He had a new wooden sword to try.

Hugh turned to the two men, standing waiting. One who

had ridden hard from Brittany, the other from Angoulême, both with satchels full of documents.

'Come, I will order food and drink. Sit and rest. The children are leaving now. They must learn their letters and their numbers.' He marched them to the stairs. 'I will tell Isabella, my wife, the queen, of your arrival.'

He found Isabella sitting in the chamber, her legs stretched out, and her feet on a low stool. She was asleep in the chair plump with cushions, her hands protectively held over her belly. He thought how tired she looked, her face suddenly beginning to show lines about the forehead, deeper creases at the side of her mouth. She was still so full of passionate needs, but her body had thickened after five children – still desirable, but older, different. And not only his children – there had been five with John. A ferocious fertility. He knelt by her side, the documents put aside for now.

'Isabella, are you sick?'

She stirred and opened her eyes.

'No, not sick, but fatigued. This time I am weary. The nights are difficult. Sleep is fleeting. I feel heavy already, and look at my ankles, how swollen they are.' She pulled up her skirt, to show him, her voice irritated. Then with a sigh, 'I must make some tincture of chestnut leaves. That can sometimes help.'

He stroked her feet and took her hands and kissed them.

'You must rest, but I have such news, from Brittany. Also plans and drawings from Angoulême. The new castle will be a marvel.'

Isabella unrolled the plans and briefly took in the deeds that exchanged land with the cathedral so the new castle could be built. She looked more carefully at the drawings of the imposing new gates flanked by two round towers: immense fortifications. She smiled.

'A worthy venture. It is what my city deserves. I will

study it in detail later. From Dreux, from Brittany, what does he write?

'That he will meet me in Nantes. Thibault of Champagne will join us and we will begin our alliance. We will be against "all men or creatures, who can be born, live or die". That is a clever phrase, as simple as it sounds. Very clever.'

'Because? My head is woolly today, explain please.'

'For we do not mention the king. We do not swear to safeguard him. Well this shows that we are directly against him.'

'Will you all ride with him on his crusade against Toulouse? He will notice your absence if you do not.'

She sounded drained, he thought. Usually Isabella was full of comments about his plans and schemes. He reassured her.

'Dreux and Thibault must follow and so must I. For the time being we are agreed we are best seen to be dutiful. But there is other news, from Paris. The letter was sent to Angoulême and now comes here.'

Isabella struggled to her feet. Hugh's voice had changed.

'Bad news?'

'Annoying news. It is from the cardinal prelate. He orders that the betrothal between Young Hugh and Jeanne must be broken. We cannot show or try for any friendship with Raymond of Toulouse now. His daughter is not for us, for I am to crusade against him!'

Isabella sank back in her chair, her face downcast. Then she laughed.

'A betrothal that lasted less than a year. It is not so dreadful this break. We may find another bride who fits our plans better.'

Hugh agreed it was not so dreadful, and changed the subject.

'Geoffroy will come here from Angoulême; his leg is too

38

painful these days for a campaign. And Agnes will come for a week or two. I will be back here by the feast day of St Lawrence and we will sit and watch the sky together for his fiery tears.'

Westminster

De Burgh, Archbishop Langton and other counsellors sat around the table in the hall at Westminster, passing documents back and forth, making sure Henry was paying attention and not dreaming about his plans for the royal apartment. This was important.

Langton said, 'We need to ask for the papal dispensation. It should be an easy one to grant. Yolande of Brittany is but a third cousin, and removed by two or three generations.'

'What is to be arranged exactly?' De Burgh wanted it outlined and clear.

But Henry knew all these plans and stumbling over his words rushed to tell them.

'That the king and the Count of Brittany will have a military alliance as well as a family one. That England will support Brittany here, where those barons who have claims to land can receive their rights. Peter Dreux will have Richmond as given. And when he says the time is right the English army will help him against King Louis.' He stood up, full of pride.

De Burgh was, as always, cautious, 'What does he give you besides his daughter? You are to help him defend and seek his rights and also, I see, to grant most favourable terms to the Count of La Marche. Again your stepfather is at the centre of trouble.'

Henry's face creased with anxiety as he thought about Hugh and his mother. She had not held true to England. Would she hold true to France? A question for all. A counsellor asked another.

'Hugh Lusignan has deserted to Louis. Do we want him back?'

'If he remains loyal to the Capets, we can make no headway in the Poitou. His support is vital. But England, Brittany, Champagne and La Marche could make great trouble against the French king.' De Burgh nodded, it might work, this alliance. Another question.

'And what have we learnt from Richard? He is there, he is mighty successful, he has spoken to Dreux. Does he recommend this treaty?'

'He does. It has been spoken of for some months, and we had hoped to hear more from our uncle Salisbury.' A long silence and long faces.

Longespée had died on his return to England. A terrible voyage home, made worse as he was already ill and weak. Three months and no news. His family mourned. A great storm in the Bay of Biscay had driven him to take refuge on the Île de Ré, but not before he had thrown everything overboard, clothes, silver plate, jewellery, all valuables lost. He had been found naked on the shore, babbling of being as naked for the eternal life as he had been when born to the earthly one. Babbling of a brilliant light, a taper at the top of the mast, shielded by the Virgin who protected it from the wind and rain. Babbling of the courage she gave him. He sheltered in the Abbey des Châteliers, fearful of de Mauléon, whose men held the island. Being warned by some men loyal to England, he set sail again, landing in Cornwall at Christmas. But his strength had gone and in March he died.

'He was granted salvation,' Henry said, finding it easier to talk about his uncle's death than the plans for his own betrothal. 'The candles in his funeral procession from the castle to the cathedral church remained alight despite the raging weather. Such a splendid house of God that will become. I have given timbers for the roof. Some others will find the necessary marble for the columns. From Purbeck.

Everyone looked around the table. Henry was about to launch into a long speech about the quantities and the costs of building. His devotion to plans for palaces and churches ran high at all times.

Des Burgh indicated that the treaty should be sealed. It would stop Louis and his grabbing at Angevin, English possessions. Henry sealed it in a dream of renewed English dominance. If he married Yolande he could see Dreux as his saviour in France. He could see himself riding into Normandy, Poitou and Gascony, at the head of an army; he could see himself sailing strong into the ports on the Atlantic coast.

So the English, the Poitevins and the Bretons plotted. Attempts were made to meld forces together again. Messy alliances were made and what would come of these?

III

France, June–October 1226

Louis had summoned troops that covered the roads and fields: a great patchwork of 20,000 – bishops, serjeants, knights, their squires, the lords, the counts, men and boys. Wagons with siege engines, carts filled with barrels of food, materials for the blacksmiths and the farriers, tents, cooking pots and tripods. Spare horses and their grooms. Cattle, sacks of corn, butchers and bakers. All ready to march down the Rhône Valley. Boats and barges were being laden, for the river was a route south too. A campaign that had been planned for months. No pillaging the countryside, no messy disorder. The full weight of the French crown and royal council was behind this crusade.

Peter Dreux wheeled about on his shiny black destrier marked with a white star, Thibault at his side, gentling his chestnut. It was overeager, its ears quivering, scenting battle. Dreux observed the crowds.

'They call it a crusade, a pilgrimage. I say it is more military than that. Louis wants to conquer this land and make it fall under the Crown.'

'Blanche will want the heretics killed. The queen has always detested them. The Albigensians should be destroyed!'

'Be that as it may, Thibault, we are here to take the south. Louis has managed to get an agreement that he is the rightful suzerain of the Languedoc.'

The lords in the south had listened, had read, had conferred and sent word to Bourges, before Louis set out, that they recognised him. And after the lords, the towns followed: Beziers, Castrês, and Nimes, all happily offered their support. Carcassonne, Narbonne, Albi, Marseilles and Arles fell into submission, towns swearing for Louis before he arrived. Before he even left.

But there would still be fighting. Louis was stern and determined, issuing his orders. *All will stay with me as long as it takes. No one who rides with me leaves until this is finished and we have crushed all heretics.*

Dreux scanned the groups where men greeted each other, knots and clusters gathering behind their banners. He could see Hugh Lusignan, Count of La Marche, riding behind his silver and blue banner and shield, talking with a well-known figure, tall and commanding sitting on his dapple grey, padded and protected.

'What can you see Dreux?' asked Thibault anxiously as he guided his horse around some ruts and sharp stones.

'I see that de Mauléon rides with Louis. Excellent. We are accompanied by many who know warfare for what it is. De Mauléon is with the French now; he defended La Rochelle against Louis and was insulted by Hugh Lusignan in the process. But look, they ride together today. For Louis. Against the Cathars. It is seen as a strong cause.'

But he was calculating how his presence, as well as Lusignan's and Thibault's, would be noticed today as he remembered his time in Lusignan, guarding the king's back. Louis had swept through the Poitou taking all the towns, one by one and driving de Mauléon to the vital port in a vain bid to hold it for the English. De Mauléon, then seneschal for the Poitou appointed by Henry to strengthen the ties between that unruly region and England. To no avail. Extra men, extra money had not arrived from England and La Rochelle was lost and de Mauléon too. He had crossed sides.

Dreux grinned and said, 'Apparently Richard of Cornwall has told his brother that English help is not needed, that Raymond and Toulouse can manage without him. Hah!

I believe Louis is happy to have this conflict.'

Thibault scowled, his plump face full of resentment. 'I could be among the leaders if I had not been passed over.'

'You did not sign the act that supported him at the council in Paris as I did.' Peter Dreux glanced back at Thibault; he was not the strongest of allies. 'So here we are, ready to show our spirit.'

'I will serve the thirty days and ten as my obligation. After that?' Thibault moved his horse behind Dreux and sulked and complained.

'Some are not even attempting the forty days. Many have paid heavy sums to Louis; those who are not ambitious for glory. The harvest months are coming. They want peace and plenty.'

There were others who wanted Louis to avoid them altogether. The nobles from Narbonne had arrived and pleaded with Louis to advance on Toulouse by another route, to avoid their lands so badly damaged, almost destroyed by a previous war. They had advised the route now being taken, to march down the Rhône to Lyon and Avignon.

The only bridge over the Rhône between Lyon and the sea; a bridge that spanned two arms of the Rhône; a splendid bridge; a bridge that Louis wished to cross with the bishops and prelates, the barons and knights streaming behind him, pennants fluttering. A king who led an army. A proud king. The bridge on its stone piers was the crossing that allowed merchandise to flow into Avignon, so rich, so full of commerce. Opulence and prosperity ruled here. A city with a great population, people from everywhere: silversmiths from Sienna, money changers from Florence, Lyonnaise tailors, Breton dock workers, Spanish merchants, spice traders and notaires from Geneva. Plenty of Avignonese in all trades; plenty of work for all. Christians and Jews; churches and synagogues; bathhouses and markets thriving with merchants who had made sure of a garrison of locals and mercenaries. All in all, around 4,000 citizens. And not part of the Kingdom of France.

The Avignonese had grown used to looking after themselves, keeping Church control and overlords at a distance. Now townspeople were hurrying up the steep Escalier St Anne, to a meeting in the Chapel Notre Dame des Doms, its ivory coloured stonework and vaulted ceiling a place to calmly discuss this problem. Their allegiance was to the Holy Roman Empire, their hearts more inclined to Raymond of Toulouse. The bishop presided and eight good, independent men made up the counsellors for the commune.

'Avignon was granted power, jurisdiction and its own liberties.'

'This city does not want Louis parading through as a victor. We have no quarrel with him, but the thousands of men, the horses, the carts and wagons, these are troublesome.'

'There will be drunkenness, disturbances, licentious behaviour. No, we cannot allow this.'

'Repugnant behaviour.'

Orders went out to build a hasty temporary bridge, to be built outside the walls, for the army to use. A polite delegation headed by the bishop met Louis and explained. 'We have provided a bridge for your many thousands, outside the walls. You may pass there unimpeded.'

The king in his prime, three years a king, wiry and strong, ready to ride through with all prestige bestowed on him. A king now taken aback. Louis turned to the nobles gathered near him with an incredulous cry.

'These merchants tell me where I can and cannot go!'

The delegation bowed and left.

'This is not good news.' The prelate Romanus, De Mauléon, Thibault and Dreux were moving forward. Romanus continued.

'If this town can bar you, so could others. Resistance to a king will be seen as something to copy.'

Louis spread his hands. 'I do not want to fight the town of Avignon. They can be persuaded to give me the freedom, and surely that is possible. I will not sneak around the back of the town. I am riding over the bridge that leads to the heart of Avignon.'

'An advance might be the best way forward.' De Mauléon was thinking rapidly. 'A party to see how serious this is, and then you can decide.'

Knights rode out of the royal camp. Guy St Pol, part of the king's innermost court, at their head carrying the royal banner. Avignon sat solid and strong in the June sun, entirely enclosed by thick walls, moats, ramparts, towers by the drawbridge.

They shut the gates.

Louis in a fury: 'I will not leave here until I have taken this place.'

'This place,' Romanus was in full cry, 'I denounce and excommunicate this place as full of heretics and protectors of heretics. A harbour for heretics.'

Louis commanded the siege engines to be set up, stones to be stacked near the trebuchets, everyone to ready themselves for an attack on a city that defied him.

The city fought back, standing across the river, well-provisioned, shots, arrows, spears, all manner of arms, heaps of stones, fighting men, horses, and food. A city almost impossible to assault. The besieging army so strong, almost impossible to repel.

June went by. The summer heat was building. The Rhône ran more slowly and yet kept the French at bay.

Louis set his face against finding another route. He was determined, stubborn. This action must be carried through. But frustration built with the heat.

Serjeants reported that there were attacks on the outer

edges of the camp. Raymond of Toulouse had sent his men to harry there, and then to plough all the nearby fields, destroy crops. There was no fodder for horses and the food supplies that had been carted down from Lyon were dwindling.

The middle of July and a fierce Midi sun was high in the sky. It beat down on the army spread out on the fields. Shade was difficult to find.

Louis sat in his tent, a wet linen cloth across the back of his neck, dictating to a scribe. Letters were to be sent to Paris, to Blanche, telling her of the continued opposition, the outrage of Avignon.

His scribe paused as a man entered. Thibault interrupting the king: impatient, abrupt and hostile.

'I am leaving tomorrow. The forty days service is at an end. My knights will accompany me back to Champagne.' He wiped sweat away from his face and swore at the flies. His hostility continued.

'The Count of La Marche leaves too. The siege is of little interest to me and should be of little to you. You waste time here.'

Louis stood and faced Thibault almost shouting. 'What you demand is forbidden. You, one of my nearest lords, and yet of all my knights one of the weakest. Late to arrive here and now early to leave. I have heard you favour the citizens of Avignon. Do you also favour the Count of Toulouse?'

'I am at odds with you over some decisions. You know what those are. I will return home tomorrow.'

'My father was a strong support to you and your mother, and this is how you repay his son? You were brought up alongside me.'

'Your father handed out no real aid; he forced my mother to buy off her foes.' Bitter words. 'It nearly ruined us. But now we climb to some peace, to some fortune, but we are beggars at your court, and constantly reminded of that.'

'I am the King of France, not of some petty fiefdom, some county that has lost its way. You forget your honour! You forget the affection that was bestowed on you.' Scorn and derision in every syllable. 'You want to go back for pretty summer feasts and fairs, to sing songs and play the lute.'

Thibault repeated. 'You waste your time here. I sing songs, but others sing better ones about you. You have turned the crusade away from the Holy Land. This is a false crusade with little hope of help from God.'

Both men stared at each other, hatred in their eyes. Thibault turned and left.

August and the sun was relentless. Food was scarce. Men sat wretched by the river, their bowels emptied. The camp was filthy with rubbish, scavenging dogs, latrines running foul. Bodies thrown in the river, bloated and stinking. Dead horses decomposing and smothered in black flies, which flew from corpse to corpse, and into the tents, into the pavilions, under the awnings, crawling about the plates and cups. Nothing could deter them. Serjeants and foot soldiers sickened and died.

'To be sat here in this heat with these diseases is not a situation that can continue.' De Mauléon was advising Louis. 'We must finish what has been started. But we cannot get close enough to scale the walls.'

'Can we cross the Rhône elsewhere? But a worry to leave Avignon as a place opposed to us. I do not like danger at my back.'

'Words; we waste time with words.' The Count of St Pol paced and turned, paced and turned. 'We should be out there breaching the walls. We have lost time and my men are chafing. There is another bridge, built for us. We have spurned it as a crossing place, but as a place to storm the walls it will provide us with a stepping stone.'

Assent, agreement, a sudden excitement.

A heavy rain of arrows, piercing sides and wounding limbs, death and injury on all sides. A carnage of stones, brains scattered, bodies black with fire and sulphur and choking on the fumes. Broken helmets, weary men with shields too heavy to carry. Just as the bridge could not carry the hundreds in their weighty armour. The wood splintered, collapsed and bodies were swept under and away. Guy, the valiant and brave St Pol was one of the first to attack and one of the first to die, a great stone splitting open his head.

Louis stood grim. He had prayed for the soul of his childhood friend, his friend full of courage and loyalty. No weeping, but sorrow seeped into him. Two friends: Thibault who abandoned the crusade; Guy who did not and was now dead.

'We will not leave.' He looked at the ring of battered knights. He looked at Peter Dreux, another from his youth, still with him. 'We sit here and they sit there. None move.'

Avignon was hurting; there were problems now with supplies, the countryside so ravaged and Raymond of Toulouse not strong enough to break through the ranks of the French and offer help. Trade had ceased and the merchants faced ruin; the town faced ruin. A winter was coming with no nest egg to dip into.

Louis knew he had used up all the good weather. After the great heat of summer September brought storm clouds, rumbling over the hills.

The end. The famished Avigonnais surrendered, hostages taken but not harmed, the great gates unbolted and flung open. The King of France rode into the heart of Avignon.

'All siege engines, all weapons are to be handed over.' A long line of citizens obeyed and the powerful group of men who had forbade entry three months before handed over bags of silver too: 6,000 marks. But there was no massacre, no reprisal killings. A new count to rule Avignon in Louis's name, to make sure that the ramparts and any fortified houses were razed and the moats and ditches filled in. The bridge was already broken in many places. Only a quarter of it remained. Without a backward glance Louis rode on to Toulouse.

A few days later the storms arrived and the swollen Rhône flooded the positions where the king and his army had held fast for so long.

It took until the middle of October to arrive outside the walls of Toulouse. Grumbles among some about the time lost in Avignon. They should be slaughtering the Albigensians now, not looking at their stronghold from the outside. A campaign that ran into the winter would not be welcome. Louis knew the army and the horses were becoming exhausted; the siege had taken its toll, with sickness striking many. He would return in the spring: a fresh attack. Now all he could do was to make sure of loyal towns and new seneschals. Good Catholic clergy, no more heretics in key churches. This took time and he was feeling weary. It was not only the army that needed rest. But it was late October before Louis turned north and began the ride home.

Within the first day he doubled up with stomach cramps holding onto his horse's neck to stop himself from falling. It was grim and he knew only too well what this meant: the sickness, fever and thirst. The bloody flux, which could end in death. He would not give in, he would struggle on, and his men must not be frightened by this. Up into the Auvergne, shepherds and their flocks dotted on the low hills, cattle being driven down for the winter. The mountains became more forbidding and it was getting colder as they climbed higher, nearing the castle at Montpensier. They carried him to a room and put him on a bed where he lay on many pillows. Men stood by with cloths and basins. Doctors arrived but could offer few remedies, a drink of fennel steeped in wine and water. They stood by helpless as the king suffered relentless voiding of the bowels. Louis's eyes were sunk deep in his face and the cramps racked his body.

Conferences were quickly made: archbishops, the chamberlain, the Marshal of France and Louis's half-brother Philippe Hurepel, Duke of Boulogne. All worried, but all making solemn oaths: to crown as soon as they could, as soon as they arrived back in Paris, the eldest son, the twelve-year-old Louis.

'We have made this oath in your presence.'

'As your son is young he must be guarded by a regent.' The Archbishop spoke softly to the dying king. He needed a name to add to the testament. Hurepel was his closest male relative. A half-brother, an uncle; the usual choice in these circumstances.

Louis looked at him and struggled, his lips dry and cracked. Doctors propped him up and one held him steady.

'I give my beloved wife, Blanche, the dignity of being regent to my son; to our son. Queen Blanche will be Queen to Louis and the kingdom of France.'

The Archbishop heard his confession, administered the viaticum, anointed with sacred oil his eyes, ears, nostrils, mouth, hands and feet and blessed him. On the eighth day of Toussaint, Louis died.

Word reached Paris of his death even before his embalmed body had made the journey to the burial place for all French kings, where his father had been buried just three years before. On a cold November day with a mix of sleet and rain chilling the mourners, Blanche stood rigid by the cortège in the Basilica St Denis. The paleness of her face echoed in the *deuil blanc*, the white mourning of queens. A heavy gown of white silk and linen covered in white embroidery, a white gauzy lace cap scattered with pearls, a thick cloak of white Flanders cloth lined with ermine. She was as white as a dove and five months pregnant, the baby conceived when Louis had spent his last night with her.

There had been no time to arrange long elaborate services. Hurepel had consoled her that Louis's heart, its love and courage had been buried with all rituals in Montpensier, that the embalmed body was sewn into a leather shroud and wrapped in a cloth of gold, a wooden sceptre in his hand, a simple jewelled coronet on his head.

Blanche knelt as the funeral mass was said. Her tears had ceased. Queens did not weep. Next to her, her son: the young King Louis. She would protect him always. The priests wrote, *maintain our Queen and save her brood*. Three weeks later he was to be crowned.

Isabella sat at the table and smiled down at the large wooden chessboard. The game had begun well two days ago. Hugh had lifted the heavy walnut board down from its peg on the wall and set out the carved bone pieces on the red and white squares. Now the endgame showed very clearly. Hugh had a king and no other pieces. She had three pawns, a queen and a rook threatening the black king. It was over. It was baremate. She had won. She reached out her hand to stroke his as it hovered over the board.

'We can leave everything, and besides, I am tired of thinking through moves.'

Somewhere she remembered Eleanor calling her a little pawn. Well, she was a pawn who had become a queen. She hugged herself and thought, this child is restless; my womb feels too small to give it room to turn. Then heard the noises outside and began to rise, pushing upright with difficulty. But Hugh was already leaving the table and calling for the door to be opened. He had heard men shouting in the yard, the unmistakeable sound of horses, bells jangling on harnesses, the dogs barking. Voices were loud and excited. Two men almost fell into the hall, the steward slammed the door shut; it would not do for the candles to blow out. The chill wind was rising, straw and leaves swirled around the courtyard. Stable boys led away exhausted horses, gentling them as their mired flanks heaved.

'Such news! Such news!'

They looked wild-eyed, gulping air. Isabella took a step forward, Hugh at her side.

'The King... Louis is dead. After Toulouse he rode north, in the mountains, into the Auvergne. The bloody flux. He is dead. There was nothing to be done. Nothing could be done. Queen Blanche and young Louis had set out to meet him at Limoges. When they gave her the news she was crazed with grief.' The messenger swayed, he looked shocked. The story was that Blanche had tried to kill herself.

Isabella held onto the back of a chair. She whispered, 'John died of the same. It is a dreadful end. Kings die like any man; they fall like any man.'

The steward hastened the men away to the fire and a servant brought hot water for them to wash the mud from their faces. Another served soup, bread and wine as they sat slumped and quiet.

Hugh asked, 'And the regent? The Count of Boulogne – Philippe, Hurepel?'

'No.' One messenger stood and brought a letter from his pouch. 'No, there is news here.' And he handed it to Hugh.

Isabella almost snatched it from him as he read aloud:

'Blanche, by the grace of God, Queen of France to her beloved citizens and the whole community of the Poitou, greetings and affection. To the Count of La Marche that

you bear sincere faith towards our beloved son, the King,
we ask you to preserve your fidelity and to attend the
coronation of Louis IX at the cathedral at Reims. To be
on the twenty-ninth day of November in the year of Our
Lord 1226. Enacted at Paris AD 1226 in the month of
October.'

Hugh looked up. 'She is to be queen until Louis reaches his majority, and she is seen as a ruler not a regent. Crowned three years ago, she is a queen.'

Isabella gripped Hugh's arm. 'Louis is dead. Dead. And Blanche, the Spanish woman, is made Queen Regent. She will be impossible. She worked hard to take England from John and she would have taken it from my son.'

'She will be defeated. The lords of France will have no desire to be ruled by a woman. I say, they will say, she is not fit to govern France.'

He rubbed the back of his neck.

'The Duke of Brittany is planning a great campaign. His daughter Yolande betrothed to your son Henry, the King of England. We have such a way forward. We have opportunities now. It is time to group and regroup.'

Isabella was not listening, her mind full of foreboding. Only one thought that ran around her head. She burst out again. 'Blanche! Blanche the foreigner, the Spanish princess, is to be queen, Queen Regent or Queen of France! So haughty she is – always was – her plans to help that husband invade England. I have seen her work, her planning and conniving. She has an energy and a passion when she wants something. And now her son is to be crowned. But *she* will rule. Oh yes, she will rule.'

'There will be many who will not attend the coronation. She seeks fealty for him and trust for herself. Who knows what will happen.'

Isabella was urgent, forceful. 'Go to Nantes, meet with Dreux. He and Thibault have the greatest power now, and we are the masters here.'

Stones cast into ponds and pools make ripples that spread out wider and wider to the edges, and the heavy fall of Louis was a stone that sent shudders through France, down the rivers to the coast and across the Channel.

IV

France, 1226–1227

All were summoned to Reims. Thibault rode out from Troyes; it would be a two-day journey, maybe a little slower than usual, as his mother was expected to witness the coronation too. She was eager to attend. Already there were rumours of men gathering against the new Queen Regent. His mother wanted to show that widows could succeed. She had also heard that Blanche was expecting a child, a posthumous child, just as Thibault had been. She, Blanche of Navarre – another Blanche; another Spanish princess married into the French nobility – she knew how things could go wrong.

Thibault rode happily. He understood so well: was this not like it had been years ago, a boy and his mother against the world? He would see Blanche, a woman he admired, a woman who only had to smile in his direction, say a few kind words, and he would be won.

'You will beg forgiveness,' his mother said as they set out, her face determined. 'You deserted Louis. Perhaps your reasons were strong, I don't know, but I do know we relied on the Jews.'

'Mother! You know very well how it was. I was not in favour of antagonising them for that reason. We made sure they were not harassed. They gave us favourable loans. It worked for us and it worked for them. Louis... well, Louis was of a different mind and wanted to strip the interest out of their loans.'

But Louis was dead. Blanche was his Queen. In his head he was writing for her a song that came from his heart, where his true love lived. She was a sweet woman, a crowned queen; he longed to sing for her. She is loved by a hundred, but he loved her more than any living man: Thibault the *chansonnier*, Thibault the *trouvère*, Thibault the troubadour.

The city gate, the Roman triple-arched gate of Mars, set into the ancient walls of Reims, was in sight. As the men guarding it saw the blue and yellow banners of Champagne, they shut each and every gate. Thibault floundered; there stood his steward, servants and serjeants-at-arms, all who had gone ahead to prepare his lodging. In the road, thrown out by order of Blanche.

The guards held their ground as Thibault blustered and swore.

His mother called to him in exasperation. 'What will you do now? Your loyalty has been doubted. My shame is complete.'

The serjeant came forward. 'Madame, you are free to enter and are welcome.'

'It is the custom for the Count of Champagne to be at the coronation: he is one of the twelve lords who attend the king. He is to hold the royal flag.' More protests by Thibault. He was turned away again and could only watch as his mother made ready to enter.

'Do not be foolish. Do nothing rash,' she warned, but Thibault had already decided to ride to Brittany, to join Dreux and push for rebellion.

Peter Dreux, Hugh Lusignan and Isabella crowded into the window of the new crenellated tower of the castle at Nantes. They were watching the boats on the Loire as they made their way downstream to the coast and the harbour at St Nazaire, carrying salt, wine, cloth, and hemp for rope – all heading for England. More goods laden onto on packhorses being guided along the tow paths.

'I can count eight, maybe nine boats. Plenty of work for those who want it.' Peter turned to the others. 'And the Loire makes a good defence to the south. Not that I am looking for trouble from there.' He gave a broad smile.

Hugh clapped him on the back.

'A fair trade to watch. You have a busy town, a busy river. River tolls, bridge tolls, customs duties, tax. Like my Poitou, mine and Isabella's, we all share a great deal. Between us we have a good stretch of the western domaines.'

Dreux agreed and mused. 'A king dead, and some would say opportunities now lost. We were keen to take on Louis, to make a rebellion, help England. Is that still the case, I wonder?'

'What I want is to make the life in our lands be in our control. A weak king will leave me alone.' Hugh stood against the light of the window, sure of himself, sure of Isabella.

Isabella turned and said, 'When there is a child, for a king there is always trouble. The counsellors can be strong, wise and clever, and they can cut out those who would get close to the boy.' This was said with keen knowledge. Had not those in England cut her ties to Henry?

Peter Dreux wondered, his face thoughtful. 'All who attend the coronation will swear allegiance to her as well as to Louis. They will reign together. We do not know her mettle, but she has Louis crowned now. Is there much dissatisfaction with the queen?'

This was asked of the man now standing at the far side of the room, puffing from the steep climb up to the tower's topmost room. Thibault.

'I suppose this will make her seem able, and she will charm them all.' He was full of hurt pride and still sulking. 'I could consider my barring from the coronation an act of great aggression if I was so minded.'

'We will continue to work with England. After all, our connections are strong there and I have sent them plans for a campaign.' Peter was confident.

Isabella looked at the men.

'Blanche will need support; she will need your friendship if she is to succeed. Who else is against her? Who is for her?'

'Hurepel perhaps will join us. He thinks it an easy thing to take the crown from a queen. And he expected more when his brother died.'

'I would be for her if she had not shut me out.' Thibault looked as if he was going to cry. 'I am not against the queen as much as others. Louis I detested. But she is a mother left with a young son. I know what that is like.'

Hugh looked at him, a relentless tone in his voice. 'We are, however, counting you as one of us. But I think for some lords it will be easier to support the crown. Those with smaller counties and fiefdoms cannot afford a great fight, however discontented.'

'They say unhappy is the land whose king is a child. Perhaps this will be true here.' Isabella spoke quietly and was deep in reflection. A woman, a boy, a group of old men to advise and counsel. How well she had known this. Blanche must be remembering it too. Ten years ago Isabella had found herself wronged at every turn. Blanche might fare no better.

She said, 'I want to meet your daughter, Peter Dreux; your daughter who is to marry my son Henry.' Isabella walked past the tearful Count of Champagne and down the stairs.

She discovered Yolande sitting with her twin brother, John of Brittany, the heir to the county, the reason his father was so busy sweeping up fiefs for himself, and entrusting Brittany to no one. For when John came of age, what then for Dreux?

Isabella looked at Yolande long and hard. Pretty enough, with a sweet face and eyes like a cat; more like her mother, she supposed, than the stocky father. The twins were attended by a priest and learning to say the Creed by heart. *Credo in anum Deum, Patrem omnipotentem, factorem caeli et terrae, visibilium omnium et invisibilium.*

'You do well.' Isabella sat down. 'You will be ready for Christmas mass.'

'I know that I must learn the Ave Maria too.' John was eager to show his progress. 'And then every time I see an image of the Virgin, I must kneel and say the Ave.'

'And we must cross ourselves and say: *In nomine patris, Filii et Spiritus Sancti. Amen.*' Yolande wanted to demonstrate what she knew. 'And I would pray to St Anne, for she looks after Brittany.'

'My favourite saint is St Tremorus. He was a boy like me.' John squirmed in his chair and the priest whispered to him that he could stand. The lesson was over. He inclined his head and said, 'A good hour of learning for both of them.'

'No whippings or beating today then,' said their father as he arrived from the stair door. 'You deserve some sweetmeats for your work. Quick, go and find the maids and say I sent you. A candied plum each.'

Isabella watched them scampering off to get their reward. She spoke very quietly, thinking aloud.

'Twins, so difficult for the mother; children so often brought to grief.'

And her mind ran on, some believed that twins were conceived in the greatest pleasure for the woman. Or that she had been with two men. But such a noble family, no, this could not be. Better to think that it was a way to salvation to have more children, as many as possible. For the priests said to bear children was a punishment for Eve's original sin and a means to be saved. She hoped Alix had been saved and her mother Constance before her, and had a sudden great longing to be away from Nantes and in her own bed, for the birth of her sixth Lusignan child. Away from gloomy thoughts of death in childbirth or babies that did not live.

Dreux watched her unsmiling face, and guessed her thoughts for every woman thought the same.

'Either the children or the mother dies. It seems they cannot all live. Too difficult an entry to the world.' And added coarsely. 'Queen Blanche had twins and they died. I would not have expected her to have felt such heat and pleasure in the bed.'

The first Sunday of Advent and the coronation was over. The young king, just turned twelve, had ridden into Reims Cathedral on a great stallion. Not afraid to show majesty, wearing the golden coronation spurs, holding the sceptre of gold with its *fleur-de-lis* finial, his slim boyish body clothed in a tunic and surcoat of purple silk, embroidered all over with golden lilies. His fair hair cut square to his shoulders.

The flask of sacred oil was carried by an abbot under a canopy held by four monks and as they processed a new motet was sung: *Gaude, felix francia*. Rejoice happy France, blessed with fresh joys.

His voice had trembled as he made his vows: to protect the Church, to give peace and justice and to defend the faith. He asked of God, courage, light and strength to use his authority well. For when his mother had told him of his father's death, she had said although beaten down with grief, 'My lord, the King is dead. You are now King. France has had three kings in three years. Henceforth, may you remember your duty.'

But already there were those who said he was too young, that his mother was weak. And the jostling, intriguing lords of France were jealous and plotting rebellion.

*

61

Blanche moved purposefully around the Palais de la Cité, taking stock of the situation. She had a good son, knighted, anointed and crowned. Louis had grown up with his grandfather still alive; a gruff man, but one who had talked to him, explained the world a little. And she had made sure that Louis always knew what was to come: to be a leader, to be devout, to be a king. Not every young king was so well prepared. Her face creased with anxiety, there were still her two younger sons and her daughter, and provision must be made for these children. She ran though her list; dowries, gifts, official titles to go with any counties or lands bestowed on them, those important royal appanages. There was much to protect. But her position must be strengthened, and in the best possible way. Counsellors, advisors, men who understood how armies worked, were walking behind her. Philippe, Count of Boulogne, Hurepel, his manner, as always, excited and edgy. Standing too close talking at her when she wanted to think. Everyone else had already spoken and given advice. Now she had to act.

'No more weeping. Although I am brim full of anxiety, tears will not drive away the worry. We must secure all authority for the king. The Count of Flanders has been a dozen years prisoner in the Louvre. His wife shall see him free again.'

A sharp intake of breath from Hurepel.

'Has she not sought an annulment once more, on the grounds of non-consummation? She would marry Peter of Brittany if she could.'

'And he her! My husband always forbade it. They would have been a powerful pair: one either side of our own royal lands. But her marriage to Ferdinand has been renewed with the pope's blessing. And in the spring this year my husband offered a ransom and a treaty.'

'I heard that she did not care to see her husband again

62

because of a game of chess. She won after a long game, fair and square, but he hit her about the head for being so clever and so bold. Her plea has always been that she found a ransom difficult to find.'

Blanche smiled.

'Yet she is so successful in Flanders with the wool trade that she does not tax the workers there. We will halve the ransom and make the terms very easy for them both. There will be no hardship. Far from it. We hope for allies there. He will be with his family for Epiphany, a new beginning.' And no marriage to Dreux she thought with grim resolve.

Hurepel continued to revolve around her; he was restless and needed to know what else was being planned. Blanche regarded him and put out a hand to stop him. He stood in front of her, not meeting her gaze.

'There are two castles, Mortain and Lillebonne. Both important and close to you. I would that you had them as a gift from your nephew, my son, the new king.'

He looked at her now. She stood so still watching him for his reaction. He glanced down at her belly, another child to be born in the New Year. She was strong, determined and not as weak as he would want.

'It is to give you greater lands, for that is always a necessity for counts and lords, is it not?' Said as an innocent question, but he knew that Blanche was no fool. He would ride with her for the time being. It was good to be seen as loyal.

And then she talked to Robert Dreux, Peter's older and more important brother. After Hurepel he was the closest relative to Louis; she needed him on her side too. Promises of lands in Normandy for his loyalty. He was secure, cooperative. Now she had support.

Christmas and the New Year could be contemplated with some serenity. She walked to the chapel for prayers. Louis was there. He heard mass every day. Blanche had decided on a great gift for him, something to help him with guidance from his personal chaplain. An illustrated bible, each scene paired with another. These pages would show the entire world: images that instructed, rich illustrations to spread knowledge. A bible *moralisée*; something all French monarchs should have.

Isabella was bored and cross. The room for her confinement was pleasant enough; everyone always made sure of that. The midwives were happy with the preparations, and Agnes was arriving next week. The children knew she had to stay in her chamber waiting for the baby. Although Guy grizzled when the nursemaid carried him away after she had given him a daily cuddle, and the little girls grumbled about not spending time with her, they had enough to do with their ideas about how to spend Christmas and New Year. Young Hugh and Aymer just rushed about and shouted all the time. Emilde worked hard correcting their manners but the boys wanted to play-fight and lined up against each other, sparring and taunting.

'Go on Aymer, sneak a blow in there.' Hugh encouraged, and Isabella called to young Hugh, 'Do not let him catch you, be on your guard at all times.' And then Emilde hurried them away stern faced and a firm grip on both.

Isabella sighed and said, 'I hope Christmas will be spent as quietly as possible.' She was standing by the cradle and pushed it gently. Hugh's voice was husky. 'Another child, a good easy birth, that is what I hope for. And you well and happy by my side.'

On Christmas Eve the children lined up and, with much prodding and tutting from Mathilde, they sang to her.

Born before the ages, son of God,
Invisible, infinite,
By whom are made the workings of the heavens

and the earth
The seas and all who live in them.
On whom the angels on high
Together always sing.

Isabella listened with her eyes closed, remembering Joan singing so sweetly the Christmas when all those plans for marriage between Angoulême and Lusignan had been made.

'What is the sea, Mother?' Hugh looked very serious as he asked her.

And that simple question brought back more memories of riding away to that harbour near Cherbourg, and seeing and smelling the sea for the first time. How often had she made the voyage back and forth from France? Six or seven times? When she had sailed home nearly ten years ago she had vowed never to leave again. And she hadn't.

Mathilde was looking happy for once and said, 'When you come downstairs and can visit the chapel, we have something so special there. Brother Francis has made a scene of the Nativity. The carpenters crafted wooden figures and a crib for the baby Jesus.'

'We put the baby into the crib tonight,' said Agnes.

'And sing again,' said young Hugh, 'and rock the crib.'

Isabella fretted as they all left, almost tumbling over each other to get to the stairs. Mathilde lingered for a minute.

'You are well, cousin? A sixth child is a blessing for all women. I am left unfortunate; some would say punished.'

'I am well, but will be glad to be delivered. It is hard painful work to push a child into the world.'

'In pain you shall bring forth children. God told that to Eve. But the pain is pain that can be offered to God.' She put her hands to her temples and massaged them.

'I fear my dull headaches and heavy eyes are not so welcome. But God helps those who are crushed in spirit.'

Isabella gestured to the table where there were dried herbs and watered wine. 'Please, take your infusion. You know it helps you. Do not suffer needlessly.' But Mathilde had already gone.

In the New Year, Agnes and Geoffroy arrived, both so welcome. Geoffroy was limping more these days, not fit to fight in a sustained battle, but still able to ride fearlessly, still commanding the knights who guarded Angoulême. He was always somewhat uneasy in Lusignan – an old enemy of his family. His face lit up when he saw Isabella come from her chamber to greet Agnes. She smiled at him and said, 'Welcome to the two people I trust most in all the world.' Agnes held her hand, turned and kissed Geoffroy on the cheek. 'I will see you in a few weeks. God go with you.'

Then they closed the door. Geoffroy climbed down the stairs, steadying himself on the stone walls. He would rest a day or two and return to Angoulême. Life was busy there with the building work. He needed to oversee it and watch the accounts.

Isabella lay on a heap of sheets and cushions on the floor. Agnes knelt beside her and whispered in her ear. 'Turn child, turn and be born.' For Alys, the most experienced midwife, had felt the baby and worried that it was upside down, buttocks where the head should be.

'You had best tell that to the child,' snapped Isabella, 'not me.' And Agnes whispered into her taut belly, 'Turn child turn. Come to the voices that coax you to be born.'

'Some would carry you to the bed and shake you to make the child respond.' A worried voice.

'No!' Isabella gripped Agnes by the arm. 'Something else, not that. The pains have not begun. I need help before they do.'

Alys said, 'My lady, you have had many births before.

I think we can attempt to roll this one. Drink my syrup first. It will make you drowsy.' Isabella sipped at the beaker of wine mixed with honey and dried powdered poppy, making a face. But it helped her to some sort of calm.

Alys washed and oiled her hands and began to massage Isabella's belly, pressing hard on either side of the dome of the womb, feeling where the head was and manipulating the buttocks, moving always up and down with long strong fingers. As Agnes and Ellen watched they could see a turning, there and there, and there again, the baby was somersaulting, settling at last with its head down.

Isabella's eyes were closed and she slept. Agnes stayed by her side and thanked Alys. 'You have learnt a great deal in your time. This was wise and successful. Let us hope for an easy birth now.'

'She has had so many births, all good. But the muscles are not as tight as they were and problems arrive. It is not for me to speak, but I would advise a rest from pregnancy.'

A week later, with no fuss and in just over two hours, another daughter, another Isabelle, slid into the world. Her mother watched her suckling noisily at the plump young wet nurse, and pushed her pillows into a nest. She reached for her present from Hugh. He had commissioned something again for her: a piece of fine Limoges enamel; the most beautiful box mirror, silver ivy leaves around the rim and on the back the red and gold arms of Angoulême with the blue and white of Lusignan. She would tie it to her belt and always know if her beauty was increasing or decreasing, and whether it was time to make use of creams and lotions. All she wanted now was to rest and dream.

How quickly everything shifted. Louis dead and back to the English went the Poitevin barons. Abundant concessions given of course. Hugh was plotting with the other rebels against Blanche and Louis and she needed to know what was being planned, but for now she would sleep. When her mind was clear again she would talk to him. Royal authority over their lands was not to her liking.

V

France, March 1227

Blanche knew a conspiracy was being hatched. She knew Peter Dreux was a man who threatened her. She knew that alliances were being born in the old Angevin realm, and that Thibault was with them! Perhaps it had been high-handed, foolish even, to reject him at the coronation.

Lusignan, Brittany, Champagne all against her and in deep at their side was Richard of Cornwall. Then there was that shifting seneschal of the Poitou, de Mauléon. Another who did not wish to swear fealty to the new king, who considered himself no longer bound to the Capets. England looked hungrily across to France again. Henry, no longer a boy king and seeking success for himself.

Philippe of Boulogne, Hurepel, held with her for now. But he could swerve – she knew his mind too well. Her other great ally was Robert Dreux, Peter's elder brother. He was loyal, she hoped always loyal, and she had promised him rewards.

If she waited for the spring to lead against them it could be too late, and there was her confinement and the baby to consider. A swift decision: she and Louis would go to Tours and make a pilgrimage to St Martin, the soldier saint. The anointed, newly crowned king would then lead the expedition. Who would dare to strike at him?

The royal army of vassals, barons and household knights made speedy progress to Tours and the shrine. They then turned west for Chinon and a few days later they were in Loudon. Just south of them in Thouars the rebels watched. Fifteen miles separated the camps and now the real games of chess began. Messengers moved ceaselessly and endless negotiations were underway.

'We have been asked to give Thibault a safe conduct.' Blanche was already summoning a scribe. Louis sealed the order.

'He wishes us well at all times,' he remarked. Even Louis, untried in many ways, doubted the Count of Champagne's rebellion.

Thibault came most days for serious talks with Blanche. The messages he brought from all was for their independence, their lost lands. He pleaded with her, impressed on her the need for recovery of what had been lost, swallowed up in the conquest of the Poitou. He sighed when he saw her: a lady so fair, who brought him so much woe.

'How he longs for her favour!' Richard of Cornwall was impatient. It seemed these negotiations suited Thibault only too well. 'How constant are his journeys to meet and discuss terms, but with never a conclusion! Does he sue for us, or sue for peace?'

De Mauléon growled. 'We can put a stop to that. They will meet again at that riverside place where they parley.' He looked around the tent; everyone was frustrated. 'The time has come to act, not talk. When they begin to make their way, an ambush, and we will show that fat fool what negotiations are.' A quick plan, and two or three set out on a drizzly February morning, trees shivering by the river, their branches dipping into the water.

The ambush failed. Thibault found out and fled to Blanche: a plea for sanctuary, a plea for forgiveness: 'Command me not to dwell far from thy side.' He was rather puffed up with pride at finding out about the ambush, he expected Blanche to congratulate him. She welcomed him back – a cautious welcome. When would he show some degree of courage, some stronger loyalty? Despite herself her heart softened when she heard his protestations of affection. But he would have to forfeit something, pay something for her favour.

'You will give up two towns to me. I do not forgive without an exchange. You surrender not only your person, you surrender your fiefs.'

Hugh Lusignan was writing to Isabella, a letter full of irritation at Thibault's desertion.

We oppose this woman but it seems the time has come for hard bargaining, not fine negotiations. We go round in endless spirals. Thibault is a dolt and cannot be trusted to move in the right direction. Dreux is holding out, as am I. We want the best price we can exact from this woman. His pen drove hard into the parchment as he wrote the last two words.

Messages were sent back and forth to Lusignan and Dreux for a meeting and a truce. Blanche offered Loudon as neutral ground. They refused and suggested Chinon. Blanche agreed, but when the day came, nobody arrived, so another meeting. Tours: still no Count of La Marche, still no Count of Brittany.

'Let them know at once that if they do not appear when I command them to come to Vendôme then the royal army will take action.'

Robert Dreux knew his brother.

'They are sulking, hiding in a shell of injured pride.'

'Be that as it may, we have begun to make our way back to Paris, but we can just as easily turn around and advance on them.'

Blanche was furious but a little scared. Robert Dreux comforted her. 'I will talk to my brother. He has much to lose, and he will be there.'

The Trinity Abbey stood tall, welcoming all who travelled into the island town of Vendôme. The Loir ran swiftly through the water gate and the monks carefully controlled the sluices, making sure that the river did not flood the people. March had seen torrential rain, leaving the banks muddy and sinking under the water.

'I would see the sacred tear of Jesus that they keep here.' Louis watched the roads that brought travellers to the gatehouse. He knew about the relic, a tear shed when Our Lord visited the tomb of Lazarus. Such precious reliquiae should be honoured. He had great longings to have some in Paris, to build a dwelling for the glory of God and to worship devoutly and fervently.

The set of rooms in the castle were large and draughty, candles flared and the fires, hastily lit, were spitting and smoking. The Count of Vendôme, full of nervous hospitality, had pointed out the Tours de Poitiers where Charles Martel had once imprisoned a Poitevin lord. Blanche wondered if she might use it for one of these troublesome men who were riding over the bridges, clattering into the courtyard and filling the room.

Here were the three Dreux brothers: Robert the tallest and oldest, her ally for the moment, very much the mediator. Henry, the youngest Dreux: the Archbishop-elect of Reims – another one for diplomacy and conciliation, placid and easy-going. Peter, his eyes cold and unforgiving, was swaying back and forth on his heels as he stood next to Hugh Lusignan, who towered over him. Hurepel, fidgeting as always, ready to prowl about the room when he became bored. Thibault, nervous, his eyes everywhere, hummed to himself. Stewards and servants milled about, everyone waiting. Louis and Blanche held themselves steady and prepared to enter.

Louis came first, his new red mantle lined with ermine, his pale face calm above the rich colour. Then Blanche, still in her mourning dress of white; a dull linen-wool mixture with faint cream thread embroidery. She was big with child and moved slowly.

Several scribes were waiting at a long table. Louis joined them, a cautious and clever boy – sweet-natured, but a little vulnerable among these men. Blanche, dignified, responsible, sat at the head and steepled her hands.

The two Dreux brothers spoke outlining the treaty, looking to Blanche from time to time for her public agreement. She inclined her head, watching the effect of the words. Peter would swear to serve the king and his mother against any creature that could live and die. He was to make no agreement with King Henry or Richard of Cornwall. He was not to ally himself with anyone at war with King Louis.

Peter crossed his arms, considering, the oath an easy one to take if, for such a promise, he would be rewarded. He nodded as he took in the intention. Now they had moved on to betrothals: a clever way to end quarrels between the king and his nobles. His face brightened as he listened.

Yolande of Brittany was to be married to the eight-year-old brother of Louis: John Tristan, Count of Anjou and Maine. Peter could continue to hold on to Angers until John Tristan came of age. Then terms and pensions would be arranged for Peter. Several fortresses which had been given into his custody would now be his outright – Bellême for one. Lands were guaranteed, provision for his future was assured. But Yolande was to be placed in custody of a council to include Hurepel, Philippe the Count of Boulogne, and Archbishop Henry Dreux. And she would remain in their care until she reached the age of fourteen and the marriage could be consummated. Blanche looked long and hard at Peter. His daughter was definitely not going to marry Henry and become Queen of England.

Now she watched Hugh Lusignan as his terms were read out. He was greedy, she knew that, and she thought his wife corrupt. She remembered her as a thirteen-year-old girl flaunting herself in the Cité Palace in Paris. The same age as Blanche, but Blanche judged her knowing and arrogant. Someone she would have to watch carefully. She regarded the conspirators in turn. They had lacked purpose, lacked a common resolve. She, however, knew exactly what she wanted: an agreement with them all and no bloodshed, not at this fragile time with her son crowned but three months ago. It might be expensive, but it was worth it.

Compensation for Isabella against her lost dowry in France, compensation for Hugh as Bordeaux did not fall into his lap. And her final move, the most diplomatic, the most flattering yet was being read out now.

Alphonse, the six-year-old brother of Louis, would marry a Lusignan daughter – the youngest one born a few months ago. Blanche's only daughter Isabelle would marry Hugh's eldest son.

Hugh glanced about the table. Everyone realised what such betrothals meant. The Lusignans would be allied to the royal family: two Capet children, two Lusignan children. Rebel barons no more. Of course it also meant that his alliance with England, with Henry, no longer stood. He would have to return those letters agreeing all treaties and terms. That was easily enough done. Turn and return and turn again. He allowed himself a smile and bowed his head to Blanche.

'I will promise you all aid possible against all threats. And I will not help your enemies or supply them with any kind of assistance: not arms, not horses, not provisions.'

Blanche signalled for them to make ready to seal. She was less anxious now. No English marriage to threaten France, Brittany's resentment smoothed over for the time being. Hugh Lusignan had been bought, as she had expected.

The treaty was sealed. Peter Mauclerc made a grim face as he fixed his seal and scowled at Thibault. If he had not defected they would not be making these agreements. What he, Peter, had just promised was all well and good, but he hoped in the future there might be more to come his way. For now he would send a letter to England: no marriage, no coalition against France.

Hugh spoke softly to Blanche as he took his leave. 'We will be most happy and most expectant to see your daughter Isabelle; she can visit us when she is a little older. Our daughter is also Isabelle. How wonderful that they will share more than just their given names.'

Blanche made a small cold reply. She wanted no more trouble from the west of her domaines. Hugh Lusignan, Count of La Marche, along with Isabella Taillefer of Angoulême, would need to show they could be trusted.

Hugh rode away with pride. This was a rich reward but he could not see Isabella enjoying the company of Blanche and her son, the King. He hoped Alphonse as a son-in-law might be more agreeable.

Peter of Brittany rode with him. They would travel to Tours together and then turn home: Peter further west into Brittany, Hugh making his way south to Thouars, Parthenay and Lusignan.

Peter Dreux spoke heavily as they parted. 'I will show that we have strength and can fight for her, but that queen must mind her ways. She likes to control the young king and the courts too much. Her words and actions are vexing.'

'And? And?' Isabella listened to Hugh and the news of the betrothals with excitement and a fair amount of glee. 'I want all the details, everything.'

'Of course, dowry compensation too, for you. Several thousand coins. And money for me because Bordeaux has not been taken.'

'What is Blanche like? Is she as pious as I remember? She

did not approve of me at all. Well, I did not approve of her. Tell me how she looks.'

Hugh considered. Blanche was not beautiful, not like Isabella, but she had grace.

'She has a very clear gaze, looks at you straight and with frankness. She stands firm and elegant even though with child. They make a word game of her name: as white in the heart as in the mind. She writes poetry, I hear, and certainly enjoys the songs of all the troubadours.'

'You mean the Count of Champagne? They say he would warm her bed for her in a trice. He likes to loll about singing and listening to verse and enjoying everything soft and pleasant.'

'He will stay loyal. His vows are full of promises about giving his heart, his life and all his lands. He will not desert her again.'

Isabella dismissed Thibault with a toss of her head and Hugh grinned at her.

'We will not be forever challenging the young king and his clever mother.'

Isabella acknowledged this and said slowly, 'Now this clever mother must write to my young king, Henry, and tell him of the large offers made. Our alliances and betrothals. No wife from Brittany for him it would seem. And what of my other son, Richard of Cornwall, Count of Poitou? Who is trying so hard to have deals and treaties. Is he still prowling about Gascony?'

News travelled down from Brittany and Paris. Peter Dreux was holding true to his vows to Blanche and had ridden out on an expedition with the Constable of France against Richard of Cornwall. Richard, isolated, swearing and full of disgust, handed over instructions and money to someone who had worked for the English crown before. None other than Savary de Mauléon. He too had again changed sides.

'You are, I think, the perfect mercenary! Sometimes with England, sometimes with France – but you will work for us once more?'

Savary smiled. 'It is a difficult time and I draw on who needs me most – who will help me keep my power here, in my own lands.' He slid the money pouch into a chest. 'I worked for your father; I can work for his sons.'

'It is indeed an inconsistent time, one of such turnabout.' Richard was impatient, these chaotic alliances made it difficult to plan. But he had to patch together a year's truce with Louis before sailing back to England. At least, he thought, there is a seneschal in place. Even if it is one who always plays a double game.

VI

'A year's truce? A year when we cannot hope to drive against Blanche and her son? This is a stumble on the way to recovering our inheritance.'

Henry could see his dream slipping away; a dream of riding out to take back the Poitou, to be like his brother leading an expedition. He scowled at Richard, who scowled back. Richard was in a high temper. He stood across the chamber from Henry, taller than his brother and looking older. The two years of fighting had toughened him.

'You were not there. For once they all united against something, against us, the English, the Angevins. The real masters of the place are all those local barons. And I was running out of resources, as you very well know. However, it means that the Poitou can be supposed ours.' A long silence as they stared at each other. 'I am the Count of Poitou, am I not?' He spoke scathingly and his scowl deepened.

'But not really ours. We flounder.'

'Well, flounder or not that stretch of lands and fiefdoms is guarded most jealously by our mother and Hugh Lusignan. But Gascony, Bordeaux and the precious wine trade still ours. Is this all the thanks I get?'

Henry drew himself up and took a step towards him. He did not like to be reminded that his ambitions needed more money, more men, more thought and planning. He wanted what he wanted: the prizes of lost land and the glory of reconquest. Richard should remember that six months ago, he, Henry had declared himself of full age. He had proclaimed that he would govern the country. He was almost twenty, time to make decisions and give commands himself. A younger brother was not going to challenge him.

Richard stepped forward too. They stood face to face. Richard could see that under Henry's drooping eye the skin twitched a little. He let out a long breath, almost a whistle, and said, 'I am pleased with the lands I have been granted: a reminder of my inheritance, as they are all dowry possessions of our mother. Cornwall and the stannaries come to me. But where is Berkhamsted in all of this? Mine too, I think'.

Henry looked at the floor and abruptly turned, saying over his shoulder, 'Follow, we should eat and you must tell me more about the campaign. There is sure to be more detail that is good to know if we are to prepare another.'

Richard strode after him and pulled him back. 'Before we break bread I need to know about that castle loved by our mother. Why is the honour of it not signed over to me? Here I am, fighting away in Gascony, dealing with the most shifting sands of alliances, clinging on to what I can with scant help from you, and now denied this. You deny me this.'

Henry red in the face, burst into a tirade. 'Do not push and pull at your king! It is withheld from you for now. It is in the keeping of a nephew of de Burgh.'

Richard lifted his hand as if to strike at Henry but did not. He dropped it and lowered his voice to an angry rumble. 'Of de Burgh? You favour him above all others it seems. Justiciar for life? Where is the sense in that? And made Earl of Kent! You are making trouble for the future.'

Henry began to protest, but Richard was not listening. His voice was harsh as the grievances poured out.

'And there is more than that castle that is withheld from me: various manors in Cornwall too. I am mindful that those are with Walerand. His brother Terric was a most loyal and fierce knight and protected our mother. I am not quarrelling with him for the moment.'

Henry crumpled. 'Terric died on a crusade. We learnt this only recently, but the story is old. He left for a pilgrimage to Compostela some years ago and travelled on further east. Remember that journey when we had to make our way to safety, after the death of our father? A good strong man, who helped to carry me when we were on the road to Gloucester.'

Richard absorbed the sad news, but then returned to the attack.

'I hear Peter des Roches has gone on a crusade too. It seems he is disgusted with his treatment. You have managed to cast him aside very easily; given no warning.' But Richard was not really concerned about the Bishop of Winchester.

Henry looked irritated and mumbled, 'Well, he promised to fight in such an endeavour as all do and now he carries out his pledge.'

They had arrived at the table laden with food. Henry went to sit, his page bringing him water to wash his hands. A gesture for Richard to join him, but Richard stopped. He looked at the court beginning to crowd into the hall, he looked at his brother and his temper flared again as he thought of broken pledges, fighting, the hardships and treachery he had experienced on the campaign.

'I would have my manors and I would have Berkhamsted. If you will not cede them to me then I must leave your court. I negotiated for you and fought for you. What has that nephew of de Burgh done for you? I will say I leave, and leave I do.'

He stormed out, calling for his men and his horse. Henry hunched over the table and watched him go. It would be possible to send household knights after him and seize him before he had even begun to saddle up. But he could not bring himself to imprison a brother, his only brother. There was a council meeting next month. He hoped Richard would attend. Meanwhile he was going to make sure that the Count of Brittany was dispossessed.

The scribes in Westminster wrote under Henry's careful gaze.

Concerning taking the lands of the Count of Brittany into the King's hand. Order to the Sheriffs of Lincolnshire, Norfolk and Suffolk and Cambridgeshire to take into the King's hand all lands of the Count of Brittany in their bailiwicks with all property and chattels found therein.

He could at least do that, as it did not seem he would be marrying Peter Dreux's daughter Yolande. He took a deep breath. Marriage was wanted now he was approaching twenty. The council had put out enquiries about other possible brides: Margaret, daughter of the Duke of Austria, for one; and a daughter of the King of Bohemia for another.

De Burgh sat with him in the hall at Westminster as he sealed the order to take back Brittany's lands in England. A scribe copied the words into the records, writing carefully on the parchment with a thick-nibbed pen. The Fine Rolls: debts, promises and inheritances. Payments to the Crown for charters, writs, privileges, licences to marry, grants of land, granting of markets and fairs, granting of tolls and customs, permission to trade and pardons or release from custody. *Hinc mittendum est ad scaccarium* – From here it is to be sent to the Exchequer. Henry approved of the lists and records. He could recite some of the dates and names from memory.

De Burgh sipped at an infusion of fennel. His stomach was growling all the time this summer and woke him in the night. He rubbed his face with one hand. He felt weary after such disturbed sleep. Henry looked at him. This great soldier and knight was now grey around the beard and temples, not yet sixty, but ageing. The man who had held Dover against Prince Louis, saying that he would not shamefully surrender, as there were sons and daughters who could succeed King John. But he was not a man for action these days. Henry listened to him. De Burgh was cautious.

'It is good we have peace for a year with France. War is costly and it seems that Blanche and her son have deep coffers full of silver. I would not be happy raising scutage now. Payments in lieu of military service comes hard on many.'

Henry roamed about the table, hitting his fist into the palm of his hand as he made forceful points. 'Be that as it may we must consider another campaign. Bit by bit the monarchy in France has taken our territory. But look how we have held on! Managed to hold off a serious effort by Louis before he turned south to the Languedoc. La Marche swinging this way and that, but still he could not take Bordeaux. And now he has given up any rights to that city. We have not been driven out.' Henry was excited, looking at de Burgh with eagerness. 'This is what I want, more than anything. This is important.'

August in Northampton and Richard was there, not shy to express his concerns, but friendly again and calm. And Henry wanted reconciliation above everything. Other lords were making demands too, and threats about restoring the forest liberties. So many conflicting claims to land, but he needed to make concessions to Richard first. The scribes wrote again, the records growing, the parchment filling up with their close cursive script.

21 Aug. Concerning the county of Rutland, committed to Richard, Earl of Cornwall. The King has committed to Richard Earl of Cornwall, his brother, all lands that

Queen Isabella, his mother, held in dower, in order to
sustain him etc. for as long etc. Order to the Sheriff of
Rutland to cause him to have full possession of the county
of Rutland with all rights, saving to the King his debts for
which he is bound to answer at the Exchequer.

Henry felt assured as he ran through the agreements made, there was more support, more money from them all. Richard standing by him again and helping him. He did not want bad temper between them. And he was pleased to know that the old Earl of Chester, and his young friend, William Marshal, Earl of Pembroke, were among those who rallied around him. Except William Marshal complained constantly about de Burgh. Henry thought, he is married to my sister Eleanor and still he grumbles. He had a sudden longing to see all three of his sisters again and be with them and Richard – a family for once. Surely their mother was more content now? She had a new pension from the French court and please, he thought to himself, please stop asking me for your dower. A rueful expression as he said under his breath, 'I have just given that to Richard. So, please, would Richard also be in a better temper from now on?'

He wondered if Isabella had any concerns that her inheritance had gone to her second son.

A journey north to spend Christmas in York. They would visit Beverley and see the rebuilding of the minster that had begun six years ago. Twin towers on the west front were planned and soaring elegant stonework for the church itself. Henry hoped for inspiration there, but he had a few grouches along the way: his room in the King's House, at Clipstone, loved by his father, needed repair. Money had been handed over but there was still much to do. A great deal of carpentry and a great deal of timber needed from Sherwood Forest.

'Such a fine lodging and it cannot be used.' Henry was

fond of a soft bed and a well-appointed chamber. 'And there is the chapel of St Edwin.' A wistful voice. He liked to visit all the places he could for worship.

De Burgh had been silent, but he explained again. 'We will rest for two nights in Grimstone – it is modest but adequate – then continue. We are not such a large party.'

'I will be pleased to have finished this journey. The north is not to my liking. But as the man at Grimstone is a good honest landowner with a decent manor house, I can grant him a buck and some hinds to stock his new deer park.' Feeling more cheerful at the thought of being generous and giving out favours, Henry trotted on and was satisfied enough with his time in York to grant the friars there a chapel and some city land.

The New Year came and went. The new pope wrote a constant stream of letters: that the Holy Roman Emperor, Frederick, was excommunicate; that Louis must restore all lands to Henry; that the kingdom of England specially be-longed to the Apostolic See; that Henry must abide by the truce with Louis; that all tournaments were to be banned in England as they could stir up unrest; and where were the promised tithes from England?

'He sees England as a place for riches and revenue.' De Burgh raised his eyebrows as he rolled up the latest letter and sent it to be locked into the manuscript chests with all the others.

'He is my feudal overlord. I am bound by special obligations to him.' Henry was sure of that and secure with that, but at times wished he could shake a little free of these constraints. He was not so constrained by Archbishop Stephen now; the rights of the archbishopric had ever been a wrangling point. Why did Langton always make him feel that he was about to behave badly? The man was a good but stern friend. He looked frail these days, no longer coming to court or travelling with Henry.

'But he is determined to take part in the celebration of the Feast of St Thomas à Becket on the seventh of July. I will never forget that year, first my coronation' – Langton showing him the way to sit and stand as a king at Westminster, making sure that all great men swore fealty – 'and then when I was the anointed king leading the procession into Canterbury for the translation of the saint.' Henry bowed his head and said a quick prayer. 'Holy Thomas of the heavenly kingdom, be received by all martyrs who hold thee in their hands. Thou art our help in England, hear our prayers and help us from sinning.'

De Burgh agreed. The Archbishop was strong-willed even if he were frail.

'Langton will be sure to mark the day again. However weak and drawn he might be, he will attend and sing the psalms.'

Then messages came. After the celebration the Archbishop had become seriously ill. He had been taken by litter to his manor house within the great park at Slindon, where he died.

'We have lost a man full of sound judgement.' De Burgh fretted and remembered the wise Archbishop with sadness. He looked up at Henry who was still silently reading the message, frowning as he read. De Burgh thought rapidly, a consoling inventory to run though, some reminders to himself: I must hold onto my closeness to Henry. An assurance to guard. I might be getting on in years but I have a title, lands and a good marriage to the sister of the Scottish king. Margaret, Megotta, such a sweet affectionate wife; an infant daughter only a year old; land and castles; a steady rise to the top. He came to with a start from musing on his family. Henry was still considering ecclesiastical matters.

'And one of great scholarship,' Henry added. 'It will be difficult now. New appointments, new wrangling.'

Letters to his cousin Frederick, the Holy Roman Emperor, who was in such an acrimonious dispute with the pope.

'He has at last kept his promise to go on a crusade,' Henry said with some asperity as he beckoned the scribe to ready his writing materials.

He dictated his letter, making sure de Burgh was listening too, emphasising points and commenting as he went. *'To bring about the peace of the Church etc. etc. we entreat you to be reconciled with the Church. For I am sure you do not despise the hand of the Church?* Not too bold from a young king? But I would have peace. And I also write to Pope Gregory to ask for permission to remove my father's body from Worcester Cathedral and place it in the Abbey at Beaulieu.'

Hubert thought back to the death of John. Impossible in 1216 to move his body across war-torn England from Newark to the south-east. Only Worcester remained in royal hands. John had founded the Cistercian Abbey in Hampshire and told those around him that he wanted to rest in the beautiful place of the king. Now his son was attempting to carry out his wishes. The Abbey's founding charter had been made out of the love of God for all John's ancestors and heirs. Perhaps that was why Henry wanted to move him there: one of the very few places that John marked with a devout hand.

'If permission is refused?'

'Then I will rebuild at Worcester. Certainly the east end needs repairs: the fire of twenty years ago left damage that I would restore. Some carving will be placed there: my mother and father together; Edward the Confessor; and King David.' Henry as always was completely absorbed when thinking about building in churches, cathedrals and castles. And when thinking about how to be a king.

Christmas 1228

Christmas in Oxford, comfortable and familiar. The Palace

at Woodstock surrounded by a park, woodland and orchards. Good hunting too. Henry and Richard followed by a string of knights and carts, their sister Isabelle and a large retinue rode away from Akeman Street and confidently over the long causeways between the lakes. They could see the mill and the smaller detached dwelling places. One was larger than the others. It had a walled garden, with a small gloriette for the summer, raised turf seats and a huge climbing rose, leafless in the December chill.

'Everswell, where the fair Rosamunde lived.' Richard was impressed with the stories of their grandfather and his many mistresses. A man who had a fiery, intransigent wife too: Eleanor of Aquitaine.

'Then I wonder who commanded that the chapel be painted with the story of the woman taken in adultery!' Henry remarked somewhat sharply as he dismounted and looked eagerly to the rest of the royal party. Isabelle was growing fast, tall and graceful at thirteen and a delight to talk to. She came towards him, calling out. 'That was a magnificent ride. I had forgotten the joy of riding here.' She hugged him and then Richard. She was looking forward to spending time with her brothers.

Stewards and servants were welcoming them all. The palace was fresh and clean with newly whitewashed walls, sweet rushes on the floor, fires lit and Christmas wreathes of holly and ivy over every door. The chief steward had organised a wooden screen against the draughts. It seemed he could turn his hand to anything. Glass panes had carefully replaced the waxed cloth in the windows. Fighting men and serving men of the royal household hustling about, men from all ranks to attend to the court.

'I like to have these useful and diligent men making the rooms comfortable and warm.' A small note of complacency as he stood by the huge fireplace with his brother and sister and de Burgh, who was to ride back to Hadleigh for his own Christmas.

'I am remembering eleven years ago, Hubert, only seven household knights to find gifts for at the New Year. How many now?'

'At least 120 and many of those have their own knights, so we see great improvements in your service.'

'What gifts do you have in store for them all?' Isabelle had seen the laden carts, the panniers on the horses. So much to bring into the yard and unpack: tuns of wine, wax for candles, almonds, dried fruit, sacks and sacks of goods. There were so many people, besides the servants, huntsmen milling about with their dogs, carters, almoners, priests and friars. Henry had already instructed payment to the men who brought food for the hounds and sent a gallon of ale to each of the night watchmen.

He stretched out his arms to show how big the bundle of gifts would be. 'Fur-lined cloaks for everyone, a good winter gift. One for you too, Hubert. The wind from the Thames blows cold along that Essex ridge, and your castle not finished.'

'True, there is still work ongoing. We have problems with the marshlands. At times the tide creeps to the base of the hill.'

De Burgh bade them all good cheer for the Christmas and New Year as he took his leave. He was glad of the warm cloak. It was no longer so easy to jump on or off a horse and his back ached. He was pleased with the gift he had given Henry: a book of short readings from the Bible, some homilies and prayers. Painted initials on each page in red and blue on a gold background and decorated with acanthus leaves. It was a costly present and one he hoped would be noted well.

Celebrations with fine food and gifts. Devout hours in the circular chapel with its paintings and oak-lined walls, the carved wainscoting dark and deep in the candlelight.

And after that the royal party looked forward to hunting. Five large forests met here: a well-stocked game park that had been fit for kings for centuries. Henry had given Isabelle not only three fine ells of Flanders wool, dyed deep rose pink, but a new hawk: a merlin. And Richard had given her stout leather gloves to wear as she flew her.

'It will take you a year to train her,' warned Henry, 'but you are patient and I will guide you.' She had tried on the gloves and talked to the hawk, feeding her gobbets of meat. Everyone was outside. A crisp morning, breath visible and frost still on the roofs. The groups of huntsman were leading horses from the stables when messengers came trotting fast across the causeway.

'A difficult river crossing at Woodstock, my lord, and the Bargate closed because of the feasting. We had to rouse the guards. These come from the Archbishop of Bordeaux who is in Canterbury.'

A packet of letters handed to the king, who took one look at the seals and said. 'The lull is over.'

VII

England, 1228-1229

The Bretons and the Poitevins were appealing again to Henry for an invasion against Louis and Blanche; they wrote that good relationships with the King of France and his mother were cracking.

'Peter Dreux makes little secret of his ambitions, he wants more than he has been given,' Henry said to Richard. He read slowly, working out the true message in the letter from Brittany. 'I am at a loss to give him all he asks for, but his alliance with Blanche has not brought about the high prestige or the rich rewards he expected. So he will oppose her, try to remove her.'

Richard agreed that this was likely, but was it not dangerous treason for Dreux to be so openly against the French queen and her son?

Henry wondered.

'Where is his power? Can he persuade others to join him? He makes noises about wanting the barons to rule France.'

Richard nodded. Who would join with Brittany indeed? Most lords enjoyed harassing Thibault and raiding the county of Champagne as a way of irritating Blanche, but would they take their disloyalty further?

Henry glanced out to the courtyard where Isabelle was being shown how to hood the merlin.

'I do not want her to hear that I think it very likely the Lusignans will be in some way against us. I hope not – but Isabelle holds memories of our mother that are rose coloured and sweet. I have some memories but I am learning that they are not as true as I thought.' Henry sighed and shook his head. He could still see his mother, standing tall with the sun behind her as she kissed him goodbye in Winchester; he wanted sweet memories too.

Richard said with a hint of impatience, 'She must be respected if not loved.' And followed Henry through the doors to the small room away from the hall, out of hearing for they must discuss in more depth what to do next.

'Richard, can we trust to Peter and make an alliance? A good time for us to embark on an expedition, to regain our lands?' Henry was now nervous with excitement. He handed Richard the letters who read them through quickly, assessing, weighing his words.

'To build on favours is of little permanent use. We make concessions, they make oaths of fidelity. Too easy. And the towns are overshadowed by their lords and counts. Look how they shifted when I was there.' An exasperated snort. 'Everyone in court knows that Hugh Lusignan always wants more. Can we trust him! Can we expect our mother to give up all that Louis gave her and then Blanche...' The question hung there, would Isabella support such a rebellion, would she see it as a blow to regain the lands swallowed up in the Poitou? Or would she see it as a step too far against the French crown, which had given her lavish compensations? What she desired, more than anything, was her independence. That vital independence, the key to her strongholds.

Henry listened as Richard continued.

'She thinks the French will wipe out what she has gained, she greatly dislikes Blanche but has an alliance with her. Children betrothed with the Capets and that is another matter, her Lusignan children, she seeks the best for them.'

'And not for us! Not for me! Not for me.' Henry was working himself into a temper. Richard called for a servant to bring wine and said, 'Henry, we can wait for counsel, no decision to be made today?' He poured a beaker for them both and stood by Henry as he drank it.

'Ah Richard, the good red wine from Gascony! Where we still have power thanks to you.' A thin smile. 'More wine.' His eye was drooping and he looked tired and much younger than his twenty one years. Richard hoped that they could forget about an expedition and leading an army. But Henry suddenly turned fierce, on his face a look of stubborn courage.

'I do not like being overruled by anyone or having the Capets lording over my authority, Angevin authority. No, it is too tempting. Call de Burgh to London. We will meet and he can advise too.'

Henry was agitated and excited, stammering as he thrust a handful of letters at de Burgh, 'Look, see what they write – reassert your rights, now is a favourable time. Discontent in Normandy, there is turbulence and rancour everywhere! They want me to lead against Blanche. A woman who tries to control them too much. The Blanche who helped her husband to sail to England in hope of the crown here! Now our turn to cross the channel, a fleet, an army, banners and flags!'

De Burgh frowned at the letters and was dismissive of the messages and pleas. He said, 'Wait, not yet, the time is not yet come. The truce is in place and we cannot be sure of supremacy there. The power of the French crown grows despite the unrest.' He folded his arms and looked very seriously at Henry who was striding about the chamber, already imagining the pageant of soldiers, ships, knights on horseback. Henry's head was full of visions of polished armour, the silks, and the glory.

'Not yet, I said,' de Burgh repeated, but he could sense a sulky reluctance to listen to him and indeed Henry set his face against these cautious words and planned. The spring and summer campaign seasons slipped away from him, but he could still prepare and plot with the Count of Brittany.

Dreux wrote that he wanted Henry to be firm and he wanted Henry to stop being full of doubts.

'All have promised support: La Marche, Thouars, even the king's uncle, the Count of Boulogne. I am to negotiate with you. They say that if they are told by Blanche to march against me they will dissemble, be hesitant and send only two knights apiece. They will not fight me in truth.'

'I do believe,' Henry was fervent, 'I do believe the time has come for us to make a deep effort, a serious effort, to recover what was lost.'

His enthusiasm was unbounded. Letters were sent to ports: Dunwich, Poole, Barfleur and London.

No ships to sail out until further orders.

All ships must be in Portsmouth on twenty-ninth of September.

Shipmasters and sailors to Portsmouth.

'I have made promises to call together an army and a fleet.' Henry sealed another letter. 'I have paid money on my galleys and my great ship, *La Grande-Nef*. Repairs made, £40 spent. It would not do for my own ship to be lacking.' He eyed his brother, the brother who had already seen France and campaigned there, who had already met the Count of Brittany. He wanted some of that acclaim.

'Where will you land?' Richard was studying the charts.

'St Malo. Peter Dreux will sail with us into his Breton harbour.' Henry unrolled a parchment and began to read aloud, 'See we have all stores ready, food for the men, feed for the horses. Beer, meat, wine, flour, all necessary provisions.'

'There are more than enough men,' Richard observed. 'Everyone who has been summoned has arrived and with knights.' Henry gathered his parchments and looked triumphant. 'Now to welcome Peter of Brittany – he has staked his fortune on this alliance and we will make sure he is granted his lands here.'

'And he will make homage to you for Brittany?'

'Of course! Dreux is a strong new ally. He will gladly make homage for Brittany.'

Richard almost spat as he thought about the man who had ridden down to meet him to set up all those meetings, pulling others into that rebellion. And who had then ridden against him. 'He is good at treachery!' He eyed Henry who was admiring a new padded jacket, a gambeson stitched with strong thread. He was ordering many for his soldiers. 'And you have given him his English lands at Richmond?'

'Oh yes, that is his prize now.'

Dreux duly arrived in Portsmouth to meet the English as promised. But the ships did not. Men were milling about, many horses stabled and others turned out in the fields, such a large muster but not nearly enough transport.

'I ordered the ships! And some forty were promised from Dunwich alone, well-armed with good sea captains and all that is needed. Where are they? And the others?'

Henry stood on the quay scanning the harbour.

'Some were provisional not firm. Some had to leave for trade, the merchants could not release them, we made them promise that they would join the royal fleet next time there is an expedition.'

De Burgh was explaining: not enough time, failure of funds, preparation was essential for this campaign with an untried ally. And, he added, to expect an army and especially a fleet to muster as late as October was foolhardy. Far too late for any fighting. Go in the spring, a much better season.

'I am minded that you have failed, you have failed me, and it is not lack of funds. It is lack of will. And the thirteenth of October is propitious. It is the feast day of St Edward, my most honoured patron saint.' Henry's anger was building, the disappointment intense. Dreux had fuelled his dream to retake the heritage lost by the folly of his father.

A Dreux observing a king with no fleet. A king who could not command. Humiliated, his anger boiled over as the reality sank in.

'But the fleet is far too small. Only six from Barfleur. Six! That is hardly sufficient. Where are the ships, de Burgh? Where are the ships?'

He was wild with rage, his dream overturned by this man who calculated and accounted and costed everything. Where was the man who had fought the French at Dover? Where was the great soldier; the most faithful Hubert, who had so often saved England from devastation by foreigners and returned England to the English? Now he only worried about his own position being at stake. Henry's thoughts began to churn. His own position, that was it, de Burgh had risen to become so high, sitting with Henry and steering him. And looking for more. It seemed men always wanted more.

'You have taken money from Blanche have you not? Taken thousands of marks from the Queen of France, she has paid you to betray me.' De Burgh protesting loudly took a step back, and then another. He put out a hand to steady himself, to ward off Henry whose face was flushed, whose body was trembling with rage as he advanced on de Burgh. Insults came pouring out.

'You are old, too old to know how to fight now, too calculating of the situation, thinking and thinking but no action! Always telling me to be patient, always telling me to wait. You are an old man, an old – traitor. Traitor! Look at me, look at me, see what you have done. Here I stand and I am shown to be a king without strength.'

De Burgh began to explain again, to deny the accusation of taking money from Blanche, to try to appease and calm Henry. All around on the stone pier the earls and barons watched, frozen into their positions. Henry in a frenzied rage was a new, unhappy development. Richard stepped closer to the pair, his eyes on his brother – who rushed at de Burgh.

'But I have enough strength to fight you!'

De Burgh turned away, he did not want to argue any more about this campaign, or look defiant in front of so many. In truth he felt confused and saddened by this uncontrolled outburst. He needed to gather himself, to find the necessary words that would bring Henry round to his way of thinking.

Henry lifted a sword high and would have driven it at de Burgh had not a warning cry from Richard sent him stepping sideways and the sword clattered to the stone quayside.

De Burgh clenched his fists and swore, white-faced, grim as he took his leave. Henry was not John, but he had enough of the Angevin temper to be a risk to his close circle; a temper that flared when thwarted.

There was silence for a minute and then a quick command from Richard and people began to move about, talking in low voices. Henry put his hands to his face, wet with tears. Richard took his arm and walked him back to the king's dwelling, where a servant brought a bowl of water and a cloth.

Richard waited for him to recover himself. He wanted to bring Henry back to common sense. Henry was shaking, already ashamed and depressed. He would make a full confession to his chaplain and there must be penance paid. He shuddered; this was how Becket had been murdered. A king's rage. He looked up at his brother, more tears in his eyes.

'I need to find some comfort. My family is needed around me.' He thought again of his mother. Would Isabella meet him when he eventually arrived in France?

York, Christmas 1229

Christmas in York, with Alexander of Scotland, the two courts together. Alexander, as foxy as ever, his mother at his side, who counselled and kept life calm. And Joan now nineteen, slender with a grave face and sad eyes, shadows under them that matched her skirt and bodice of heathery blues and purples. But she could not stop smiling as she stood with Henry, Richard and Isabelle.

'Henry, is it possible that we are together? And will Eleanor join us with her fine husband? And you are now of age, a full twenty-one. A man.' She added, 'Of course, a king too.' She stood on tiptoe to kiss his forehead.

Henry thought, she is guileless, still the sweet Joan he had missed when she was in the Poitou, in Lusignan. It did not matter that their young lives had been spent in separate households; she was always his beloved sister.

Joan looked at her brothers in turn, a determined but friendly look. She knew how they quarrelled and made up and quarrelled again. The sparks had flown even when nursemaids had been in charge. She also knew that there had been an old arrangement that Alexander would marry a daughter of King John and that a sister of Alexander would marry a son of John. The first part had come about, but now for the second part. Which one might marry her husband's sister?

'Henry, it is time you married, and you too, Richard.' She linked arms with them and called to Isabelle. 'Come, join our chain. See how we match each other.'

Later in their chamber, Joan sat with her sister, patting her hand and asking question after question about her life. She exclaimed over the answers and praised Isabelle's skills.

'So many accomplishments! You have a way with you, Isabelle, which is special and good to see. I wish Eleanor was here. Is she grown tall like you?'

'She is not the baby of the family anymore! But no, she is not of my height. But she is slender, her looks are fair. Full of impulses, like our brother the King, darting here and there.

Her thoughts can be wild at times.'

'She is well cared for?' Joan worried about her little sister, married to the great soldier.

'Well cared for, fine clothes and an admirable woman, Cecily Sandford, who guides her in all things. She approaches womanhood and needs that.' They both knew what the other was thinking: no mother to turn to.

'My turn to ask now. How is your husband?' Isabelle was candid and curious. 'Does he have a red pelt all over like a fox?'

Joan looked amused. 'A fox? No, I have not married a fox. You have listened to too many stories. He is a man like all men. And he is considerate to me, his English wife.'

A wife who has not produced a child. The thought hung in the air.

'His mother is kind. She has made intercessions to St Edward, for I seem unable to conceive. I am honest with you, for I do not want gossip while we are together. I am not yet called barren. There is time for that.' A fleeting, unhappy look crossed her face. Barren queens were set aside. 'But it is hard to hear that our mother still has more children, year after year.'

Four days celebrated with splendour. Lavish gifts from Henry: two heavy silken mantles for Alexander, a jewelled chaplet for Joan. She set its golden filigree flowers glinting with their tiny ruby hearts on her barbette for the Christmas feasts. She wore it when she danced a carol with Alexander to the strange reeling music played by the pipers he had brought from Scotland. The little rubies echoed her red and violet shot silk skirts and she glowed.

A late December morning as the court of Scotland readied for the journey home. Joan shivered even though she was wrapped in a long thick grey cloak lined with otter pelts. Henry helped her into the covered cart and onto the broad seat piled with cushions and arranged a heavy wool quilt over her.

'You have given us a safe passage across your lands, through Northumberland to the border.' She teased him. 'Am I so much of a threat to you? Your little sister?'

He kissed her hands and tucked them under the quilt.

'It is the way it must be, and no, you are no threat and nor is your husband, for he has gifted me money towards the just cause that is the campaign to reclaim lands that are ours. We will set out in the spring.'

VIII

France, 1228–1230

Isabella moved restlessly from Lusignan to Cognac, to the chateau there at Merpins. She would go back to Lusignan when news came from Hugh. She needed to feel safe. Merpins was strong and well positioned between Poitiers and Bordeaux. Taken from that fierce man who had been so against her when she had arrived in Angoulême twelve years ago. Renaud of Pons. She had found the money to pay for knights; she had driven the plan through. Hugh and Terric and Geoffroy had ridden out with a keen force and won Merpins back for the Taillefers. Her family, her possessions.

The journey there had been slow. Heavy-wheeled carts rumbling along the road, full of everything that was needed, chest after chest piled high and strapped on, followed by the lumbering covered carts for the children, their nursemaids and the governess Emilde. New babies, two more sons: Geoffrey last year, the smallest boy Isabella had delivered, a scrap with skinny limbs. Alys and Ellen had tutted over his size, but he thrived. The other born at Valence, covered in dark hair. Christened William; William 'le Brun' Valence, 'a little brown bear of a baby', his wet nurse crooned to him as they jolted along the dusty tracks.

At Merpins there was a sense of peace with an Abbey and the monks who worked the land provided solace if troubled. And Isabella was troubled. She would have to bide her time before the new castle at Angoulême was finished. The chateau much fortified with a defensive city wall around a huge park, limited only by the edges of the plateau. She thrilled to the way it would dominate the land. But now she was on her own once more. Hugh had been with Peter Dreux. Several lords stirring up trouble again, plotting to seize the young king and make him see the error of allowing his mother to rule him and to rule France.

'Queen Blanche ought not to govern so great a thing as the kingdom of France. It does not pertain to a woman to do such a thing.' This was what the lords decided to write and send to those would listen. And then they told Louis to his face as he rested outside Paris. That a woman should not be sitting alongside him. Louis replied that he needed only his good and wise councillors and promptly left Orleans and rode back to his capital, thinking: I must be seen to be a king in my own kingdom. He rode tall; fair hair, open faced, and everyone saw their young king, their anointed and crowned king. Travelling with his mother who was with him at all times. Blanche heard of a blocked road, a strategic road for the king and his knights, she heard that here in a small town, the rebel lords and their army stood concealed ready to ambush him. She sent to Paris for help. Twenty miles south of Paris and crowds arrived, great crowds, the road lined with people, shouting and crying aloud, God give the King long life and save him from his enemies. The crowds saved him. The rebels had failed. Hugh held back from the leaders, the arms of Lusignan not flying proud and obvious. There was a treaty to remember. Marriage betrothals and a very rich annual payment to Isabella. Peter Dreux might consider it something he had sealed with reluctance and lack of faith, he might consider that there had been no reconciliation but Hugh wanted to watch how the wind blew. He sent messengers to report back to Isabella. Some embroidered the story, others enjoyed the scurrilous details. But all were agreed, Blanche had acted promptly and Louis was showing his mettle.

'He is but thirteen years old but is a prudent young king.

He sheltered in a great castle and his mother called on the people of Paris to save him.

'And did they?'

'They did, and all the towns of the Île-de-France went to his rescue. The road, the way to Paris, was crowded with knights, students, merchants, townspeople – armed and unarmed, everybody turned out to guard him.'

'The Count of Champagne is in thrall to her. They say she is with child by him and must appear naked to show that she is not.'

'He poisoned her husband! That is what I hear.'

'Now they call Blanche, Dame Hersent, after the she-wolf in the story, for she is accused of adultery, but speaks for herself and defies them.'

Isabella dismissed the gossipers from her mind, but thought harshly about the queen who was able to command such loyalty. She might be despised as woman trying to be the regent of France, but Isabella recognised Blanche's proud and haughty ways. She had Angevin blood after all and Isabella knew all about that.

Hugh would be wondering what to do now, who to make an alliance with as this plot had failed. Isabella mulled over the treaty made in Vendôme. Hugh had been pleased with the terms but Dreux had dismissed it all easily. He was proving difficult to keep track of, and she prided herself on knowing how such men worked out their moves.

Thinking about it made her fractious and she walked to the Abbey for vespers. Mathilde was there at the door. She had not stopped praising the Cistercian order since they arrived.

'Such straight and solid beliefs! They have returned to the rule, as it should be. And this is the perfect place to serve God. I will miss them when we return once again, to Lusignan. They pray through the night. Such devotion.'

'They are also mainly silent.' Isabella wondered if

Mathilde would ever be quiet. But now they would both stand side by side and listen to the psalms being sung. O God, be not silent as to my praise, for the mouth of the ungodly, yea, the mouth of the deceitful, is opened upon me.

Hugh lay back in his bath, relieved to be in Lusignan. He reached for the beaker of wine that stood on the board. Isabella had a jug ready to fill it again: this year's pressing. She sat behind him, rubbing his back and massaging his head. He had been tight with anxiety. Now he looked more at ease. Mud and sweat washed away, clean clothes waiting.

'It is as dry as an almond,' he gulped and wiped his mouth, 'and as sharp as lightning.'

Isabella sipped the clear, light golden liquid.

'The steward called it frisky and quick, like a squirrel, he said. But I think I might boil some sugar and berries. A little softness added would make a good syrup.'

She stood and moved to face him as he lay soaking. A strong man, his arms still muscled and his shoulders broad, but the beginnings of grey in his beard and dark hair. He was weather beaten and more lined in the last few years. She watched him as he regarded her. They both knew each other well and nothing could surprise them. But Isabella was unsettled. Hugh had been away looking for conquest, while she had been travelling around the county with the family and the household, worried about not being with him as plans and decisions were made. She always craved the power of that: which way to proceed, who to trust, how to judge a situation.

She burst out, 'I am tired of doing nothing but reading my psalter, listening to stories, checkmating Mathilde at chess, feeding the hawks, trying to work in silk threads to add to the hangings!'

'You? Working with silk and embroidery?' Hugh roared

with laughter. 'Your boredom must be at a level never seen if you are stitching with a needle!'

Isabella laughed too. 'The last might not be true,' she admitted, 'but what now for Lusignan and Taillefer?'

'We must make sure that the counts, lords, and barons of France rule France. Any alliance is good against Paris!'

'Would you join us with those in Anjou and Normandy?'

Hugh nodded.

'It seems that no one here or there wants the young king or the Hersent to control us, so yes, it is to be thought about. An incompetent king is a blessing for us.'

'In truth it has always been easier when there were men who had no resolve. These two, mother and son, we have to break them.'

Hugh stood and Isabella handed him linen towels to dry himself. She slipped her arms around him as he stood naked and they kissed. He stroked her swollen breasts and belly, the thin linen gown taut. She rested against him and then pulled away. He looked at her gravely, her eyes were tired these days, and her mouth creased. He knew she was weary from travelling and did not sleep well with the kicking from the baby.

'Can you feel it?' Isabella said and he nodded as he folded her again into his arms. His Isabella. He felt her familiar warmth and weight, smelt the scent of roses and lavender that she sprinkled on her clothes, stroked her head with tender love. She was his wife of a dozen years. Their first meeting had been stormy, but they had known as soon as they circled each other in the chamber high in Angoulême that their marriage was meant to be. And now here they were, secure, comfortable with their lands and revenue, their children growing straight and strong. There was nothing he would not do for her. He rocked her gently and exclaimed.

'Such a wonder, these children who flourish within you.'

She whispered, 'We are capable of so much, you and I. Come, let's to bed and dream.'

Word came from Brittany. Blanche had seized lands from Peter Dreux – lands that had been given to him in the Treaty of Vendôme. She had ordered the fortress castle at Bellême, granted to him outright, to be besieged, and it had capitulated.

'A feather in her hair and a blow to the Count of Brittany, who wants always to ride high.'

Isabella read the letter aloud to Hugh, a letter confirming how the Count of Brittany was no longer a vassal to the King of France.

'She acts with great speed, all are astonished by her. And the king's uncle, Philippe, Count of Boulogne, has said he is with her. That the king is his liege lord. A fine new story! Hurepel at last worries about being called traitor. So Peter Dreux is without that man.'

She folded the letter along its creases and sat back in her chair and said very slowly, 'But Dreux has thrown in his lot with Henry.'

Hugh frowned and said with exasperation, 'And he is intent on remarrying.'

'Well, he has been looking for a new wife for more than three years!'

'He says he has found a match. Margaret of Thouars, the handy widow of the Count of Thouars.'

He bucked his belt, pulled it tight and swore.

'She is made bold by the intention of marriage and is claiming land around La Rochelle, land that is ours. So now Dreux plans to ride into the north of the Poitou and makes a great deal of trouble for us there.'

'He would threaten us?' Isabella helped him on with his cloak, pinning it on his shoulder. She jabbed at the material.

'Such inconstant loyalty, he has no regard for you or for me. He only cares about his own advantage.'

Hugh nodded and began to laugh. 'In truth Isabella, do we not all take that view? But I am sending word to Vouvant, Geoffrey Lusignan will move against this sudden unfriendly man.'

'A most unfriendly man,' repeated Isabella, and wondered if he would prove to be more trouble as they all shifted and contrived.

And indeed he was trouble. Geoffrey Lusignan was captured along with thirty of his knights and imprisoned in Brittany, waiting for ransoms to be paid. Dreux was triumphant and in full possession of his new wife's domaines. Hugh snarled as he heard the news. Dreux had overstepped the mark. He threatened everybody. Blanche, local lords, allies and friends.

'What news of Henry? He makes deals and pledges with Dreux.' Isabella was impatient. She wanted her son, the English king, here making war against the French king and his mother.

'Henry and Richard, the two of them together, that would be even better. Both of them here, my two sons. And their allies – even if Peter of Brittany has to be counted among those.'

She stopped and looked thoughtful, 'Would he fight us *and* Blanche?' And then she worried away again at the idea of an invasion, 'They must come, they could put paid to this powerful ascent by Blanche, her son – the Capets on the rise like never before. We could be with Henry, with Brittany, some of the lords of Normandy. We could reclaim everything together. '

Hugh listened to her, but shook his head. 'It could be a danger to us to fight against Louis and Blanche. We have a double betrothal; we have some ties beginning to knot together. We have a rich pension in recompense for much of your dower. I would not want you to forfeit that.'

'The Count of Brittany is too arrogant for me and for others,' retorted Isabella. 'I can feel alliances breaking.'

'We need to be on the winning side. I do not see Henry leading a victorious army.'

Isabella looked at him with fury. Was her son not able to take back these lands that had so long been part of the English Crown? His father had lost them. Could not the son regain them?

Hugh put an arm around her shoulders and said, 'I am asked to be at the Christmas court this year. Blanche wants to make sure of all of us, and I will go, but Peter of Brittany will not.'

A startled cry. 'You will go and be counted a friend there?' And then a look of understanding. 'Of course you will, you have been pulled in, because of the treaty at Vendôme and because of the prospect of Lusignans marrying into that family. Well, I see some sense in that. Marriages are important.' But she fretted that he would be roaming about taking casual pleasure where he found it, while she stayed here, another child to be delivered. She did not look forward to being confined again. Her face darkened but Hugh reached out a conciliatory hand.

'Isabella, we have frustrated England with our union. Let us take stock again, decide later which way to go when Henry has landed.'

And with that she had to be content.

IX

England and France, 1230

Easter was over. The Holy Week had been spent in the Abbey at Reading. A great place of worship built on a spur between the Kennet and the Thames, with piers and wharves providing easy transport. The town prospered; under the Lord Abbot there were fisheries, mills and woods. Henry came by road, a route he knew and liked: Westminster, Windsor, Reading. He had his chapel furniture carried with him, the altar chest and curtains. And his crown. For at Easter he wore his crown to remind the world that he was King. And he decided he would order much regalia – the crown, sceptre and a baton of gilded silver, gauntlets and a royal mantle of white silk – to be packed to take to France.

'I will ride into Nantes wearing all the marks of a king,' he said to his steward, 'Make sure of it, everything stowed with care. The voyage could be rough.' He looked directly at de Burgh as he gave this order, they were reconciled for now but Henry found it difficult to forget how he had been blocked from invading France last year. However, he had lost no time during the winter, ordering vessels and men to be ready.

Now he stood on the stone wall of the dock at Portsmouth watching the ships and the muster. The wind was slight, the harbour full: a forest of masts. There was shelter here whatever the tides.

Clerks and shipmasters sat marking payrolls, writing dates of service and checking against the requisitions. It would take some days for supplies, horses and men to embark. Hurdles were being set up in the holds to make stalls for the horses. Provisions had been secured for months. De Burgh stood next to him, keeping his thoughts to himself. Richard of Cornwall was explaining that over a hundred ships would return to their ports, not needed. The problem this year was not too few ships but too many. He thought 230 sufficient. Henry was impatient with this careful consideration and reeled off a list.

'The muster roll shows 275 barons, knights and men-at-arms. The foot soldiers we cannot reckon, in the thousands. More than a dozen horses in each ship. And I will take chests full of silver with me. I intend to enlist more men when we arrive.'

He shot a triumphant look at de Burgh who turned away and scanned the harbour for the king's own ships: two or three of those for knights and all royal supplies. He would sail in one of them, but perhaps not with the king. There was Henry's galley with the royal arms painted on the sail in brilliant vermillion. He hoped Henry had some idea about taking on the French on their own soil, but he doubted that he did.

'I am waiting for William Marshal to see this.' Henry was more than a little proud of his fleet. 'Eleanor our beloved sister is coming too. Richard, we might all meet our mother together?' He shifted his weight from foot to foot and laughed. 'I am trying to understand what it will mean to balance on board.'

The commotion at the end of the pier meant that the Earl of Pembroke and his wife had arrived. Eleanor walked quickly and lightly, all smiles, and her face lit up even more when she saw her brothers. Her heavy travelling cloak blew in the wind and under it a richly embroidered mantle could be seen. Henry embraced her.

'It is good to see you, and you are well I trust?' Everyone knew that now she was fifteen she would be at her husband's side at all times, for a child must be conceived. Henry had already recognised her maturity and was pleased that he had granted her ten manors to remain with her even if widowed. He wanted all his sisters cared for and she was the youngest.

The ships moved out of the harbour. The sea was choppy with gusts of a north-westerly wind shaking the square sails of the sturdy cogs. Henry stood under the forecastle in the prow, his face set and determined. The long-awaited expedition was under way. A king of England had not sailed to France at the head of an army for seventeen years. Four knights stood by the mast and watched his back as the ship sailed on. The wind was strengthening and the large sail billowed.

Eleanor huddled in the aft castle, her face pale, her smiles vanished. Pembroke stood by her, one hand on her shoulder. She retched and turned to hold onto him. The captain swung the tiller and the open sea stretched wide and empty, the fleet leaping forward into the morning.

A cold night, a chilly moon, and stars overhead bright and hard in a clear sky. Rough waves lapping and breaking at the sides of the ships. Men moving about adjusting ropes and everyone intent on a task. Henry sat with his sister and held her hand. She was asleep, her head back on the planking. There was scant shelter below. He had been up on top of the fo'c'sle, watching the wake of the ship and seen the rest of the fleet making its way steadily in the strong wind.

The captain approached.

'It is going to be a fast run. We will be in Brittany, if not St Malo by the second day of May. The men have worked hard. I will give orders for beer and bread when we see the dawn.'

'We pass close by Guernsey, do we not? Ships from there ply the Bordeaux wine trade. And pay tax.'

'And charge silver for landing.'

Eleanor stirred, her voice faint. 'There is land soon?

I would be on land again. This marine voyage is full of misery.' She wiped her face with a damp linen cloth and held it to her mouth. 'Henry, I cannot take more of the sea. Can we shelter somewhere?'

William Marshal loomed out of the shadow, a cup of water in his hand.

'Drink this. You have need of water.' A tough soldier and stoic, he was fond of his young wife and she had quite faded from the merry laughing girl since they had been on board.

Questions were asked and decisions made. The captain said it would be possible to spend a day in St Peter Port. There was a good harbour.

'It has a rocky approach and the tides are never still. But give me anything but calm. A stiff breeze will help us around the danger. Hidden rocks, seldom seen. With a high tide we can anchor near the jetty. Look out for the castle on the islet to the left as we approach.'

In the early morning the cog dropped its sail and the men rowed to the rough stone jetty. Either side of this were sloping sandy beaches, high tide covering all but a strip of coarse grass where the beach met a track. The royal group climbed ashore and Eleanor staggered. Henry and William held her and guided her to the small church and mill built at the end of a valley facing the sea. The little town was surrounded by steep cliffs. Two roads ran north and a gatehouse could be seen with a few houses nearby. Everywhere there was a powerful smell of fish. Nets were draped over rocks and fishermen sat gutting mackerel and conger eel. Dunes and shingle stretched all along the shore.

'We will sail again on the next high tide, in the small hours of the morning.'

The church was a sanctuary, cool and calm. Water and victuals had been found, Eleanor slept on the floor guarded by her husband and brother.

The English army clattered across the granite causeway from the island town of St Malo to the mainland. Horses restless and nervous and men bleary-eyed and tired. Henry led them, his desire to be on the road halted by the need to stop and let the horses feed and the men adjust after such a rough crossing. Most of the fleet had spent a night to the west of St Malo blown there by the north winds. The thirty ships that had taken refuge in Guernsey had caught the very early tide and made a swift crossing. Henry was exultant. On to Nantes.

Peter Dreux met the royal party: Henry, Richard, the Earl of Pembroke, the Earl of Chester, the Earl of Gloucester, de Burgh. Eleanor was recovered but still pallid as she bumped along the rough road with a small retinue around her.

'We will rest here for a few days,' Henry reassured her. They climbed the hill to Dinan and the flat land that spread out to the north where a camp was made. Henry proud and pleased: his first sea crossing, a camp struck, already important men arriving. Norman barons and their knights approached, swearing fealty.

'We have a great wish to stir up independence in our duchy, we urge you. Invade Normandy now.'

'Now, immediately – it is true Blanche has snuffed out some seeds of rebellion. But with your army – now is the time to attack.'

De Burgh shook his head. 'Very rash, very rash to propose this. How do you think we can divide the army with any hope of success? A steady pace through Brittany is what is wanted and with help from La Marche and Thouars we will strike into the Poitevin lands.'

Henry looked down at his feet and up after the departing men, he had wanted to lead the army with them at his side. It was all exciting and new, this tumult of being here in the middle of the noise of the camp, his pennant flying high. That reminded him.

'And Bordeaux. We must get to Bordeaux to show ourselves there.'

Isabella dried herself carefully. She was trying not to think too much about meeting her children, John's children, again. Her long soaking bath had helped to relax her and she had used a poultice of herbs soaked in wine and wrapped in a muslin bag to cleanse her face. It had tightened the skin and she hoped would smooth the deepening lines around her mouth. Marie brought her the round wooden box with its precious ointment: almond oil and jasmine to be rubbed into her face and hands. Isabella fretted as she looked in her hand mirror. Her hair was not as bright as it had been. Each pregnancy seemed to make it duller and thinner. She slipped on her chemise, light cream silk and cotton with fine gathers on the skirt. Hose next, rolled to the knee; and then a free flowing kirtle of dark green fustian, the tight sleeves buttoned from elbow to wrist.

Agnes came into the room carrying a new surcoat. Gold thread picked out the pattern in the deepest blue silk brocade, medallions and roundels holding deer – all interspersed with stars.

'From Italy, the very best, and a colour that is true.'

'It is good to have a coat that covers me. I am still plump in the belly from Marguerite. Pleasing though it is to have another daughter I am weary of being heavy with child. And my nights are disturbed with such sweats and dreams. I would sleep in the day if I could.' She looked into the mirror again and pushed her mouth into a smile. In the corner of the room a new wet nurse rocked the cradle. A wet nurse whose full breasts were signs of good milk.

'But she is so sad about the face.' Isabella had said. She and Agnes were concerned; a melancholy woman might make the nursery a dismal unhappy place. Ellen had reassured them, 'She is sad because her own child died. This is the second time her child has died. But she will nurse yours well and heartily. She has two needs, to give succour to a baby and be rewarded well for this. Her husband has sickened and she needs to provide for him and all the family.' And Marguerite, all crumpled with a creased forehead and a wail that set the teeth on edge, nestled into Béa's arms and latched on, suckling like no other baby had. *Sleep little cuckoo, sleep on my breast, sleep little cuckoo and find your rest.*

Isabella clutched Agnes's hand. 'It has been three months and the necessary bleeding after delivering Marguerite stopped within the month. My milk dried up very quickly this time.' She let go and fastened her girdle, smoothing down the sweep of her skirt and then glancing up. 'No flux has returned. Hugh joins me in our bed but there is no sign...' she broke off and fiddled with her rings; she half knew what the reason was, but could not face it. 'I am not yet forty, so this is strange.'

Agnes considered and spoke bluntly. 'The sweats, the bad nights, and now no flux. It is likely that it will return but not every month. There comes a time when that is that. It is possible that you will not find yourself with child again.'

'Then I will watch my Lusignan children grow and rejoice in their advance. I can do no more.' Isabella's tone was fierce and uncompromising. 'And now I must finish all preparations and see those other children from that other time.'

Agnes settled the surcoat over Isabella's head and held her gently by the shoulders.

'You look magnificent. You can be proud of everything. Geoffroy will be with you to guard your well-being. I wish you Godspeed on your journey north.'

Dinan was a long journey. She wanted to see them, yet it

would be hard. And she wanted to show them that she was still a queen.

'It is a favourable time for the English.' Hugh was helping her into a covered wagon for the early part of the journey. 'The army of Blanche is busy helping the Count of Champagne. So many lords despise him and their jests and oaths have turned into an invasion of his county.'

'I heard the song they sing, saying he has no friends except the Queen of France, and calling him a vile hill of flesh. But I also heard that Louis is already at Angers, waiting to fight. What an encounter that will be!'

Geoffroy rode near Isabella, watchful and protective. The first part of their journey meant cart tracks through the woods before they reached the road to Niort and Parthenay. This old way would lead them towards Nantes and Dinan.

'We must skirt around with care, some of the Poitevin lords are looking to Henry again.' Hugh and Geoffroy were in accord about this, they wanted no trouble from them as they crossed their lands.

'Better to move now before they consolidate.' Geoffroy urged on the group.

Niort came and went with its inland port and harbour, marshy land that often flooded falling away to the sea. There were hidden causeways but these were risky. Then past the Abbey St Pierre of Maillezais on its waterlogged island, a burial place for the Dukes of Aquitaine.

'The Abbey can be seen from the sea,' Hugh told Isabella, whose cart had stopped to change to fresh horses. She looked about her.

'It is a dark place to build, such dense growth all around. But they have chosen well; higher ground.' She thought longingly of Angoulême and its rocky cliffy heights. She was glad to get out of the gloom and into wooded hillsides at Parthenay. Here pilgrims walked the narrow street that climbed away from the river and passed through the arch of the Porte Saint Jacques on their way south to Compostela.

The last stretch of their journey now. The long straight route that led to Nantes and then on to Dinan. But first she must bid goodbye to Hugh, who wheeled about with his company of knights. He was riding on the better road that led to Angers, for he was joining Louis there. Her visit to see her children was maternal, curious, but she was not necessarily going as an ally.

X

'She has arrived. They tell me they have crossed the bridge with a great company of men and horses. She is riding too, very tall on her palfrey. Look, can you see there, the ferraunt grey? Iron grey for Isabella Taillefer.'

Henry was nervous, pulling at the sleeves on his tunic, buckling and unbuckling his belt, remembering to stand tall. Richard was feigning indifference. He had met La Marche, and he was not worried about meeting his mother. When had she last seen him? A dozen years had passed; he was not a child any more. Neither was Henry. He shot a sharp glance at him. He hoped he would not cry.

The door opened and Isabella was there: splendid, beautiful and unsmiling. Not throwing her arms wide to embrace them. She walked to Henry and made as if to curtsey, although she had no intention of doing so. He stammered, 'Mother,' and stopped her. He knelt and stood when he felt her hand on his shoulder.

She saw a young man of twenty-three, muscular and strong, a good head and beard of brown hair, friendly eyes; the left one drooped. A look of his father about him, but a kinder mouth. He embraced her, the kiss of peace, and called for refreshments to be served at once. Servants obeyed with speed and the room filled with people. Richard stepped forward and also knelt to Isabella. She held out her hands and he kissed them. She saw here someone tall with long legs, dark red hair: an Angevin. She smiled at last. Satisfaction at seeing such fine sons.

'You have been here for some weeks. You have turned

117

away from Normandy and would meet the son of that Spanish queen near here?'

'We think Normandy is not possible, Mother. It is better to make our presence felt strongly here and further south. The possessions that were ours, taken back into our hands again. ' Henry clasped his hands behind his back, trying to appear more confident than he was. 'Although we cannot use La Rochelle, it is true, and the sea journey from Bordeaux is mighty long. I am glad we have St Malo. The Count of Brittany has secured us a good harbour there.'

Henry was eager to talk to her about his strategy.

'De Burgh's advice? It will be followed no doubt.' Isabella regarded him again. He seemed unsure of what he was doing here. Not a king who made a good soldier. Richard now, there was more in that son. She thought he was not so easily persuaded by others.

'Who else is here with you?'

'Ranulf, Earl of Chester, a man who has fought for England over and over again.' Henry was full of admiration as he spoke of this veteran. 'Also William Marshal's son, Pembroke. The Earl of Gloucester and diverse others. A good army. We have come prepared.' And then eager to tell of his arrival: 'I will ride into Nantes in my regalia, Mother; I wish to show that I am King here, not Louis.'

'No, not Louis.' Isabella regarded him keenly. Someone who liked the trappings of royalty. She sighed as she thought of that coronation in Gloucester and her hand went to her head, her chaplet, her gold collar given as his crown. She turned away to hide her face. Tears were welling and she needed to hold them back.

'Mother?' A new voice, light and sweet, a hint of roses in the air. Isabella turned and saw a young woman so graceful, so slim, so like she had once been that she caught her breath. Eleanor curtsied low, her thick red damask skirts pooling on the floor. Isabella lightly touched her daughter's head and sighed. Royal daughters, beautiful and clever, or not, had to be married into alliances.

Henry had married her to Pembroke, had granted his younger sister to him. She studied the forty-year-old William Marshal. For me he will always be the young William, she said to herself, watching as he followed his wife into the room. A tall, heavy man with a broad face, a great deal like his father. She had heard that a long poem, a family history, had been written about the great William Marshal. Something to bolster and gratify the family no doubt. This eldest son of his had commissioned it.

Be that as it may she thought and drew herself up, making sure he recognised her as a queen of England. As he knelt to her she was thinking furiously, he had better remember he is only a subject of the crown, his chase after a royal marriage was met by Henry and his impulsive choices. And turned over in her mind the useful fact that Henry was indeed impulsive.

'You are well, Mother?' Eleanor was unsure how to talk to this striking woman; a woman she did not remember at all. Isabella inclined her head. She was well and for how long was Eleanor staying in France? Her daughter shivered slightly. 'I will return to England next month. They tell me that June is a calm month to travel on the sea. I am not a sailor.' William Marshal heard her words and beckoned her to his side and she stood there, demure and still. Isabella noticed her stance and thought she is good at playing games that one. She will be whatever he wants her to be.

Henry was at Isabella's elbow. He stood there glorying in being a king standing next to his mother, the Queen of England. And suddenly she was glad to have him with her in the company of all these men who reminded her of an earlier life. Hubert de Burgh was now kneeling to her, and murmuring a greeting. He brought back unwelcome sharp memories, being pushed out of everything important in England; the endless disputes about dowry lands and money.

'It was a long time ago,' she whispered to herself, 'and I have done so much more.'

She was gracious to de Burgh who was guarded with her. She listened to him talking about the duties and responsibilities of the king and his counsellors of whom, of course, de Burgh was the most important. De Burgh now married to the sister of the King of the Scots and Isabella's daughter Joan married to that king himself. She gave de Burgh a sharp look; she hoped he did not think this made them some kind of kin. He had a great deal to lose now he had climbed so high – a soldier who was also a statesman.

'And you will not march to Normandy, not begin an advance?'

De Burgh pulled at his beard. 'No we will make our way to Nantes and wait there. And then south to show the king the road to Bordeaux.'

'Not Normandy,' Isabella repeated, 'no alliances there.' She hoped her voice did not betray her dismay. If Henry was to come all this way and only intended to show his face in the south west she knew too well how the Poitou and Gascony would play him.

'Normandy is made of very strong stuff, and I would not advise an assault.' De Burgh said, as he flicked some lint from his sleeve, he was dismissing her already thought Isabella. He continued, 'Of course we will recruit soldiers from the duchy.'

'And from Brittany too. I believe Peter Dreux is riding through his lands and brings men to the alliance?' She sent a keen searching glance around the room, the lords, the knights, Henry animated, a little preening and obviously enjoying his first foray in France.

'Yes,' de Burgh was curt now, this woman had badgered

the council in Westminster for more than ten years, kept her own daughter almost a hostage to make sure of her demands, written endless letters about her dower and then had the temerity to marry Hugh Lusignan without asking the English court for permission. Uniting La Marche and Angoulême. He pressed his mouth into a tight line.

She looked about the room again. Where was that bishop, that man from Anjou, who some thought a Poitevin, but he was not and never would be. The man of the Church, who was more a soldier than he was ever a cleric. He had held such power as Bishop of Winchester, with Henry in his charge but managed to insult her over and over again. Full of fine silky words and a manner that insinuated.

De Burgh smiled thinly. 'Des Roches is on a crusade. He left two years ago, the most lavish of crusades. But we all think he will be safe from death in battle. A man of such renown.' De Burgh almost openly sneered. 'He seems in no hurry to return to England.' And he folded his arms across his chest, pushing his hands into his sleeves. Complacent, thought Isabella. He thinks he has the ascendant forever. He is grown slow and too careful for this expedition.

And then Henry was taking her arm and escorting her about the room, his face proud. He wanted his mother and her husband Lusignan with him; he hoped de Burgh had spoken well about the campaign strategy. Richard joined them.

'You have my lands and keep them strong, I trust. They will make you rich if you can hold them for long enough.'

'Richard has much indeed.' Henry strutted a little for they had been his gift. 'But he has ideas of more than wealth. He wishes to find King Arthur in Cornwall. Tell our mother, the Queen, about your trade for Tintagel.'

Richard looked for a moment like someone younger and more vulnerable than the stern knight with the cool head that he wanted to show the world.

'It is difficult for the people of Cornwall to accept me. Suspicion lies between them and outsiders. I will have Tintagel in my holding and will build a castle there. There are tales written about Arthur and that place. The scholars wrote the story of Arthur in their ancient books: all the deeds of all the kings.'

'But you are not a king,' said Henry, and looked hard at Richard, who looked away.

Two days later Isabella kissed her three children goodbye and began her journey back. Her horses and carts picked their way down the steep narrow streets away from the walls and ramparts, away from her son who had looked so overwhelmed by what he was doing, despite his excited words and plans. She spoke to Geoffroy when they safely reached the long road south, away from Dinan, eventually to cross the Loire and on to her county, her domains: the Poitou, the Charente, Lusignan and Angoulême.

'I am pleased to have seen them all, my children, but also glad to be leaving. I see no point in throwing in our lot with my son. Hugh knows. Does Louis know? I am sure Blanche knows. Henry does not. This campaign is going to be disastrous.'

Blanche sat in her chamber in the chateau at Clisson, that well-fortified castle built on a rocky outcrop and protected by a shallow moat. Two round towers, strong walls, bastions, a place of safety. The view was down to the river Sèvre where it joined the Loire and rushed on over banks and weirs to Nantes and the sea. Blanche approved of the family and its lords, a family she could trust. They had fought alongside Philippe against John at Bouvines; they wanted to keep Peter of Brittany at bay. Their name might come from a trellis of branches, but now they built defences of stone.

She prayed quietly that the meeting with Hugh, Count of La Marche, and his wife Isabella would be a calm and successful one, and then stood to admire and wonder at the hanging on the wall. Foliage, flowers, violets, early lady orchids, pomegranate trees, a spangled grassy space, and in the middle a pure white unicorn wearing a gold collar. The Clissons had brought it back from Flanders, a fine piece of weaving, good wool, gold and silver threads, Italian silk. Blanche ran her hand over it, the metal twists caught the dawn light that began to shine through the window.

Louis would be in the chapel and her steward would be arranging food as well as organising the clerks and scribes. Blanche wanted today to be smooth and trouble free. It was to make sure that La Marche stayed with them and did not turn to support Henry. She had no real concerns about Hugh, he was enjoying the money too much, enjoying the fact that he was being paid to be as independent as he wanted to be. It was a delicate balance for while she and Louis bought his support they could not influence the Poitou. Blanche considered her options. Hugh had been part of the group that had attempted to kidnap Louis. Oh, he had held back, been less than forceful, but he had taken part. So she had summoned him to the Christmas court and made sure that everyone saw him there, swearing fealty again. But everyone knew that he and Isabella had a small powerful estate of their own, almost a principality, and that no sovereign could enter the Poitou without their assent and support. So she would continue to buy that support and block a rapprochement between them and Henry. To keep Henry from becoming a real threat. Hugh had tried to trample on the treaty made in Vendôme. Well, now the treaty would be made anew, it would be reinforced and Isabella would seal it too.

But she mistrusted Isabella; she had watched her intrigues

and skilful conspiracies for years. She thought back to the meeting at Bourges. Blanche had not attended but her husband reported back about the couple who had pivoted to the French when offered enough. That had been the first time the Capets had bought La Marche and Angoulême. Blanche considered the widow of her uncle John, Isabella, the Countess of Angoulême. She put some papers down on a table by the window and turned them one by one, studying the treaty and its provisions. Isabella, she thought, above her extravagance and desire to live like royalty with revenue flowing in daily, was also very proud and wilful. She always wanted to be thought of as Queen of England. It was not all about dowries and pensions.

Louis came in and walked across to her, kissed her good morning. 'My boy,' she said, and marvelled again at his fair, delicate face. It had been an honour and a burden to be left the administration of the kingdom by his father, but she was able, she knew that, and she was the mother of the king and Queen of France more than she was a widow. Forty-two years old, married for twenty-six years, mother of five children, the last born after Louis's death. Charles, a baby she had carried while wearing the white dresses of mourning, while putting down the rebellion by Dreux and la Marche and the Count of Champagne and facing off her husband's half-brother Philip the Count of Boulogne. Called Hurepel: rough haired, bristle head, a nickname he did not mind, it seemed. She knew they called her the She Wolf, the Hersent. And Isabella called her the Spanish queen because of her Castilian father. Rude names. But her mother was the daughter of Eleanor of Aquitaine and Eleanor had brought her across the Pyrenees all those years ago to make sure she safely met Louis and married him. And they had been so happy, no secrets, no rivals, his love was for her alone.

'Mother,' Louis gently interrupted her reverie, 'Mother

we should go to the hall and talk about the day.' Blanche shook herself and smiled agreement.

They sat eating quietly, bread and a thin soup, some early peaches. Louis remarked, 'Henry has been in Nantes for ten days or so. He rode in to hold court and has shown off his silk mantle and gauntlets and carried his baton of gilded silver through the streets. A veritable parade!'

'He prays as well as parades I am sure, he is devout, unlike his father. And the man de Burgh plans the movement they will make?

'He does. We will not attack though. I am sure he wishes we would and wear the army to shreds. I am not besieging Nantes. It is a waiting game now.'

'And I think a bidding game is about to begin,' said Blanche. 'You must watch for the movement of the army, I must watch to see the negotiations with our guests who arrive today.'

'Is everything packed? Do you have all my jewellery, all chemises, the skirts and bodices I chose? They are carefully folded and placed just so?' Isabella frowned as her mind ran over the preparations for the meeting that was to settle again the treaty of Vendôme. But the new sealing and affirmation of that was not what made her anxious, overwrought, her colour high and her voice sharp. She was to meet Blanche, not seen since that visit to Paris when Isabella was the new young bride, married to John. Blanche's uncle. Well, she thought grimly, I was Queen of England then, and I am still Queen of England, a dowager queen – as she is too.

'You have the vials of scent and lotions, the pots of ointment?' Isabella whirled about as Marie closed the lid of the small iron bound chest. The chest that had been with her since childhood, taken to Lusignan when she was first betrothed, and with her ever since. It held her most precious objects. Her queen's matrix for sealing charters and treaties nestled in its pouch, her emblem of power.

'I will guard them all,' reassured Marie and exchanged glances with Agnes who whispered, 'You will be much needed in the days to come with your skilful hands.'

'What was that? Do you talk about me behind my back?' Isabella was on edge and suspicious. Both women began to protest, they were simply making sure all was well for the journey. But Isabella had gone, speeding down the stone stairs, joining Hugh in the courtyard. And they set their horses on the road to Clisson where Blanche and Louis waited.

They arrived in the courtyard with their retinue spread out behind them, horses, baggage carts and a covered cart for Isabella. She waited as Marie stepped down and helped her out, smoothing her skirt and straightening her cloak. Hugh held out his hand and they walked slowly into the chateau. Isabella held her head high; pleased to think how well they looked together. Her skirt of deep damson red with dull gold embroidery that traced a pattern of roses and lilies, the plain tight bodice trimmed with fur, its long sleeves ending in a heavy gold button. She showed herself to every advantage as Hugh, by her side, escorted her into the hall.

Blanche, grave faced, was looking at her directly. Isabella pulled herself even taller and met her gaze. There would be no dishonest or ill-intentioned gestures today. But neither would she kneel at the door or again in the hall. They were equals. She was not going to be humble or meek before this woman. A pause, and then from both a small bow from the waist, an incline of the head, carried out in unison. Eyes lowered and then met again – they both knew there was mutual distrust and mutual jealousy.

Hugh was kneeling to Louis who was his liege lord, Louis, awkward but dignified as he commanded him to rise and then approached Isabella to give her the kiss of peace. She took a small step back and then moved towards him. A queen and a king, just as it had been when she had met his father. Blanche said, 'Welcome. Most welcome. Please sit and take refreshment.' Gracious, careful in her speech.

Isabella walked to the massive oak table, with benches and stools of the same wood. At the end of this table, a large arm-chair, overhung with a canopy of padded silk. The stone floor carefully strewn with the scented herbs of summer. The walls hung with tapestries: fields and woods and cattle, the story of Troy, a jousting tournament. She thought with a small imperceptible toss of her head that the tapestries were dull; the ones in Lusignan told far better stories.

A servant brought water and linen for them to wash after the journey and then everyone sat, Louis in the canopied chair with Isabella next to him. She was pleased to see the fine dishes on the table, capon and rabbit with dried plums, small flat circular loaves – the very best bread, a large fish bright with a green leek and parsley sauce. Strawberries in sugar baskets, small creamy cheeses. The knives and plates gleamed, the linen tablecloth fell in generous folds and wine was poured into bright gold goblets. A feast for a queen.

But none of this stopped Isabella from being distrustful. Although for now, she had every intention of supporting Blanche and her son, it would not be a gift. She was guarded as she walked alongside Blanche, who moved so quietly through the rooms, taking her to see the unicorn in the meadow. And this, Isabella had to admit, was a wonderful piece. As she stood gazing at the tapestry, Blanche stalked ahead trying to hide her animosity. Isabella's face hardened. She would not run after her. Very slowly she made her way down the passage to an open door, the chamber she and Hugh were to use, plain and simple but a comfortable bed heaped with cushions and covers. Marie sat in the corner unfolding and shaking out a chemise. Blanche, distant, polite, asked, 'It is to your liking?' and moved away, not waiting for an answer. Isabella's mouth curled with distaste, she was already thinking of the journey home, she did not enjoy the company of this queen.

In the afternoon they sat at the table, cleared of the meal, now clerks and scribes joined them, writing materials set neatly to hand.

'As you know,' said Louis, 'my lords and knights will only stay with me for the necessary days of service. I cannot hold them to more.'

'Henry shows no sign of leaving Nantes,' said Hugh. 'And when he does he will make his way through the Poitou with noisy mercenaries. He will pay them with the chests of silver he carries.'

'Indeed. I would let him march about as long as someone watches the roads at all times. And the important towns.'

Blanche steepled her hands, the Count of la Marche and Isabella of Angoulême could say yes or no to this. She felt a sudden spurt of anger. They were much too strong. And then she noted to herself, at the moment they were too strong, but in some future plan perhaps they could be weakened?

It was her turn to speak.

'We are offering you more land, St Jean d'Angély, the Saintonge, lands around La Rochelle. Which I believe you disputed with Peter Dreux and his new wife not so long ago.'

Isabella said, 'Domaines, fiefdoms, they can come and go as the seasons come and go.' And looked around the table at each person in turn. The air was suddenly tense. Everyone knew what she meant and wanted. Blanche beckoned to her chief scribe who brought a sheet of parchment to her. She wrote a sum of money with a clear hand, gave it to the scribe who gave it to Isabella. Who smiled and folded it into her lap. She was implacable within her position and meant to keep it that way.

'I accept the conditions to which my husband and I will agree.'

And Hugh swore he would make no peace, no truce with Henry without their agreement. That he would shadow Henry and keep him from moving east.

'And when that is clear, the marriage betrothals will be properly sealed within the month.'

Blanche nodded towards the clerks. Hugh beamed. Isabella rose from the table. Blanche quickly followed, that spurt of anger again. Would Isabella continue to act as if she had all precedence? For both of them the formal leave-taking could not come soon enough.

XI

Henry fretted and moped. There was no alliance with his mother and stepfather. Isabella had had ridden away and taken his hopes with her. He was sure she had considered the possibility of supporting him, but no; she and Hugh were not on his side. Neither were the Viscount of Thouars and his nephew. The people that de Burgh had counted on. He thought about de Burgh and his strategy. It seemed not to be working.

'Shall we march south at last?' A slightly desperate note in his voice, for how was he to keep alive his dream to retake what his father had lost? Even Henry was getting tired of sitting in Nantes, nearly a month of idleness.

'As always the Poitevins are swaying this way and that. But yes, we can pick up support if we pay them.' And the commands were given to be ready for the roads. The French army gathered just a day's march away seemed to be slowly disbanding.

Henry rode at the head of his army but already there were those around him thinking it a long, pointless progress from Nantes to Bordeaux. A few friends made, Mirambeau holding out, but besieged and captured. Nowhere else resisted so strongly but nowhere else helped him much either.

'My father rescued Eleanor, his mother from this place,' said Henry with satisfaction. It was a small triumph for him, even if Gascons had to help and Bordeaux to send a siege engine.

Bordeaux. Where many rushed to make homage and this boosted his pride. But the homage came without an offer of funds. So after this useless march to Bordeaux, after one week's rest, he ambled back again, never seeing Louis – but someone shadowed them and threatened all the time to the east. So the English army kept out of the way. And that way was difficult in the heat of August. Through the marshy lands of the Bas Poitou, insects that bit day and night laid men low with sweating and fevers.

'The way has been very hard,' he complained when they were back in Nantes in the middle of September. 'So many small towns and small lords all swearing loyalty, but what does that mean in reality? And those small lords write letters wanting help because the Queen of France threatens them if they fall in with me. I do believe they will turn against me once more. And I have paid them! It is not good, not good at all.' Henry looked at his armour being carried away by a page to be oiled and mended, his banners and pennants being cleaned and folded. He did not want to dress again for a march that meant riding all day; long hours in the saddle were not for him.

'Nantes is a good place for us all to rest, do you not think, de Burgh? It is comfortable here, even luxurious.' And he looked longingly at the bed with its cushions and curtains. De Burgh agreed.

'No more military efforts. We have men who are sick and groan without ceasing. We cannot pull an army together to fight.'

Richard made a sardonic face. 'We will rest and then?' But Henry wasn't listening; he was already in bed and had pulled the covers over his head.

The autumn brought a slow meander through Brittany: a good place declared many, a place where the nobles learnt how to drink deep when the English court arrived. But even that palled and Henry and Richard were ill, tired and short of money.

'This cannot continue. Many of the knights are selling their horses to support themselves.' Richard said.

'I will write and tell those lords in Gascony and the Poitou who look to us that I have ordered our ships to St Malo. We will return to England and leave the Duke of Brittany in charge. He has guarded the Breton borders at Brest very ably.'

And so, in late October, Henry was on his knees in the church at St Pol de Léon, praying fervently for a safe Channel crossing.

'The first Christian King of Brittany is buried here.'

He knelt at the altar and shrine, pleased that he had managed to visit several in the last three months. Richard knelt beside him and reflected that Henry had been saved from a reckless adventure to take Normandy, but that it had been an expensive lesson to learn. And that the progress to Bordeaux had proved nothing. They had lost men and nobles too, not to combat, but to sickness. The Earl of Gloucester died as they made for the coast; another man struck down by the sweating fever. Richard prayed hard for his soul and tried not to let his thoughts slide away onto worldly matters, but it was difficult. Henry was running out of resources and pledging far too much to Peter of Brittany. The money just slipped through his fingers as his campaign dragged on. Richard would be glad to sail back to Portsmouth, and glad to leave Dreux and the Earl of Pembroke in charge in Brittany. Eleanor had returned to Portsmouth in calm summer seas and now she was summoned to sail back to France to stay with her husband. Richard hoped she would not suffer on the crossing again. But the sister of the king, the wife of the earl, would be a presence, a reminder of the ties of loyalty to the English as her husband attempted to carry on with Henry's blundering war. Which in Richard's opinion had been full of hopeful arrogance.

*

Christmas celebrations in Lambeth, with all the usual cere-
monies, but it was a subdued end to the year. The return to
England had not been the expected triumph. Henry seized
his small personal seal in a petty show of defiance and began
to use it for sending messages to de Burgh. He wanted some
more independence and now he sulked.

'I was invited to France. That should have meant
something. To see the realms of England and Normandy
united again, is that too much to want? But no, we did not
fight for Normandy and we could not take the Poitou back
entirely.'

'The French resisted and blocked, skill there, but I agree
we had many chances, lost chances.' De Burgh knew how
unwelcome the failure was to all. He said nothing about
the lack of support from Lusignan and Taillefer. From
La Marche and Angoulême.

'So why did we not win back what was ours?' Henry
wanted someone to blame, he did not want to remember all
those cautious words about how his mother might prefer
to hold onto all she had gained in the Poitou and not fight
the Capets. That she might think the allegiances there more
worthwhile than anything England could offer.

'Your plans were wrong, not well thought out. It was
a collapse, a sorry collapse of all I wanted.' Petulance crept
into his voice and he glowered at de Burgh, who was mindful
that he had just been given custody of the lands belonging to
the recently dead Earl of Gloucester. He was to hold them until
that earl's heirs came of age, and so with this in mind he held
his tongue. The scribes had written what he was to pay for
that privilege. Several hundreds of marks, but worth having.

'We must look forward to the spring and new beginnings.'
Platitudes in an attempt to change the subject.

But there were no celebrations that spring. In February,

William Marshal and Eleanor sailed back from Brittany. William Marshal was very sure of himself and determined to make the best for his young widowed sister, Isabel. The late wife of the Earl of Gloucester.

'You mourn him deeply but there is one who would be your husband.'

'I loved him deeply too; it is but five months since he was buried. I will not love another with such feeling.'

William snorted with impatience. 'I know how the world works and so, I think, do you. Richard of Cornwall will be a good second marriage for you.'

Fickle March sunshine blessed the couple as they stood in the chancel at the simple flint church in Fawley. William and Eleanor listened to their exchange of vows.

'I, Isabel take thee, Richard, to my wedded husband, to have and to hold from this day forward, for better for worse, for richer, for poorer, in sicknesses and in health, to be honoured in bed and at board, till death us depart, if Holy Church will it ordain; and thereto I plight thee my troth.'

'The widow Isabel to my brother! That is rich! Another binding to that family who is keen to oppose me if it suits their purposes. My brother makes influential friends everywhere. He is getting closer and closer to the Marshals. My friends, my kin! My lords of Cornwall and Pembroke!'

Henry glowered and roared. The shadow of his father, but capable of an exploding temper.

'He has six stepchildren to act for now. He will want children of his own.' De Burgh was all too aware of the rights of these particular heirs. Henry could only kick out at the dogs that had slunk away from his anger.

April began cold with a cruel north-east wind and then it turned and the rain was ceaseless. For two weeks it poured and made the rivers overflow their banks and the ditches fill with mud. City streets became streams. The young sprouts of crops in the fields were washed away. And everywhere people coughed and shivered, huddled and morose.

And suddenly, William Marshal, so sure in his position, the first son of the great Marshal, was dead. A blow, an unexpected blow for all. Eleanor a widow at sixteen. Henry reeled and lamented next to her in the Temple church, where the young Marshal was buried next to his father.

'Is not the blood of the blessed martyr Thomas fully avenged yet?' Henry cried these words as he gripped the arm of the Master of the Temple, a stern figure in his stark white surcoat with its blazing red cross. For the Temple Church had supported Becket and now it seemed that everyone was against the English Crown. Eleanor was praying, had been praying for hours, her face ashen. She had been married in this church and now she mourned her husband. By her side knelt her governess, the woman who had schooled her for marriage but not for widowhood.

In the king's chamber, at the Palace at Westminster, the two sat close together, and Cecily Sandford explained to Eleanor that it was important to watch and see if she was pregnant.

'You will know by the early summer, will you not?' Eleanor nodded, wordlessly. Would there be a child who could inherit the Marshal estates? There was so much wealth from these in England, Wales and Ireland, and then her own manors too.

Henry turned to his sister. 'I will send instructions; you will have your rights, and places to live, revenues, forest provision. The law is very clear.'

His face was full of shadows and Eleanor looked exhausted. They must gather themselves.

'Come. We will walk about the grounds in the fresh air and think of all that is to be done. At last the rain has ceased, even if our tears and grief still have a tight hold on us.'

Eleanor gave a weak smile and followed him, her heart full of sorrow and anxiety. She trusted that Henry would be true to his word, but the inheritance was sprawling and complicated. And if she were not pregnant then Richard Marshal would be the new Earl of Pembroke, and he had been no friend of his older brother and would not be hers, she knew that already.

Within a week of William Marshal's death, de Burgh had persuaded Henry to block Richard Marshal from succeeding to the earldom of Pembroke.

'He has Norman lands; he is the liegeman of Louis. A Marshal and the French king is too strong an alliance.' De Burgh thought grimly how the Marshals had held onto land in Normandy through every twist and turn, whereas others had lost theirs. It would be sweet to deny them this wealth in England.

So Henry agreed he was not going to allow the succession, and besides, his sister might be carrying a child. But she was not. And then Richard Marshal came back from France and paid homage. Henry thought him such an honourable man, a reminder of his great father, someone strong, and someone who could be a friend. So he changed his mind and swiftly granted Richard his title and his lands. But despite this Richard furiously contested Eleanor's share. He saw a sixteen-year-old girl who could outlive him, and tucked under her belt a great deal of his inheritance.

The court was a tense and frustrated place. Disappointed knights returning from Brittany were adding to the vexation. The Welsh were raiding the Marches, no brave and bold William Marshal to check their attacks. The churches were grumbling about the papacy and the way it enriched itself within the English Church. Efforts were made to suggest marriages to Henry. His younger brother was now married. Henry needed a wife, and he needed heirs. The youngest sister of Alexander of Scotland was being pushed towards him.

'My brother Richard thought of marrying her and de Burgh is married to another sister,' complained Henry. 'Should I not have some better wife than my justiciar? It seems he lacks nothing of royal power except the crown.'

Yolande of Brittany's name swam into view again and was dismissed. Henry was embarrassed.

'I attempted to be a serious ally of that family; I attempted to be with Brittany in that invasion. And both betrothal and battles came to nothing.'

He read through the truce again, in a way it helped. He did not have to plan another invasion or a marriage to a woman whose name would forever remind him of his failures. Perhaps the three years of peace promised were to be welcomed?

And who had helped negotiate the truce? A sudden excitement, ripples of news spreading. Peter des Roches on his way home from the crusades. He had been sent by the pope to parlay with the French. The Bishop of Winchester now seen as many things: a statesman, a soldier, a churchman, a crusader. And he was back in England.

De Burgh watched, as his most hostile enemy was welcomed back to court. Not only des Roches, but his supporters, none of them to be trusted.

Courtiers stood in knots, feeling the cross currents that were beginning to swirl about Henry. Richard Marshal observed.

'This is not good for the king, too many Poitevins here at court.' He wanted none of it. 'I see he has a nephew now, what does he call himself? Peter de Rivallis. Not much to commend him is there?'

'His nephew, or some say his son; whatever the relationship, he will prosper.'

But for Hubert de Burgh, what was far worse: the return of de Maulay. He scowled and turned away.

'I know what de Maulay is capable of,' he said under his breath. 'I would put him in a place so dark he could not see his hands or feet, not have him in the brightness of the court. A man who would help murder Arthur of Brittany. There will be plenty of plotting now all these are back.' He swallowed his angry words and thought: I must balance what we have here and so must the king.

Des Roches held Henry spellbound and his face lit up as his old guardian and tutor, the man who had been like a father to him, told his stories of the crusade.

'You worked with the Teutonic knights to strengthen the hospital that my uncle founded? Richard was a great crusader!' Henry's eyes were fixed on des Roches.

'Indeed, and there was much to do in Jerusalem, it needed new fortifications.' More tales of expeditions to negotiate between the pope and Frederick, a dynamic, forceful emperor, who put himself above Church and State. Admiration plain to see in Henry as des Roches recounted these meetings. This was how a ruler should be.

De Burgh listened and felt snubbed. His careful patient work to restore the king's revenue had always been difficult and there were eternal problems with bailiffs who slipped profits into their pockets. And too many royal manors were not leased out on proper terms. He worried and scrabbled over the accounts and explained again to Henry, 'The failures in France have led to weakness in the Exchequer. You pay Peter of Brittany huge sums of money all the time to keep him as your ally.'

This was said with a raised incredulous voice. For de Burgh knew that Henry's ambitions ran him into debt. And this was a weakness that de Burgh could not counter. The King liked extravagance and his resources were never sufficient.

'You advised me on matters of warfare.' Henry was surly. 'It cost too much? Who says that? I am not content with what I hear. I hear chatter about the place that there were no gains in France. Why do so many grumble? I am not content,' he repeated. 'And you constantly tell me we have no money, constantly.'

De Burgh explained with barely concealed impatience.

'And another drain is that we still pay pensions to the Italian clerks and clergy whom the pope sends here. As fast as the Exchequer brings tax income to the Crown, it is spent.'

'And they are attacked! Their stores stolen. Why are you not arresting the men who would bring about such ill feeling? Letters written to the bishops saying that men are ready to die rather than tolerate the foreigners. One papal messenger killed.'

Henry was working himself into a passion, ever mindful that the pope was his feudal lord. England must be honourable towards his representatives. Every time he talked to de Burgh these days he felt irritated and bored.

'His Holiness the Pope expects a great deal from us,' de Burgh said with a grimace and took his leave.

Now it all began to crumble. Des Roches lavishly hosted Henry and his court for Christmas at Winchester, and then in January des Roches smiled and nodded at Henry's complaints and said he was sure he could help. He could check and balance the accounts, there was sure to be money found. Henry was full of expectation. He had something to look forward to.

Worcester, spring time and in the cathedral Henry stood gazing at the new tomb for his father. The effigy was bright with its paintwork, blues and reds and a gilded cage over it all. On the far left a statue of his mother Isabella standing with one of her husband: his parents together. Nearer to the tomb, Edward the Confessor: a saint to guard his father.

'Is he at peace now? I promised not to follow his ways for he imposed his will most cruelly on others and some claim him a bad king. I would not be as he was.'

De Burgh agreed and wondered about his own position. He must keep Henry with him, and resentment was stirring all the time. He felt a continual unease now des Roches was back in England. That he was influencing Henry, there was no doubt, for Rivallis, des Roche's man, had been made the treasurer of the King's household.

Henry was aware that there were undercurrents at court, but chose to ignore them. He made one of his impulsive decisions. It would please his justiciar; they would spend time together away from the intrigues.

'We will make a pilgrimage to your county of Norfolk. I would visit the Holy Rood at Bromholm Priory again.'

Henry prayed for guidance in front of the fragment of the True Cross. He must not be a tyrant like his father. He longed to be honoured as a man who was full of saintly deeds and thoughts; he wanted to build soaring churches to show his devotion; and he wanted the pope to approve. But then there was the world clamouring for him to be a strong, decisive ruler.

Early July in Norfolk was clear and sunny, the huge skies cloudless over the flat land and the sea stretching forever. Henry was happy in de Burgh's company, amused by his young daughter, pleased to be with the family. The manor house was comfortable, a generous table, a good chamber to sleep in. A footbridge meant he could walk peacefully to the riverside church for daily mass and gaze at the arcade of slender pillars supporting the elegant carved arches. Above these rose another arcade with tall, narrow windows set between each arch. He felt such exultation for the beautiful simplicity.

The next day, before they would ride to Walsingham and then south to Woodstock, Hubert decided to speak. His sense of foreboding was troubling. He knew des Roches was determined to bring him down. He wanted to make sure of Henry. They sat in the hall, men standing close by. His family were near. A source of strength, for what he was to ask was risky, even desperate.

'I would ask you, my lord, to take an oath, a personal oath, that all the charters you have granted me and my wife be maintained for life.'

Henry looked at his most trusted and oldest counsellor, who had been with him since childhood, and a great rush of affection came over him.

'I have given you many manors and their lands. You have much private profit. Why, I have made you Earl of Kent to help your family rise! You would have me swear to keep you forever in all your ennoblement and riches?'

He smiled at his host, and made a sweeping gesture around the hall. 'I will swear.' His voice almost exultant.

De Burgh looked at him hard. 'You will swear on the pain of excommunication if you do violate this oath.'

Henry, at his most pious, nodded.

'I will swear on the Holy Book.' A bible, bound with a vellum cover decorated with gilt and gold, was handed to him, and Henry put his hand on the book and swore the oath, and kissed the bible.

De Burgh watched as he did so and the clerks wrote that the King had made an oath on the Gospels: ...*all grants, gifts and observe all the charters which he has granted and has made God his surety...*

'I would make an oath too: one that prevents you from ever going back on your word.'

Henry listened as Hubert explained. He knew was being bound tightly by de Burgh, but de Burgh was one of those who had given him his kingdom, helped him to rule. Henry began to feel nervous; there were no other great men in the hall. But he did not hesitate, he would accept de Burgh's oath.

Hubert de Burgh has made an oath by the King's order that if the King, of his free will or at any suggestion of any, should desire to invalidate the charters, he, the said Hubert, will take care to impede that purpose and do all in his power to preserve the said charters inviolate.

Woodstock stood bathed in summer warmth, harvests safely gathered, hay barns full and fruit ripening. The kitchen was busy with salting and preserving meat and vegetables. The smithy rang out as nails and horseshoes were made for the stables. The buttery was well stocked with barrels of new wine. In the almonry the friar was quietly dispensing money to a family with a sick child. All was prosperous and should have been peaceful.

The chief steward, anxious and alarmed, hesitated at the door of the King's chamber for the shouts and clamour had been raging for over ten minutes. The King's voice was harsh, his words stuttering in a fury.

'I have documents here which show that you have encouraged... Encouraged!' An emphatic thump on the table. 'People make moves, begin riots, yes riots, indeed riots, against the Italian clerks. You are responsible, you! De Burgh, I remind you we must provide for them. They are the beneficiaries sent by the pope.'

'I do not believe it is right for England.'

'I do not believe you are right for England! You lost the Poitou and did nothing to help our campaign to take the lands there. And the money we had, you spent on the siege of Bedford! You wanted that above all else.' Henry was flailing, his face in a dark fury. 'I have raised my sword to you once before, when I thought you a traitor and by

Saint Edward, I will do so again.'

Hubert glared at Henry and said in a voice rough with emotion, 'You are so innocent, whoever turns your head with promises of this and promises of that, you follow them. A boy king once, and still not sensible after more than ten years. I would box your ears for you.' The words hung in the air. De Burgh defended their rude message with an accusation. 'Your words are base. Harmful and base. I am no traitor.'

Henry growled back, 'You are no justiciar!' A long pause and then ice in his voice. 'And now I demand that you make an account for everything that you have done since my father's death.' A few second's grim silence and he began again. 'You will be held to your record. And that record will include all your actions that have been against me.'

De Burgh's temper broke. 'You treat me like some cur and push me to the edge. I have upheld you at all times, but now–' He made a sound of disgust, turned his back on the king and rode out of Woodstock at a gallop to London, to Merton Priory, to necessary sanctuary.

October: Richard Earl of Cornwall and Poitou to Henry III
We have received the charge of Hubert de Burgh.
January: Gregory IX to Henry III
The oaths you have taken not to recall your grants are null and void.

XII

France and England, 1233–1240

Aunis-Saintonge-Poitou-Angoumois-Limousin-Berry-Auvergne. A great territory that straddled from the western coast to the foothills of the rugged mountains in the east, and controlled the roads that ran from north to south, and from the west to the centre. All fought over and troubled, but now peaceful and prosperous. It was easy for Isabella and Hugh to ride from town to town. They knew that the independent lords of Barbezieux, Aubeterre, Niort and Confolens might toy with the idea of supporting the English against them, but it did not last. Why would it when everything worked so well? Everyone was happy with the way they made the money flow. No need for France or England to be involved here at all. This was how it should be. And they were building, thinking about their spiritual lives and their need for some inner peace. A convent in Angoulême. A Cistercian abbey at Valence to be the burial grounds for all Lusignans. But also making sure of strong castles with formidable defences: thick walls, ramparts, sturdy keeps and round towers added to overlook plains, rivers and valleys. And Isabella's name given to the best: the tower of Isabella of Angoulême.

She sat now in Lusignan, watching the youngest children who were everywhere. Servants had set green pottery jugs and dishes on the table, dogs scratched and bit at fleas, a kitchen boy yawned as he carried in a big round of bread. Emilde chided Guy who was teasing Geoffrey and took them both by the hand insisting it was time for their lesson; they must learn their words for the day by heart and recite them properly by the end of the week.

'You like the story,' she reminded them, 'about the giant who is mighty and strong.'

Guy shouted, 'And fully thirty feet long.' Agnes, Alice and Isabelle looked demure and a little smug as they followed them out, chanting softly, *her visage white as lily flower;* they knew their lines from the poem.

Mathilde sat down heavily next to William who was tracing letters in the dust on the table. He knew his letters and more, his mother had promised him lessons in Latin. He was bored with the poems that Emilde taught them. Mathilde looked crossly at Marguerite who was fidgeting.

'Keep still,' she grumbled as Marguerite nearly fell off the bench. Isabella chided the two of them.

'Have you eaten? No? Yes? Well, leave the table and go outside. See if Hugh and Aymer are home from their ride.' They went without a backward glance, William pushing Marguerite through the open door and shouting, 'Where is everyone?'

'I would talk with you.' Mathilde looked drawn. She had aged these last few years, the constant upheaval as the household moved from Lusignan to Angoulême, to Merpins and back again might suit this large energetic family, but it did not suit her.

'I am listening.' Isabella gave her a keen look. Mathilde spread her hands on the table.

'I am to take vows and live elsewhere, quietly. In the convent of the Cordeliers in Angoulême. Not as a cloistered woman, but as someone who desires to go where there is solace. No, do not speak.' She held up a hand. 'I am decided. And content. But I must arrange for my lands and dower lands in some way.'

Isabella was thoughtful.

'My daughter Eleanor has done the same. Did I tell you? But she lives in her estates, widowed and as chaste as nun, a vowess looking for no husband; a woman of some wealth whose dowry lands will not be disputed now. Indeed I think she feared des Roches would marry her off to some Poitevin and wanted none of his plans.'

Isabella remembered how des Roches had made sure of the plan that she should sail away from England. Seeing her to the port and smiling as he watched her board the ship that just happened to be ready for such a voyage. It was what she had wanted anyway. She shrugged. They had both won.

Mathilde saw the shrug and was wary. She was not to be dismissed so casually. She must be clear.

'I will of course need an annuity for my lands.' Mathilde folded her hands in her lap and was looking very proper but gazing cold and hard at Isabella. Isabella laughed, her eyes bright with amusement.

'Lands that are to be assigned to me?'

'And I suppose to Hugh. But an annuity from you both,' Mathilde put her head on one side and slyly continued, 'something I know you can both afford. I am diligent and I know that both of you,' she repeated, 'can afford to pay me. An annuity.'

Isabella put her arm around her.

'Hush, there, there, hush. Of course, and you will have it. We will arrange all. Do not fret.'

It was remarkably easy to make everyone happy. At the end of August a charter was drawn up and the Archbishop of Tours confirmed it.

Agreement between Mathilde, daughter of Vulgrin, once Count of Angoulême and widow of Hugh, once Count of La Marche. And Isabella, Queen of England, Countess of La Marche and Angoulême. The former Countess abandoning to Isabella and her husband, Hugh Lusignan, her rights in the County of La Marche and her dower right, in return for an annuity.

Isabella insisted that she help with the arrangements for the departure to the convent. She packed Mathilde's baggage chest with small packets of herbs, for she knew how her head throbbed and how her eyes could not bear the daylight. She believed the potions helped. She also believed that once living quietly and not forever looking for something to complain about, Mathilde's headaches would stop.

'She must visit us for the feast days if she wishes to.'

Isabella felt generous and she folded a length of fine linen into the chest before adding an old winter cloak of long plush. Grubby and water-stained it needed to be brushed and made clean by shearing the nap. Agnes would work hard on this to make it ready for three or more seasons. And here was a big square of perse, dark blue wool, some striped silk, three pairs of cloth shoes for the house. Two pillows and three pillowslips with drawn thread work, five towels and a pair of heavy linen sheets embroidered with her initials in red. A quilt with a pattern of crosses. A prie-dieu. Two green Saintonge jugs. Heavy damask bed hangings. A small book chest. Mathilde might be going to a convent for the tranquillity, but she needed three carts, five chests and six great horses to take her there. And an escort of two knights.

The priest blessed the collection of carts and wagons and the farewells were brief for Mathilde was anxious to be away. Isabella watched her covered wagon bump down the hill and hoped she would have an easy journey.

Orders were briskly given and the chamber where Mathilde had spent most of her time was aired, swept, the walls dampened and new white lime wash painted on.

'Agnes, Alice and Isabelle can sleep in here now.' She surveyed the room and called the carpenter to make new beds, servants to make new rush mats to be strewn with herbs, the maids to cut and hem new sheets from the store of linen. Everything to be new and fresh for her daughters.

Royal messengers were riding throughout France, every road busy in all directions. A young squire arrived, his journey from Paris to the Archbishop of Tours, then the cathedral in Poitiers, and now Lusignan. All the great and powerful were informed: King Louis was to marry Margaret of Provence at the end of May, in the fine cathedral at Sens, to the east of Paris.

'A good match.' Hugh sprawled in a chair, Isabella packing again, this time for their journey north. Maids brought in their clothes and sprigs of lavender to place in the chest. Isabella had chosen her dress of deep ochre and scarlet, the colours of Angoulême. She had made sure that Agnes provided good wool cloth for Hugh's tunic and surcoat of rich dark brown, flashed with blue and to be worn with a cross belt. New gold buckles. Fine knitted hose and buffed leather shoes.

'She is a clever woman, Blanche,' he continued grudgingly. 'Pulled the Provence into the centre with her.'

'Marriage one day, crowned the next. Margaret is how old? Thirteen? I was twelve when I was married and crowned. But her husband is twenty. As you say, a good match.' She shut the lid of the chest with a slam.

The wedding was magnificent. The money poured into the town, on barges, in carts, for there was much to spend it on. Coronation jewels, a filigree crown and a gold loving cup. A present of a sable cloak with fifteen precious buttons. A three-day feast. Scaffolding and platforms built for the banquet tables. Silken damask seats set in an arbour to shade the king and queen while they watched the entertainment of jousting, tumblers, minstrels and juggling. Trumpeters for each dish as it arrived at the table. Louis, in gold mail, riding to meet his bride. Margaret in a heavy silk gown of dusty pink and silver, her cloak trimmed in ermine. And all the men of France bending their knee and pledging allegiance.

'She speaks Provençal and is learning the language of the

Île de France,' Isabella observed. 'Well-schooled.'

'She has sisters,' teased Hugh. 'Perhaps we could find a bride for Young Hugh among them.'

Isabella was unsmiling. 'He was betrothed to one much finer, the king's sister Isabelle.'

Hugh nodded. It had been a good treaty that made that arrangement. Isabella gave an exasperated sigh.

'But she refuses to obey the betrothal and refuses to marry; a young girl of the greatest piety, all are full of her praises and of course she is supported by her mother. I think Blanche is pleased to deny us that alliance.'

Another sigh, another reproach.

'In fact she is very pleased to deny us *all* alliances! I know, I know.' She put up a hand to Hugh's protest. 'So that betrothal broken. And I cannot bear that he was once matched with Jeanne of Toulouse, we could have made a strong link. But that quickly came to nothing too.'

Hugh continued her sentences, he had heard this many times.

'For now Jeanne is to be married to the brother of Louis, Alphonse. Alphonse who was to marry our Isabelle!' And he drew a circle in the air, 'Around we all go.'

Isabella reprimanded his attempt at humour.

'These royal unions were a way of keeping the Capets with us and now I see stresses and strains.'

Hugh reached out and drew her to him. 'Isabella, we may have to look north of the Loire. Will we do that?'

She considered and smiled, kissing him lightly. 'There may be some merit there. I would not see that Spanish queen and her son gain everything so easily.'

The Palace of Westminster

A more settled court, a calmer palace. Clerks, stewards, household knights, valets, grooms, pages and even the laundry maids were all too aware of what had happened since the Bishop of Winchester had returned. Everything he did was underpinned by a spirit of revenge. There had been three years of a triumphant des Roches who had attacked de Burgh, had hounded him, harried him and could not rest it seemed unless he pursued his vendetta against him.

'He persecutes anyone who might challenge him,' said de Burgh, dragged out of sanctuary and giving up all he had gained.

'He puts Poitevins in every state office possible, and tightens his grip on the court and government,' said grumbling courtiers who were arbitrarily dismissed.

'And influences the king. Leads him on,' wrote the chroniclers.

But not everyone was controlled and coerced. One who was full of defiance was Richard Marshal; he had risen in the land, to become the leader of the barons, for the old Earl of Chester had died. A man who remembered King John, who had seen Henry crowned as a boy, a fighter from forty years ago who continued loyal in service, leading the campaign in Brittany.

'He did his best,' even Henry admitted. 'He was determined, but we could not press hard enough. He supported me well. Men do not always support me when I have need of them.'

Richard Marshal, the new Earl of Pembroke, back from France, and sure of one thing: he did not want to support Henry surrounded by Poitevins; he wanted nothing of them and said so with great force. He left court and refused any summons to attend.

'If you want those foreign men about you as advisors and counsellors, then so be it. Call me a traitor, I worry not. I am mindful you may have plans to seize me as you seized de Burgh.' And he rode away, careless of being branded treacherous.

*

A messy, chaotic time followed. Des Roches insisting that Marshal must be compelled to submit. Everyone else calling on Henry to make peace with Richard Marshal. Henry shuddered as he heard again the insolent voice of des Roches scoffing at Magna Carta, taunting him, his presence looming over everything. Henry sank into himself, weighed down in confusion.

'I am tired of these men who would dominate me. My entire life these men have told me what to do.'

He saw them all. William Marshal, long gone but wise, calm and making sure that des Roches did not grab him. De Burgh explaining, cautious, but gradually seeking higher and higher status and trying to bind Henry to him forever. The papal legates offering blessings and paying debts for the Crown, but always turning back to Rome. Archbishops who counselled and reprimanded. Older men, who hoped to win him round, keep him tractable, promising to guide him and support him. And two were such enemies he could not have them both at court, and he realised he could not completely trust both either.

'I need time to think; a pilgrimage again – Bromholm to pray once more before the Holy Cross.'

And he was much consoled in Norfolk, happy to return to Westminster only to arrive and be admonished by Edmund of Abingdon. The new Archbishop of Canterbury sat in his carved chair and waited for Henry to approach, kneel and kiss the ring on his right hand. Henry, full of devotion, listened to his gentle words. But the words became harsher and Edmund frowned as he listed grievances. Henry began to protest, he was full of goodness and mercy, he had prayed for grace.

'The problem, I will not waste time, the problem always comes back to the Bishop of Winchester and his mischief making ways.'

More protests.

But the archbishop frowned again and dismissed these declarations. 'He is quite worthless to you or the court. He would persuade you that you are above the law. It was through his counsels that your father lost the love of his subjects. We have struggled long enough with the men who are strangers in England.'

Henry began more objections, but the archbishop interrupted him.

'You must dismiss him from this place. There will be no peace until you do.'

Henry struggled with this. How could he rid himself of Peter des Roches, Bishop of Winchester? Edmund gestured around the hall, bishops and barons watching, waiting for some sign that Henry would do what was asked. Henry, who did not enjoy battles or raised voices, but who could burst into a rage and be vindictive. Who could also be so devout, so meek. Would he explode? Or fall to his knees?

Edmund spoke with great clarity.

'And if you do not then I will excommunicate you.'

And a king who was so often seen as weak, only a boy, suddenly became resolute.

'And I will' Henry was insistent that the clerks record his intent. 'Look, I will. I will order Peter des Roches to go back to Winchester and stay there or leave England. I will tell him to meddle no more. I will tell all those Poitevins to remove themselves.'

But the man who had wanted them gone, who wanted to see England free of the men from the Poitou, had died in Ireland: Richard Marshal, injured while taking back castles there that had fallen to his enemies, defending his estates. But he was outnumbered, betrayed, captured and wounded. Dead. Again Henry was mourning the death of a Marshal son. He prayed into the night: 'Bless thy Holy Name for all thy servants departed this life in thy faith and

152

fear, beseeching thee to give us grace.'

The soldier bishop, Peter des Roches, who had taught the king to pray, who had arranged tutors to teach him to ride, to fight, to read and to write, who had held him in his keeping as a boy, who knew him first as Henry of Winchester sat heavily in his beloved Hampshire garden. His face more weary than it had ever been, devastated more than he dare admit by the total loss of the king's confidence. The king had yielded and given him up.

'I am not wanted here. I find no comfort even in this place, Winchester, where Henry was born, where he was given into my charge. Given to me by his father and then again by William Marshal. His mother bade him goodbye in this garden. Isabella, so sharp tongued, so interfering!'

Des Roches squinted at the sky, he could see her now, hear her voice. Well, he had escorted her to the ship that had taken her back to France and there she had stayed. But not quietly. He made a wry face and returned to thinking about Henry.

'He makes a great deal of fuss about how this man is the one to follow, and then this one or that one. And those who were his strength are pushed to one side.'

'The question is, what to do now?'

'His anger may pass, I can hope for that. You are safe, de Maulay, in your castle at Devizes, how clever and tactful you have been with the king! Or has his brother looked out for you all this time? After all you kept him safe at Corfe when he was young.'

De Maulay smiled and made a mock bow; the fall of des Roches had not harmed him in any way.

Des Roches frowned into the sun, twisting his bishop's ring and folding his hands into his lap.

'I will leave England and turn to Europe, I have money, I have military experience, I have friends there who can use my help.'

Henry had new friends, new advisers, but he was nervous; being seen to be independent was difficult. Conflict would surely vanish as his father's men would vanish? They had been the problem, he reassured himself. He comforted his anxiety with another mass, to be humble before God, to ask for forgiveness if he had been rash.

And for one man came the kiss of peace, the man who had been with him and with his father, who had held Chinon, fought a great naval battle against the French, but always doubted it possible to recover the lost lands in France. Hubert de Burgh standing calmly in front of Henry and being welcomed back to favour, but not to power, not to position.

'I will have no justiciar again, but you will be remembered always as my great minister who steered me through so many treacherous times. Beloved and faithful.'

De Burgh had been glad to retire from court and begin a life less disturbed by a king who was not consistent in his dealings. A king who had listened to des Roches and pursued him relentlessly with charges and accusations, a king who had cast him into prison. A king from whom he had to flee, to escape rough justice. The shifting sands of royal favour were tricky. Henry watched him walking slowly away and straightened his shoulders, glad to have a free hand; he could manage the government now, could he not?

So those decades were gone, nearly two decades of De Burgh and des Roches. Henry strode into the Palace at Westminster, Richard at his side, up from Wallingford where he lived with his new wife. Henry grinned at him. He felt in command, the turbulence of the last few years had died down at last.

In the Great Hall, they both threw off their cloaks despite the February chill and Henry peered over the accounts, searching for funds, money. His finger moved down the columns and he was adding under his breath. Two clerks stood by, anxious.

Richard looked at him and reached for a scroll. 'You live well enough day to day. Are you worried about the future? No Justiciar, a new Archbishop. Have you found some fine in there you can ask from Bishop Peter? He had his triumph! A long time he waited for it too, but a short-lived victory.' Richard wondered, for he had not liked des Roches. 'Yet you gave him permission to cross the sea, to leave the country.' He dropped the scroll. 'But it seems he did us some good service when in exile.'

Henry thrust the parchments at the clerks and spread his arms wide. 'I have to find 30,000 marks for Isabelle's dowry. You know very well that our sister is to marry Frederick the Holy Roman Emperor! Not only a dowry, but new clothes and more for her and her retinue.'

Ambassadors from the Emperor's court had arrived, letters sealed in gold, written by Frederick who declared he wanted Isabelle as his third wife. And Isabelle brought to be interviewed from the Tower of London where she lived in the royal apartments. She was declared very beautiful, very poised, a well-educated young woman with a fine voice, low and gentle. And they had doffed their hats and called out *Vivat imperatrix! Vivat!*

'I have written to Joan for I am keen to share this news. She will greatly rejoice that there will be a marriage for our beloved sister. Our sister is betrothed to the emperor.' Henry was almost prancing around the table.

'And who persuaded Frederick that our sister was such a good match?' Richard caught Henry by the arm as he came past. 'I do believe des Roches had some personal ties to the emperor. I do believe he may have called on him to find favour with our sister.'

But Henry was not really listening. Des Roches had gone.

'Frederick says he will take her as his wife and keep her with all the dignity of an emperor. And the pope advises it is a proper thing for us to agree.'

He had great hopes for this new alliance: help, more help against the French. This marriage could be a way, a stepping stone to recover Anjou, Normandy and the Poitou. There was no doubt that betrothals, marriages, pacts and understandings were on everyone's mind. Children were growing up, bonds had to be forged or strengthened and this is where they were put into play. Another sister ready for marriage.

'It will be worth asking for a tax or two to help with the dowry.'

Henry was eager. Surely this could be done. All it needed was consent from the council.

Irritation greeted his request and a voice called out, 'Why do you resort to taxes on knights' fees and clergy income when you have rents and farms? Should not your sister's expenses come from those sources?'

Henry was jolted. He began to stammer. The pope would act as a guarantor. It would not become his sister to go to her husband looking impoverished. She must be a symbol of England's strength. The council frowned. Money given to Henry seemed to trickle away. He was over fond of fine things. Henry sulked and chewed his lip. He must not rage like his father had done. He gripped the edge of the table.

'It will be paid in instalments, over two years, so the sum must be possible.'

The council set a condition: there would be no precedence. There would not be, he assured them. And the tax was collected.

'Although it is the very devil to extract and account for,' grumbled the clerks and sheriffs.

The first instalment was heaped into dowry chests: 3,000 marks in silver pennies; thousands of sterling silver pennies. The marriage contract signed.

'My dearest Isabelle.'

And there she stood: tall, intelligent and gracious. Twenty-one, not a child, not a bride only just arrived at the age for marriage. A beautiful young woman. Henry heaped on her everything he could to mark her transformation from princess to empress.

A chapel service of gold and silver plate. Her private chapel to be provided with priest's vestments from a bolt of Spanish cloth of gold, and from Genoa, a matching cloth to hang before the altar. A fine bed of silk and muslin drapes. Three dresses of gold silk: one to be her wedding dress. Bed covers of sheer woollen cloth in dark carmine red. She held up a robe dyed to match, pretty little sleeves and lined in minever.

'It will be good for the bedchamber. And see, I have a long mantle to wrap myself in to keep out the cold draughts.'

'And something for the long journey ahead. You will ride for days.' Henry gestured to the padded jackets and short waxed rain cloaks. Her old nursemaid and young maid bustled about sorting these into sizes. A practical pile of clothes.

'Margaret and Kathrine have been busy and packed chest after chest of garments and goods. And Margaret knows me well from when I was a mite. I am pleased to have her with me at all times.' Affectionate smiles and nods.

A new livery for her household servants: plenty of stout linen and wool, red and blue and brown cloth marking them for what they were. A horse marshal for the forty-four horses being sent with the party. Cooks, tailors, maids and washerwomen, with the blue cloth of their trade but trimmed with lamb fur; better than the washerwomen who served Henry's household.

'You must be shown to have the clothing of an empress. You must be magnificent!'

Now Henry called the goldsmith in and the man unwrapped a crown engraved with images of four English kings, martyrs and confessors chosen by Henry.

'To take care of your soul, here is Saint Edward the Confessor. He has my devotion and will have yours as he is the saint who guards us all: me, Richard, Joan, you and Eleanor.'

In the first week of May after a service in Westminster Abbey, Henry, Isabelle, the Archbishop of Cologne and the other escorts and messengers sent by Frederick set out for the coast. Their journey took them to Rochester and Faversham and then to Canterbury. Henry and Isabelle knelt and prayed before the shrine of Thomas Becket.

'Fifteen years since his body was translated to this shrine. I led the procession, a newly crowned king. After my second coronation in Westminster. There was no Crown of England in Gloucester, only my mother's gold circlet. But you have a fine crown, Isabelle, to keep you safe.'

Then all arrived at Sandwich, and thousands of knights gathered on the shore near the port, the high tide up to the town walls and the cogs bobbing and pulling at anchors and ropes.

Isabelle and Henry embraced and wept. She said goodbye to her bother and he watched her sail away to Antwerp, his face wet with tears. From here, sitting at the side of the old William Marshal, he had watched the victorious sea battle, the Battle of Sandwich, led so brilliantly by de Burgh.

'Richard, it is good to be married?'

Henry was restless. He missed Isabelle, his brother was often busy with his own new family and sometimes they were estranged, hot heads clashing and each thinking the other not as great as they thought they were. But now there was a sense of security and he was beginning to recognise that he had needs beyond the spiritual. They sat together in the mews in the Tower of London. Henry had a newly trained goshawk from the lands to the east and could not stop admiring it. It had fierce yellow-orange eyes and a pattern of wonderful barring on its breast. He wondered how Isabelle's merlin had managed the journey to her new home.

Ships were arriving up the Thames and one of these was bringing a present from Frederick: three leopards to match the ones on the shield of England. He was also sending back all Isabelle's household except Margaret and Kathrine. Henry felt sad for his sister, so far away. He bit his lip. If he had a wife from a far country he would let her have her friends and family about her. Had not his mother also been friendless in England? He remembered her standing lonely in castle rooms, forever looking through windows to a world where she could not find her place.

Richard snorted with laughter and punched Henry's shoulder.

'It is indeed good to be married and not just for the marriage bed! Although that is a realm where, if your wife knows how to make you happy, every man can be a king.'

'And you enjoy more than that? Companionship, devotion to each other and to the church?'

'Oh yes.' Said lightly, but then more seriously, 'It is time for you to be thinking of having sons, an heir: a royal family. Twenty-eight! The oldest of us and the only one not married.'

'Eleanor is not married.'

'But she was and I know, we all know, she has taken vows of chastity. That is all well and good; perhaps for her it is the best way of life. I do wonder if one day she might be persuaded to make another alliance. But you, Henry, still pure. Very noble indeed. Why any princess or fine lady would be happy to alter your state of innocence!'

And so Henry looked across the Channel, to Ponthieu, at the mouth of the Somme. A wealthy heiress, a great-granddaughter of a French king: Joan, Countess of Ponthieu in her own right. A county that bordered Normandy and what better place to be, to use her wealth to launch an attack, to re-establish English rule and control Normandy again. But her father had fought with John against Philippe Augustus, been captured, exiled and only allowed to return with conditions hanging over him. One of these was to promise that he would not marry off either of his two eldest daughters without the permission of the King of France. Blanche knew this and moved swiftly: this was not to be allowed. She gave no permission for the marriage and appealed to the pope not to grant the dispensation Henry sought.

'The pope refuses to help me!' Henry was astounded, 'I have already paid him for this dispensation and he says no.'

'It seems that Blanche has called checkmate as you search for a queen. She is very clever at making sure of alliances – or denying them,' Richard said with some admiration.

'Perhaps I will follow what she has arranged for her own son. If it is good enough for Louis...' And Henry, looking at the French court, had another idea.

'The Capets looked to Provence for a wife. A splendid move for them, their power to the south grows all the time. Good not to have everything centred on Paris. They say his wife is very beautiful.'

He counted on his fingers. 'And she has the most beautiful devout sisters: Eleanor, Sanchia and Beatrice.'

'Would you have Louis as your brother-in-law?' Richard mused. But Henry was seized with determination. He wrote letters, many letters eager for approval and acceptance. The first asked for a large dowry sum and then he wrote another asking for less. The scribes recalled once more and now another letter. Each time the sum reduced until with careless generosity he wrote that he would marry Eleanor without a dowry, if necessary, for he had heard so much about her charm, her grace and her beauty.

The King to his beloved Beatrice, Countess of Provence, greetings with sincere love...

We have revealed our will in every way, to marry your daughter Eleanor...

We therefore, with the Lord authorising, make known to you that wishing to take your aforesaid daughter, given to us as ours, to wife, we will send you our ambassadors who will meet you in Savoy, and your said daughter and your friends. And to deliver your daughter to our aforesaid ambassadors which will bring her, honourably as is fitting, to us.

XIII

France, 1235–1240

Yolande of Brittany felt very fortunate. She was sixteen and travelling through the countryside in some style. Her horse, the most beautiful sorrel palfrey, was a present from her father, and from her brother a new cordovan leather saddle embroidered with white and gold. It was luxurious, padded and comfortable. The two carts that were rumbling along towards the end of the trail of riders, knights and servants, had all her belongings packed tight. After nine years of moving from household to household, promises made and then broken, she was at last making her way to a husband and a home.

As the entourage wound through the lanes and tracks, Yolande thought about how her fortunes had changed over and over again. Ten years ago she had been ordered to live away from her family with guardians: very grand guardians – an Archbishop of Reims, King Louis's uncle, Phillipe Hurepel; her own uncle, Robert Dreux. Her ambitious father always quarrelling and fighting with Blanche over his choice of husband for her. He wanted to marry her to his English ally, the young King Henry, and a contract was sealed. Blanche lost no time insisting that this marriage was impossible and forced her father to change the betrothal to one where Blanche could be in control. So she had been betrothed to John of France, Count of Anjou and Maine, Blanche's son. A year older than her. She had been schooled by her guardians and governesses to think of herself as a royal countess. They kept her close in their care. Peter of Brittany was not to use her as one of his chess pieces. She was not to be surrendered to her father until John reached

162

fourteen and she could be married to him: the age of consent under canon law. And then John had died as he reached his thirteenth year. And so her father made more plans.

'You are well, Yolande? No fevers? Nothing for anyone to be concerned about? Good, good.' Peter rubbed his hands together as he sized up his daughter. She always looked cheerful and had both the charming nature of her mother and her heart-shaped face. 'I would not want you to be weak and succumb to the bad air as did your fiancé.'

Yolande looked away. She had met John so rarely and he was always shy with her. Her hope of living alongside him in Paris had kept her daydreams alive as she obeyed orders from this guardian or that. But now he was dead there was no need for her to be with a guardian. And, in fact, two of them were also dead. She shivered at her morbid thoughts, quickly said a prayer and crossed herself. She turned to face her father. He was in charge again but not to be trusted. She had heard too much from the stories that everyone told about him to regard this man with anything but a suspicious eye.

'I have made a new friend of an old enemy,' he said cheerfully, 'and you will benefit from this. Of course you will.'

Yolande tried to stay calm. She clenched her hands. 'I am listening, Father.'

'An escort will take you to the Abbey Prémontré. You will wait there for the Count of Champagne. He is to marry you. You are to marry him. It is an excellent match, puts an end to the troubles between us.'

Yolande felt her stomach lurch. The Count of Champagne was twenty years older, had already been married twice, and was fat, puffing as he walked. Full of sighs and laments, a blundering fool of a man.

'I have the interests of Brittany to put first, Yolande, and for him it... well, for him, it gives him fewer enemies and safer lands.' A brusque tone and he turned on his heel.

She rode with the escort into the place called Valsecret near Château-Thierry, where Thibault lived. A large clearing in the thick forest, sloping wooded hills on either side of a collection of buildings: two cloisters, a dormitory and refectory; the abbey church all very peaceful. She sat waiting, almost sick with apprehension.

But the Count of Champagne never arrived. Messengers rode after him as he trotted heavily towards the Abbey. They handed him a letter. A letter full of warning.

> *The King now learns that you have agreed with the Count of Brittany to wed his daughter. The King bids you to renounce this plan lest you lose all you possess in the realm of France. And you must know that the Count of Brittany has worked more ill upon the King of France than any man alive. Would you outrage the Queen and her son?*

No hesitation. Thibault turned around and rode home.

Yolande rode home too, her heart singing, her face alight with relief. Her father was casual.

'I had hoped for some help there, but I have other plans stirring too. For a moment it seemed Henry of England might be interested once more, but he is looking elsewhere. The Hersent queen keeps everything as she likes it. We will have to think again.'

The Count of Champagne had to think again too. He sighed over the poem he had written to explain his attempt at marriage to Yolande. The words said it all. *Why should she marry a suitor so far away? Her father had the heart of a traitor and the face of a thief. He would save her from exile to a cold desolate England.* Perhaps he could set it to music? How he hoped Blanche would hear it recited in one of her castle halls and understand. But she proved to be impervious. Before the year was out he was bustled into a marriage with the daughter of someone close to the Capets. Blanche made sure of that.

Thibault decided, 'I am to take the cross, a prudent idea to assume the cross. To be a crusader will surely make Blanche and Louis look on me with kinder, more forgiving eyes.'

His young pregnant wife smiled prettily and he patted her shoulder.

'But no expedition to the Holy Land for me until I journey to Navarre to claim my inheritance. You will be Queen of Navarre, Margaret, and I will be the most powerful baron in France.'

He looked forward to a kingdom tucked under his belt; he would be richer, happier, more secure.

Peter Dreux also thought security was important, and as his son was only two years away from becoming the Count of Brittany, it was time to find him a wife. He had not managed to marry Yolande to Thibault, but Thibault had a daughter, another Blanche. *The name of the Lady who dost weave such love in me*, wrote Thibault. More sighs.

Father and son skirted Paris in the middle of the morning, riding in from the south before the August sun grew too high in the sky. It had been a long dusty journey from Brittany. The last night in Orleans and now Château-Thierry would be reached by nightfall. In the distance the huge bastion towers built into the high city walls of the capital, Paris. Closer to their track, marshes and swampy ground, hovels and poor villages of thatch. They would not linger here.

'Where the river and the wall meet, there is a tower.' Peter admired the fortification but had no desire to visit the Île de Paris while he was intent on this new alliance. John Rufus of Brittany at his side, a boy who had grown into someone very like his father. They spurred on their horses to the town on the banks of the River Marne, where the Counts of Champagne had made a grand and comfortable seat for themselves.

The two of them sat with Thibault in the richly furnished hall of his castle. Deeply carved chests of walnut wood, coloured brocades and silks from Navarre draped everywhere. Silver gleaming on the long white linen cloth and Thibault lounging in a high-backed canopied chair. The meal had been cleared away and only beakers of the local wine were left, very pale pink, light and easy to drink down with gusto. He was beaming as he pushed himself back from the table that stood proud on its dais.

'She is fair, is she not?'

And his nine-year-old daughter was fair, with plump cheeks, all dimples and smiles. Her blonde plaits hung heavy on either side of her face and she wore a hyacinth-blue tunic and skirt trimmed with pearls. Her constant companion, Alba – a small, white, long-haired dog, snuffled by her side. She was a good bride for the fifteen-year-old boy who watched her with an acquisitive stare.

'And the pope will grant a dispensation for this marriage! We need not be concerned about that.' And casually he flung an arm about his wife who had taken Blanche by the hand and brought her to the table to be sat next to her father. Thibault looked at her and then at Peter Dreux. Boastful and expansive.

'And I am granting the right of succession to Navarre as her marriage portion.'

A standard reply.

'We will grant her one-third of Brittany.' Peter and John both bowed slightly towards Blanche who bobbed her head.

'An agreement here which serves us all well.'

January 1236 and the marriage ceremony was over. Blanche pulled the hood of her thick wool cape up over her head and holding hands with John Rufus of Brittany walked from the chapel into the snow. His father grinned at him and he grinned back. Their retinue was ready to travel back to Nantes, horses shaking their heads and the men mounted already. Thibault kissed his daughter goodbye. Margaret, pregnant again, longing for a son, squeezed her hand and murmured a prayer. Blanche's maids helped her into a low cart with Alba, all wrapped up together in a quilt. Then they squashed in next to her. Thibault watched the entourage make its way to the road and reflected that this alliance must surely bring about some peace for him.

But Louis was not pleased; this did not suit at all. It was almost as if those two were intent on a new league against him. He threatened to lay siege to the Count of Champagne, but Blanche stepped in. 'He must renew his oath of fealty at court in Paris.'

And Thibault, portly and sweating, dressed in his finest silks, crocus yellow and azure blue trimmed with ermine, arrived to bend his knee to Louis and Blanche. He readied himself to enter the room where he knew they would be sitting. He coughed, he shifted from foot to foot, and he took a step forward, whereupon the king's brother Robert declared, 'I have never liked you', and flung a basin of curdled milk over him.

'At no time before has an earl or baron or count been so dealt with!' Blanche was furious and aghast at the poor man all dripping with the sour milk. 'That boy, son of mine or not, will be locked up for such a poor jest.'

Thibault crept away from Paris, and thought that his own kingdom might be the better place to live. He sang no more songs of love for Blanche, vowing, 'Never, please God, shall I go against you or yours.'

'He was doused with milk! With sour curds of milk!' Isabella rocked with laughter as the tale that had spread out across the countryside reached Angoulême.

167

'You think it funny, Agnes? You must do.'

Agnes's face twitched as she supressed a smile. 'I can't help wondering about the fine clothes and how to make them clean again. Curdled milk would be very greasy. And the rancid smell, so difficult to get everything fresh.'

'Oh, Agnes, always so practical, and for that I love you.' Isabella patted her friend's arm.

They were working together in a small chamber in the new tower. Maids had swept it clean and a fire was ready to be lit. The bedstead had been carried up that morning and the carpenter had carved the headboard with the arms of Lusignan and Brittany. The oak was polished with beeswax and it was golden in the spring sunshine that flooded the room. Agnes was testing that the bed curtains ran smooth. Isabella unfolded the quilt, two sorts of silk in a checkboard pattern, well-made and richly stitched with threads of gold. She put a pillow on the bolster and pulled a linen sheet over both. Next came a woollen blanket and over that she spread the quilt. On the far wall stood an armoire, its two arched doors open, and on the shelf another bolster, cushions and linen towels.

'We have only to pick the flowers to strew onto the quilt and all will be ready for the nuptial night,' Isabella said in a satisfied voice. Agnes, her hands on her hips, looked around the room. The final preparations were complete.

'She will no doubt bring happiness to this place.'

'It is a marriage we had not expected, but the houses of Taillefer, Lusignan and Dreux, this union strengthens us all.' Isabella hoped this was so. Peter of Brittany, a man who had come into their lives and twisted and turned with them and against them. Isabella remembered Yolande as a little girl carefully learning her catechism. She remembered her as the possible bride for Henry. Her daughter-in-law. And she would be but married to a different son. She looked forward to seeing her tomorrow, and welcoming her to Angoulême.

An alliance made that no one frowned upon, a true alliance between Peter Dreux, Count of Brittany and Hugh Lusignan, Count of La Marche and Angoulême. Both now swearing fealty to the French king. Peter Dreux had happily taken great sums from Henry but he had been beaten down by Louis. And Henry could not afford to invade Brittany again.

They were powerful though, in their own regions, those two men. And she reminded herself, there is also a powerful woman, who never forgets her titles, her status, who is a queen who now sees her son joined in marriage. And I do rejoice in that, thought Isabella as she closed the door of the chamber and fastened the latch.

The next day a blessing in the cathedral and after that the feasting and dancing. And then the songs of love. The minstrels and troubadours sang pure and high. The language of the Poitou full of sweet desire.

> *O wise, gentle lady may He*
> *Who fashioned you so beautifully,*
> *Grant me that joy which I await.*
> *Come to me in the night*
> *Or I will come to you*
> *And when you undress let down your hair*
> *And make me a necklace of your arms.*

The evening turned bawdy with tales told of men climbing into high windows, others being thrown into the moat or pond, their *braies* stolen by women who laughed to see them naked. Then came the ribald cries of those who escorted Young Hugh and Yolande to the room. The priest blessed the bed and Hugh and Yolande sat there holding hands as all stood around and drank from the loving cup.

'Time for us to dance and sing some more. Come, friends, we shall leave now.' And Isabella took charge, shutting the door of the chamber. No doubt in the night the crowd would throng in again, but now let the pair have time together. She watched her guests stumbling down the stone steps, but did not follow, for she too wanted some peace. Hugh was swaying slightly and she took his arm.

'Come, my dear, we need our own rest.' And wearily they sat by the fire.

'What do you see in the flames, my heart's love?' Hugh was full of mellow sweet wine and reached out a hand to hold hers.

Isabella looked up from the fire and he saw that she was crying.

'The wine is making you sad! Why this wine is as clear as your tears and better than any other. Our good drink should not bring about unhappiness.'

'I am mindful that this year both my eldest sons have married. Henry at the turn of the year, and now Hugh.' She wiped her eyes and said dully, 'News comes from London of magnificence beyond words. Weddings and coronations are costly. I wonder at Henry's skill in finding money whenever he wants it, but I think he will forget me. He still chides me about my marriage to you. And that is why I cry.'

'Hush, Isabella. You are not forgotten, and we have a new daughter, new ties. And Young Hugh is our son. *Our* son, Isabella! A young man in whom we can have pride. Strong in thought, strong in body, a loving loyal son.'

'He is all those things, that is true.' She sighed and sat up straight. An intent look now.

'I must remember we have other marriages to plan. Hugh now married to Yolande and that is that. I am content. But we had hopes for a daughter as a wife for Alphonse. Not to be. How those resolutions crumbled. He marries Jeanne of Toulouse. How galling for us! Blanche, Louis, they are intent on gathering the south into the crown.'

170

'And we must do the same! If not the south then to the east, to the west, to the north!'

He stood, finishing his wine in one gulp, opened his arms wide, deomonstrative, rocking on his heels.

'For our children, we must make sure of alliances for them all.'

Isabella stood too and walked to the window, looking down at the cathedral.

'Today was a marriage of some joy. I could see how they looked at each other. Is it not to be wondered at that two young people can see each other and know at once that they will be content?'

Hugh stood behind her and held her, murmuring, 'I can still sing a song for you. Listen.

> *O love which I so covet*
> *Your body fashioned by God*
> *Smooth skin and gentle hands*
> *I have always wanted you,*
> *For nothing else so pleases me,*
> *No other love so tempts me.'*

By the grace of God, Queen of England. Isabella took her seal from its pouch turned it over, looking again at the images on either side. It was an uneasy peace that kept the Poitou free of trouble now. It seemed as if Louis and Blanche were looking to hamper her in many little ways. Louis was of age, but did he pull away from his mother? No. The rhyme was true: Louis, King of France was made, and in everything truly obeyed, Blanche the Queen.

'Why is she so successful, so able to grab every opportunity? They call her wise; I call her the Spanish queen. Others call her names, Hersent, she wolf. Perhaps she learnt wisdom from her grandmother and has that devious streak and cunning from her grandfather. The Angevins were of the devil.'

More grudging thoughts from Isabella. Blanche was adept at encouraging some alliances and blocking others, using her connections with great skill. She had stopped Henry marrying Yolande. She had stamped on any alliance England might have made with Jeanne of Flanders, broken the betrothals with the Lusignans, and now she was putting obstacles in the way of others. Simon de Montfort, such an ambitious man, gave up his lands in France, found his way to England and claimed his inheritance there, the earldom of Leicester. Then came back to France sniffing around for a wife. A very daring de Montfort who made overtures to the Flanders heiress Jeanne too. Blanche, infuriated stood over Jeanne and made sure she refused and made sure she married another. De Montfort shrugged in exasperation and courted the widow of Philippe, Count of Boulogne, Hurepel. Blanche promptly betrothed her to someone else. Twice Blanche had nipped his ideas sharp in the bud, and a furious and proud man had ridden back to London, still looking for a betrothal, a marriage.

XIV

The breezy Thames ran past the Tower of London and under London Bridge, the only river crossing, so plenty of work for the many ferrymen and boatmen carrying passengers from one side to the other. Buildings, houses and shops crowded all along the bank. Churches stood behind the waterline like tall trees in a forest, and near them the fine residences for men of wealth. The Templars' church was both a place of worship and a treasury. Henry kept his personal treasure there and now he and his queen stood by one of the chests as she carefully wrapped her new book in a linen cloth. It was a fine volume with its gilded cover, studded in flowers of turquoise and jade, and placed here for safekeeping.

'A story of the Crusades; a very precious story.' And he leant down and kissed her cheek. His happiness was centred on this young woman who delighted him. Had delighted him from that January day when he first saw her. Rushing to claim her from the entourage that surrounded her at Canterbury, marrying her there and then, crowning her the following week. Making sure that London was fit for a queen, silks and tapestries, candles and lanterns – it might be winter but Henry turned the streets into a mass of summer gold. And she had been dressed all in gold for her coronation, a shimmer of a gown, tight at the waist with wide pleats falling about her feet. Long sleeves lined with ermine against the cold. She walked into the abbey taking tiny steps, a bishop on either side, escorting her carefully to her king and husband.

Here in the Templar's strong room she gazed up at Henry,

her mind full of stories about King Arthur and Guinevere and Lancelot. And sighed with happiness as Henry kissed her again. He adored her and she willingly gave him support, loving attention, the hope of his own family.

Three days later they left for York. There was a need to talk with Alexander once more. The King of the Scots was demanding Northumbria. Better to have it out with him face to face.

'He is bringing Joan with him. I would see her again with the greatest pleasure. She is not content or happy, I fear, and yet writes me letters that keep a link between her household and ours. She is watchful for England at all times.'

'As I would be, dear heart. Could she travel south and stay in England for some weeks? Your beloved sister Eleanor often lives alongside us. Joan came to the coronation and we were all together: you and Richard, your sisters. It was a happy time. A family is so important. We must always be loyal. You are content that I have my uncle here?' Eleanor prattled on, but Henry loved to hear that sweet voice and kissed her and petted her, and agreed.

'I am. He is a man of great learning and will help me manage my affairs. As to Joan, I have given her manors and money to improve them. I would not have her think she is neglected in her own country.'

In York the two queen consorts sat together, Eleanor watching Joan who was so skilful as she spoke to Alexander or Henry. No raised voice, calm; sometimes just repeating what they said so they could hear their voices as if anew, to make them think about their words. The council was aware of the difficult matters that had to be agreed and she was a welcome presence. Eleanor tucked her observations away to ponder on later. This was a queen consort who knew how to intercede successfully. And it was successful. So many details listed and to be dealt with. Northumbria, promised as Joan's dowry for years and never given. Alexander dour-faced as he finally renounced his claims. Henry beaming for he had avoided offering Scotland a fiefdom within England.

'The north of my kingdom is not to be broken into pieces and I will find you other lands in lieu. And no burden on you at all! Only homage and fealty. Oh, and an annual gift of a hawk, is that not a fair price?'

Alexander accepted. 'We make this accord as equals, Henry.' For him this was all-important. 'And I gladly give you the hawk.' He looked forward to managing what he had gained.

The charters were drawn, lines and boundaries frowned over and agreed. The border with Scotland set down on the maps. Clerks scurried from chamber to hall and back again and all the while Joan watched carefully and Eleanor watched her.

In the queen's chamber Joan slumped in her chair. The doctor had been called and had bled her. An anxious Eleanor stood by, stroking her head. 'You are very tired?' she ventured. Joan's face was grey and her eyes sunk.

'I am tired and at the same time content, for the agreement is reached between my husband and my brother. When I was married they called me Joan Makepeace. There is no gladness in quarrels between families. And I am the person who must try to make all well, to continue to weave the peace.'

'I have no knowledge of quarrels in families.' Eleanor spoke simply. Her Provencal family was close and loving. Sisters and a mother who cared and showed they cared.

Joan roused herself. 'I will sleep now. My night-time prayers are to St Anne for as you see I have no child. The King my husband tolerates me as a mediator, but as a wife...' Her voice died away. Eleanor crept out and to her own bed where Henry sat waiting for her.

Curled in his arms she said, 'I would that Joan comes with us. We could make a pilgrimage to Canterbury. I would pray for a child too. It is eighteen months since our nuptial bed.'

Henry held her tight. 'We have all the time and all the nights. But yes, prayers are powerful in such matters.'

Henry rode south with his young, so young, so beautiful, queen, and his sister rode with them. Joan had packed her pastes and infusions and pessaries into her own small coffer, everything the doctors recommended for a woman declared cold in the womb: cloves, nutmegs, artemesia. Her marriage was unravelling, the reality of it hollow and sour. Alexander barely said goodbye even though she knew he would demand her return if he felt the need to show his wife to the world. But now she would go to Canterbury. Eleanor wanted to make this journey too. They could talk and pray together.

And then equable Joan, peace-loving Joan, made a decision; she would linger in England for the rest of the year. It was a time of gentle pleasures. Despite her fatigue there was company to be enjoyed. Reading romances with Eleanor. An Eleanor who was only just with child and revelling in her fertility. Playing chess with Henry, embroidering kerchiefs for her maids. Planning Christmas gifts and festivities for the court at Westminster with the family gathered. The first time they had all been together for fifteen years, except for Isabelle. Joan missed her. So elegant, so graceful, her voice full of melodies. But she beamed at everyone and tucked away her observations. Her widowed sister Eleanor, Countess of Pembroke, somewhat distracted it seemed. Richard, happy with his new wife and the children from her first marriage. And now they had a son of their own, named for Henry, two years old, chubby and gleeful, toddling over the stone floor with his arms stretched out to one and all: 'Carry, carry.' Joan lifted him onto her lap where he squirmed and said, 'Down, down.'

Eleanor, her sister, sat with her as they received their gifts. A splendid new robe of violet damask for Joan and a humbler one of wool dyed with madder for Eleanor. The cloth of simplicity.

'For you have taken the vow, have you not, and here we both sit without children. For you that is an offering to God, and for me it is an offering I would not make.'

Eleanor turned the talk away from her vows and her chastity. 'But we are both given venison and wine and those I gladly accept!' She picked up her nephew and sat him on her lap, tickling him under his chin and kissing the top of his head. Joan watched and observed. 'You look like a woman who would be a mother.' Eleanor blushed and hid her face, how she longed for the marriage bed and a child.

But for now she must be seen as Eleanor, Countess of Pembroke, quiet and modestly dressed, even though all knew she was a wealthy woman, very busy with her estates. She needed to manage them as well as any lord. Henry gave her oaks to mend her mills and houses, and she built and restored as best she could. For she had her own new residence and moved into it with some relish. Odiham, a fine manor and castle a present from Henry. Her unseen father had built it and hunted here, and so did she. Another gift from Henry, a fine black palfrey, so she could ride out in style in the forest and make the two-day journey to Windsor or Winchester. She enjoyed the court on feast days with its mix of laughter and solemnity, and the chance to see family and friends. And, she hugged the thought to herself, the chance to be with Simon de Montfort, who had been such an important part of the queen's coronation. He had danced attendance on her. And dancing in her heart ever since.

The Christmas court grew to a close, everybody making their way home. But some stayed on: Eleanor's uncle, William of Savoy, to whom Henry deferred for every decision. Joan.

Simon de Montfort. And Eleanor.

Together they came to Henry in his great Painted Chamber, standing together, fingertips touching. He listened as they made their plea, for a marriage and soon. He shook his head at them. 'No one would agree to such a proposal. There was enough trouble when Eleanor was promised to William Marshal. Delay after delay.'

Angry tears and protests from Eleanor. An exasperated Henry said, 'Richard, your brother, would never countenance this, you know that. And the Church will be full of horror, for you are pledged to Our Lord. Have you forgotten your vows?'

'I have not. I was too young when I made those. My life seemed over. My schooling pointed always towards marriage and then a meek and humble widowhood. I am but three and twenty and I would not be sad and barren as others are. I have seen what that means.'

Accusing.

'You have a loving wife now. See what happiness you live. Would you deny me this?'

Determined, so fiery in her manner that Henry was reminded of their mother. Yes, that is who she was; not only in her beauty, but in her pride and her passion, and her air of arrogance.

'I will have what I want,' she stormed at him.

'Eleanor, I want you to be happy, but this is very sudden.' He grew suspicious. 'Is there some reason for the haste?' Eleanor swore there was not and de Montfort looked straight at Henry and denied any seduction. More tears, more pleas.

And he suddenly capitulated. He would make this decision. She was his sister, he was the king. Why should he consult with anyone?

On the seventh of January in Henry's private chapel in Westminster he took her hand and placed it in the hand of Simon de Montfort. The widowed Countess of Pembroke was now the Countess of Leicester and had risked her immortal soul to marry the man she had chosen for herself. She would not gain a crown as her sisters Joan and Isabelle had done, but she would have the man she wanted. She would not be a bride promised to a foreign ally to make sure of loyalty to Henry. She followed her mother, Isabella, and made her remarriage to a man close to her own age, whose presence enraptured her, who would give her children. She turned to him with great joy.

They knelt for the nuptial mass but after the ceremony Henry suddenly worried, reminded the few who were present of the importance of keeping the marriage secret. He had told no one.

But Joan had guessed and was glad.

'I have a gift for you.' Joan handed her sister a pair of the most beautiful embroidered bed cushions, red and silver thread with an edging of pearls and coral beads.

'I wish you happiness,' she continued, 'for you have been bold in this marriage and there will be those who will frown heavily when they hear of it. Not least the Archbishop who heard your vows of chastity.'

Eleanor hugged her and whispered, 'Simon will seek to validate the union by making a journey to Rome. He knows it needs support and we do not want gossip and trouble.'

'You are the most beautiful of all of us, and I must say this, Eleanor, the most like our mother. So there will be gossip and trouble.'

Richard exploded with warnings and threats when he discovered.

'Firstly, you consulted with no one. Well, did you? Perhaps with those foreigners you keep again at court, first the Poitevins, now the men from Savoy.' He sneered as he said Savoy.

'I wager this marriage is not valid. Have you sought approval from your council? I thought not.' Richard banged the table. 'The king's sister married to a man of lower rank and that man barely a man of England? He rode here to take what he could in the way of lands, but to take our sister too is an insult to the family.'

Henry twisted a ring around on his finger and watched Richard storming out. He seemed often to storm out when he disapproved of Henry. Richard felt his brother's gaze and turned around to shout back at him. 'Coward that you are! You know very well this will be protested, not only by me, but by Eleanor's family from her first marriage. For who controls her inheritance now?'

Henry shrugged awkwardly. Richard warned him.

'The Marshals and others will meet together and you may find that they will rule England.'

'I do not trust my own brother,' Henry explained to Eleanor who was walking about the Painted Chamber as the sleet fell all over London and turned the city into a drab, grey, sullen place. This was so far away from the sun and warmth of Provence. She was singing a song from there to cheer up the gloom: *I do not sing for bird or flower, nor for snow, nor for ice.* She wanted to help her husband; she wanted to strengthen his resolve.

Henry was furiously dictating a letter to all the ports. *Receive no orders from my brother Richard, who has risen against me because I have married our sister to Simon de Montfort.*

But Henry needed to ward of this rebellion, Richard and the Marshal family.

'I assure you of my brotherly love,' he wrote and by dint of sending a huge sum of money to Richard in February they were all reconciled.

Henry and Simon. Richard and his new brother-in-law, de Montfort. Richard and his brother, the king.

They were reconciled just in time. News came from the

household at Havering where Joan was waiting to travel back to Scotland. Henry had already sent venison, a cask of French wine, and expenses for her escorts. Men he trusted to see her make a safe and comfortable journey. As he had arranged all those years ago to bring her home from France.

Now in the first week of March, the brothers hastened to Essex. Galloping fast to the king's house and park. Havering Palace, all set within the great forest, high on the ridge overlooking the valley of the Thames.

Riding together: Henry white faced and anxious, Richard urging on the horses. Arriving in a flurry of servant's laments, a stern, grey steward leading the way to a darkened room.

Joan lay there, grievously ill, weak and distressed.

The steward said, 'My lady planned to travel from here to her manor at Fenstanton: easy stages on her way north to Scotland. We made all the arrangements. But yesterday morning the pain stopped her from moving from her bed.'

She held Henry's hand and Richard's too. Her maid took a linen cloth to moisten her parched lips with water.

'I have always been happy with you both,' she whispered, 'with my family. So many years apart.' As Henry cradled her in his arms she raised a hand to stroke his face, and then with a strange sighing noise, died.

Weeping, he gave orders, his voice choked with tears.

'We will bury her where she wished to be, as her will asks, in Dorset. Not in Scotland, not near cold indifference, the reminder of lost hope and failure.'

And on a drear March morning, two brothers standing side by side, both mourning deeply, as her coffin was lowered into the ground at Tarrant Abbey. Joan, twenty-seven years of age. Henry offered woven silk cloths, some of gold, as gifts for her soul, a marble tomb to cover her body in its coffin of gold, and paid for masses to be sung. Careful commemorations made with love for his favourite sister.

'In her memory, I will honour that all my life,' he vowed as he lit the two candles that would burn constantly: one at the high altar, and one in front of her tomb.

XV

France, 1240

A daughter dead, her eldest; no children. A daughter shut away in seclusion, far away in Sicily; three pregnancies and one living child named for her brother Henry; her husband the Emperor rumoured to have a dozen mistresses and as many bastard children. A daughter whose second husband had to scurry to Rome to plead for dispensation to make the marriage valid, and a baby born in unseemly haste; another Henry. Three grandsons named Henry: Henry Almain, Henry Otto and Henry de Montfort. And this de Montfort child was in England, left behind by his parents as they fled into exile to France.

It seemed Eleanor and Simon were ambitious but forever in debt and looked to Henry for funds, who apparently was generous but not a fool. Although it was more than foolish for Simon to name him as security, not seeking permission, against a great sum of money. Money owed to one Thomas of Savoy – yet another uncle of Henry's young queen. Isabella had heard that the king erupted in a rage to match the size of the debt: an exhibition to behold. And it all happened in the most public of places: the full court assembled for the churching of Queen Eleanor. She had been delivered of a son, born in June and baptised Edward, for the Confessor. Simon happy to be one of the many godfathers. Six weeks later after the birth, 500 tapers burning before the shrine of Saint Edward, the choir ready to sing *Laudes Reginae,* waiting for the procession. The noble ladies in fine new robes and surcoats, figured silk shimmering in the August sun. All splendid and ready to walk with the queen to Westminster

Abbey for her purification ceremony. Now halted by Henry's anger. Eleanor and Simon, the Leicesters, stopped from attending.

Henry was in a passion, in a fury. The ceremony for his beloved wife was not to be sullied by this couple. The slur of the taking of his name without asking, the slur of the taking of his sister not to be tolerated. His voice was harsh, unloving.

'De Montfort, you stand there brazen. You are excommunicate! She may not have assumed the habit with the veil, but she had worn a ring and betrothed herself to Christ.'

His anger mounted and more insults poured forth. 'You are the most wicked of men – and I am told you secretly defiled Eleanor before marriage.' Words now whispered with venom. 'I allowed your union most unwillingly only to avoid such scandal.' He came close and jabbed at de Montfort. 'I would throw you into the Tower.' A move to summon guards, but Richard stepped forward and held his arm and said something that calmed his brother.

And the pair had fled. First to the refuge of the bishop's palace at Southwark, where the king's guards drove them out. A return to the king, Eleanor in tears.

'My humiliation. I am overwhelmed in disgrace.'

Henry was stony-faced.

'The crowning wretchedness of all of this is when your husband pledged me for his unpaid debts. And did not ask me!' His face darkened, as he looked at them both, so visible, so guilty. Eleanor turned away from his wrath, anxious now to escape. Whatever else happened they must get away from England. She was with child again.

A hasty assembly of a few servants, a boat secured at Dover, to France, to Simon's birthplace, the strong fortified town near Paris. And a son, ten months old, left behind in Kenilworth where he had been born.

*

Isabella turned over the pages of her breviary. She was only pretending to read, it stopped people talking to her and she wanted to think – think about both her families. Henry happily married, with a son and heir; strong, she had heard, a fine baby, doted on by his parents. And Richard had his firstborn, but now no wife: Isabel Marshal had sickened, turned yellow and died giving birth in Berkhamsted Castle, the baby dead too. Her heart had been sent in a silver gilt casket to be buried with her first husband, while Richard mourned at her tomb in Beaulieu Abbey before leaving on a crusade.

I was happy in Berkhamsted, thought Isabella, with Terric my dearly mourned knight; a good practical man who looked after me well; the castle, me, the children – those children by John who now try to forge their way in the world. Joan has gone, a sweet girl. Isabella sighed. Such a sweet girl. My namesake Isabelle, they tell me, is a beauty that befits being an empress. And Eleanor, well she is in my image, perhaps the most like me; a determined, passionate woman who will challenge those who cross her. She was learning how the world turns when I met her with her Marshal husband. No matter that she is now married to a man of lower status. That can work well. I see cleverness there and some cunning. I see John and the Angevin temper still at work in Henry, the cool Angevin strategies in Richard.

What of this family who are all around me now? Young Hugh and Yolande, a couple on whom the sun shines at all times; a granddaughter, Alix, the most beautiful child I have ever seen, and now a grandson, another Hugh who is as dark and strong as all the Lusignans.

She looked up with delight as Yolande and her two children, Emilde and the nursemaids following, walked through the door. She held out her arms for kisses and hugs and dandled Alix on her knee. Such eyes, such a wonderful smile – a heart-shaped face but Isabella's colouring: dark tawny hair. Isabella stroked her head and murmured, 'A pretty child is she who sits on Grandma's knee.' Alix patted her grandmother's face and Isabella kissed her and set her down. Emilde called, 'Come Alix, we will play. Clap, clap little hands, here is a fish, here is a dish, one for you and one for me. Are you ready?'

Yolande said, 'Baby Hugh is still teething hard. I have rubbed his gums with the coral stick you gave him. He bites down on it.'

'And he drinks a little of the liquorice water? That will help.'

Isabella watched her *belle-fille*, so tranquil with that measured air and so truly loved by Young Hugh. It was good to have her about the castle now that two of the Lusignan daughters, Agnes and Isabelle, were betrothed and would soon be living with their new families, in Chauvigny and Anjou. Alice and Marguerite yet to be found husbands. The four boys – Amery, Guy, Geoffroy and William – forever out on their horses, practising at the quintaine, hitting at the shield and dummy as it swung and twisted. Amery was the fiercest: a tall young man and tough, difficult to keep indoors whatever the weather. Guy followed him everywhere, his doting shadow. Geoffroy an easy-going twelve year old, and William different again, keen to learn, keen to be schooled.

'Have you news from Eleanor and where she might be?' Yolande was curious about the Countess of Leicester. Her own father was riding back from the Holy Land with Thibault of Champagne and she blessed the day over and over again when the fat count had been warned not to marry her. News was that Simon de Montfort and Richard rode through France under separate flags, one making for Brindisi and the other for Marseilles, then the sea voyage to Acre. Simon would fight under Richard's command. Where would Eleanor be?

'She is travelling with her husband. He brought their small son, not yet two, back from England – a hasty visit to fetch him and money for the crusade. And there is a new baby born this spring, so a family reunion. No doubt there will be more babies!'

Isabella reflected with some bitter amusement that this second marriage had brought about the need to fend off accusations. For my daughter, the Church in England disapproved; she should not marry again, they wrote with frowning faces. And the pope and his cardinals had to be begged for support, and paid for it. And for her? Why, when she married Hugh what did Henry do in one of those petty acts of his, but call on Rome to make an enquiry into her marriage. Letters from the pope calling her marriage unseemly. She muttered indignantly to herself, 'Was it to be wondered that we sought friendship from the court in Paris?'

Then she realised Yolande was talking to her. She must stop shaking her head at too many thoughts: so much to remember, all those decisions. Isabella stood and smoothed her skirts.

A proud woman, proud of her life here in the Poitou.

'More babies are to be welcomed.' Yolande was smiling as she gathered her family together. 'We hope for more.'

Hugh and his son strode in, flinging down cloaks and gloves, the room a sudden uproar as Young Hugh caught his daughter and threw her in the air, catching her and setting her down to chase about.

Yolande remonstrated, 'She will be too excited to sleep, and look you have woken the baby. He has slept so badly with his teeth.' Fretful wailing from the corner.

'We will go to our chamber now,' he said, a little abashed, but then grinned at her. 'You will not scold me anymore?' She moved to him for a kiss and then holding his hand they made their leave-taking.

'Fare the night well.'

'And for you, fare the night well.'

The port and harbour at La Rochelle were busy, trade brisk and men working long hours to load the ships with wine and salt. On the quay, a man standing with his back to his house, prosperous, a fine wool cloak and tunic, the leather belt buckled tight. Estienne Savy: a merchant and ship owner. The house had been built by his grandfather and was in a good position. Estienne thanked him every day in his prayers for setting the family on the road to wealth. Wine, salt and orchards: a trio of productive harvests. Wine and salt stored in the cellar ready for a shipment on the next tide. He watched as shop fronts were let down, servants helping their owners, and women carrying baskets to set on the counters. Another busy trading day.

Estienne sniffed the air, a good strong onshore breeze, and pancakes frying somewhere. He tucked his thumbs into his belt and strolled down to see what might be arriving from England. He passed the coils of rigging ropes, barrels of pitch and canvas, all needed for the cogs. No doubt that the trade to and from the north was steady. His grandfather had told him the story of the English king fleeing from La Rochelle. The king had been liked well enough because he granted the port charters for a market, allowed the trade in wine at favourable rates and the right to collect taxes to build the quays. But La Rochelle found the struggle for power after his death difficult. The burghers, his father included, wrote for help to the new King Henry because counts like La Marche were riding out and demanding tithes, taxes and dues and not giving much back. But at least the city walls were thick and strong, strong enough to hold out against the French king when he besieged the place. But when La Rochelle capitulated and he won, there was La Marche again, strolling about the town very full of himself. He seemed to have fingers in all the bowls of pottage.

Estienne had grumbled then, a discontented seventeen year old watching the burgess asking vainly for the right to hold the control of the port, to build more walls to defend the outskirts where the vines grew, no one listening. But six years later when King Henry rode up and down from Brittany and the townspeople laughed behind his back at such a wasted campaign, someone listened. The French king had sent his army to take back everything Henry thought he had won. A knight who came to the quayside to find wine and provisions for his men stopped and spoke to Estienne about the problems his port had, and wondered out loud if Estienne would be interested in helping the Queen, Blanche, who was a strong leader but good and wise too.

'It is in Poitou that the trouble always rises. Always a threat here, and the main thrust of that comes from Lusignan and Angoulême. Of course, the countess is the mother of Henry, but that is of no consequence to her if she chooses it not to be. They think to have powers here against Paris.'

Estienne, who hoped to be elected to the town council, ordered a barrel of the good local wine up from the cellar for his new companion, who, sampling a beaker, had suggested, 'It would be useful to make friends with the pair who sit so proud.' He raised a toast. 'The Count and Countess of Angoulême and La Marche.' They both drank and then the knight winked and said, 'You are lettered? I thought so. To keep your bills and accounts straight a man needs to write. Do you know their household, who comes here for the market?

'The stewards and servants and others who trade with Flanders, buying wool cloth and furs. Plenty of goods travel back to their castles. Then there are the salt and wine taxes to collect.'

'Just report what you can: movements, conversations; visit them, take some of your wine as a gift, be quiet and discreet. It will take time. The French queen has been watching Isabella for years. She is patient.'

Blanche was brisk and efficient with her network of spies and agents, all necessary as she worked to keep France supreme. She had them within her palaces and castles too, as she wanted to know where the young queen was at all times, to keep her from distracting Louis. He should be at his devotions or attending to matters of state, not walking in the gardens with Marguerite, picking daisies for her as a token of his love.

She frowned now as she saw them riding together, frowned even more as they listened to music with such pleasure or shared books, standing close as they pored over the texts, Louis helping his wife with the Latin translations. Marguerite had quickly learnt the language of the Île de France, her Provencal only used occasionally. So a bright, beautiful girl had begun to blossom.

But Blanche was determined that Marguerite was a wife for one reason only: to provide a son for the Capets, not for companionship. And yes he could sleep with her at night because that had to be to produce the child, but apart from the nights his attention must be elsewhere, and she, Blanche, should be the centre of it. Try as they might, meeting in courtyards, and secretly on staircases that connected their rooms, Blanche won. The young Louis still obedient to his mother, listening to her advice, allowing her to be at his side all the time. And she made the policy and dictated the letters sent in their joint names.

'The duties of the state must come before feelings.'

Louis bowed over the parchments his mother had stacked on the table. He was anxious to please her and today she brought his attention to his father's will. Her dower was in good shape. It was time to look at the lands that should go to his brothers.

'I am pleased that Robert has the Artois. Now he is married he needs a county to steady him.'

Blanche looked cross. No son of hers should be accused of being unsteady. But Louis was laughing. 'Mother, he threw curdled milk over Thibault. That was not steady! And he is reckless often, loving to us all, but reckless.' Reluctantly she agreed.

'So we have the one who would be a brave knight and full of such deeds that the troubadours would be proud to sing of his valour, and then there is dear Alphonse, not cut from the same cloth at all, but a difference we can all cherish.'

Blanche approved of her third son, not as strong and thoughtful as Louis, but precise and neat. He was frugal too, a good Capetian like his grandfather, but not dull. She had managed a good marriage for him, not to that Lusignan daughter, but to Jeanne of Toulouse. Raymond of Toulouse had conceded defeat and the Languedoc was no longer as independent as once it had been. Blanche had gradually destroyed that. There was still trouble there but she felt in control of the south. So she looked to the west now, where so many counts, lords and castellans were rebellious whenever they felt the need to make demands, or ignore commands from Paris.

Bailiffs and treasurers entered the room, clerks bringing more parchments and tally sticks. Blanche began instructing a clerk to make a fresh notch in one to mark money spent on building a covered market, and Louis reached for what he hoped was the last document to seal. He was eager to slip away. But Blanche saw him move and called out, 'There is much still to discuss – the lands left by your father for Alphonse: the Poitou. We must invest him with the Poitou.'

Louis turned, his face all smiles. 'I would give him a feast and the most sumptuous celebration, and a saint's day to be chosen. A summer saint; John the Baptist.'

Preparations began with invitations being sent to all. Three thousand knights, the entire court, every baron, count and lord. No matter that Richard of Cornwall had been made the Count of Poitou some fifteen years earlier by Henry, who still saw the Poitou as his; no matter that Richard was away on a crusade and could not protest. He was regarded as careless of his inheritance and spent no time in the Poitou, which suited everyone there.

'The Poitevins bend their knee to you, Louis,' Blanche observed, 'and then to England. Homage to both and proud of it!'

'They have a strong leader in La Marche, Hugh Lusignan.' Both his father and grandfather had warned him about the Lusignans; each one as bad as the next, his father had said.

'And his wife lurking all the time, or pushing herself where she is not wanted. I have watched her for years; a minx when married to my uncle. And arrogant now, how she struts! '

But Blanche had to admit, it was that marriage that had given Philippe all he needed to make war on John and take Normandy, the Lusignans furious at the kidnapping. John had not been devout, not good and not kind. Isabella's second marriage was distasteful, to another Lusignan, the son of her former betrothed. Blanche shuddered and said a quick prayer. But it was infuriating that many in the Poitou seemed to like having a Queen Dowager of England as part of their elite. Hugh Lusignan needed to be curbed. France needed to gain the upper hand. Isabella might have ties with England but England had no place here. And the sooner everyone realised that the better. In Saumur next year the Capets would show just how powerful they were.

XVI

Saumur, Poitiers, Lusignan, 1241

Between the Loire and the Thouet, lies the town of Saumur. On the edge of a steep cliff, overlooking the river, the great castle. Built by the warrior Count of Anjou 200 years earlier and rebuilt by Henry II, the Angevin king, when he was at the height of his power – the place where he took refuge when sick and dying. Now the wheel turned and the Capets rode in. It was their castle fortified, their domaines controlled.

Isabella and Hugh had travelled north on the old road. A two-day journey, one night in Fontevraud where they ate a simple meal with the abbess. The Abbey was as calm as Isabella remembered it from her visit all those years ago, when John had brought her to see Eleanor, his mother, the Duchess of Aquitaine and Queen of England. She walked into the church to light candles for her. A large echoing space, stone and arches and tombs. She knelt by the effigy of her *belle-mère*; so strong and powerful in life and here she lay serene, holding a book; a woman of great learning and courage. Isabella prayed for her soul and for the memory of that twelve-year-old girl: Isabella of Angoulême, just married and about to be crowned queen-consort.

'I have no fear of Blanche. We have met and agreed to be polite. It was uneasy for us both I think. But for now we will not snarl at each other,' she said to Hugh as they wended their way through the forest roads leading to the banks of the Loire and the bridge into Saumur. 'No fear of that French king, making his brother the Count of Poitou. It will not matter to me. It might matter to my son Richard, but it is my title as Queen of England that gives it to him.' She looked up at the sky, midsummer blue and cloudless, and continued. 'And you have knelt to Richard, which is at it should be, for he is the son of a king and you are the Count of La Marche.' The word *only* hovered in the air.

'What are you trying to set out for me, Isabella?' Hugh was getting tetchy. This great gathering was going to test his patience with protocols and rules. Alphonse to be knighted and others with him. It would be a long day or two before they were done.

'I am saying that I am a queen and I do not kneel to counts, and I do not kneel *even as a symbol* to Alphonse invested as Count of Poitou. Not even through my husband, who is also a count and a powerful one.'

'I will have to swear liege to Alphonse as my overlord. Will you accept that?'

'I do not like it, but it seems we must show some loyalty and we will do that, alongside the others who show their loyalty.' Her voice was acid. They followed their knights holding aloft the banners, blue and silver with the five red lions, flying proud to herald their arrival.

All the bells were ringing and all the townspeople were out on the streets watching the procession as the lords from every quarter rode to the church. Hugh, stern and tall in the saddle, his palfrey wearing a caparison of the deepest damson, edged in azure and argent. Isabella was proud of him and his knights, so brilliantly equipped. They had grown in power like no other; no one else matched them. She looked forward to the feasting and the opportunity to show their strength.

After the long and solemn mass all made their way to the great covered hall. Arcades around the sides and spacious in the centre. Here were huge tables covered in linen and silk cloths. Everywhere the new arms of Alphonse of Poitiers; his serjeants-at-arms in sendal, that finer richer silk; a mark of an important ceremony. Alphonse in the most glorious purple tunic of Spanish brocade with a pattern picked out in dark gold thread. His fellow knights wearing robes of samite, cloth of gold, some with sable trim, others with civet. Louis in the celestial blue of France, his cloak of vermillion silk lined with ermine, but on his head a simple cotton cap.

'He shows his piety and humility with that. I wonder if he wears a hair shirt.' Isabella was amused and narrowed her eyes as she took in the young Queen Marguerite. More splendour in her brocade tunic and skirts of deep violet and ermine. 'But she prefers her luxury.'

The royal couple sat together and Blanche was at her table facing them, smiling at the crowd of nobles, the banquet so huge with so many to serve it was difficult to see them all. Young lords presented platters, carrying the heaped-up chunks of roasted meats that had been carved by the squires. These boys were kept busy and thronged about the sideboards, not only wielding knives but pouring wine, local Saumur white and red from the Auvergne, barrels and barrels rolled into the hall. Estienne Savy, observant and discreet, saw with pleasure that his quiet supervision had kept it all flowing.

They were shown to their places, Hugh to sit with Peter of Brittany, the two of them being reminded very clearly of where their loyalties were today: close to Alphonse and his wife, Jeanne of Toulouse. She sat unsmiling, determined to hold her head high.

Isabella was grim-faced as she saw where she was to sit, not with Blanche, not with Louis, lower than his chit of a queen and the new Countess of Poitou. No, she was at a table near the Count of Champagne, whom everyone knew was out of favour, despite the fact that he was now the King of Navarre. A fool of a man, she thought, sitting there on some kind of a throne, his ample body all satin and gold clasps, and his head covered in a hood of cloth of gold. His wife sitting next to him looked uncomfortable. With child again, Isabella thought, running her eyes over her belly. And so pale and tired.

Well, she is married to a man who strays at all times, in love with the romance of being in love.

Isabella drank her wine and picked at the venison, watching the tables and the loyalties that were in place today; watched Blanche making sure that the world noticed her sons. It could not be denied that the glory of the Capets put everyone in the shade.

Alphonse went straight from Saumur to Poitiers. Blanche had told him in no uncertain way, you must be seen in possession of the territory left to you by your father. And he agreed, now he was knighted, invested with his title, he would demand fealty from the local Poitevin barons. It was time to put an end to the swivelling from one king to another. The Poitou was his, belonged to the French crown, and this needed to be sealed very publically. In July, in Poiters, another few days of feasts were to be organised with Blanche firmly in control of the planning. She had four extra cooks on hand and the tableware bought for Saumur was already loaded onto carts to be reused. Another careful piece of housekeeping: the investiture had been very costly, more so than Louis's wedding. But it had been important to show friends and enemies alike that there was a royal family and a king of France who intended to rule over all.

Louis and Alphonse and their wives settled into the palace. Elegant chambers in the tower of Maubergeon for them, and other rooms for the rest of the court. The Great Hall echoed with footsteps and then the sound was lost. Carved blind arches decorated the walls and in between these hung the tapestries, so brightly coloured, but no sun shone onto them. Candlelight flickered and revealed the stories of the hunt, of the myths, birds and deer, trees and unicorns. Their borders made precious with gold and silver trimmings, ivory hooks holding them on to the rods. When Blanche pulled one across, small bells threaded through the top chimed, making her smile. Her grandmother had built this, the largest hall in Europe. Eleanor of Aquitaine had loved Poitiers. It was only right that her great-grandson should be here. Blanche sat on one of the stone benches and gazed up at the barrel vault ceiling and around at the painted plasterwork. The central hearth would not be needed in the height of summer. But if Alphonse wanted to spend Christmas here, firewood must be ordered. She stood up, no time to daydream; now to command servants to set the tables on the dais. The family must be ready for the arrival of the local lords.

For three days she had waited, her fury rising as each dawn brought no invitation. But now Isabella was dressing with great care, everything to show her status. This was important, as the fealty Hugh had to show would hand over so much to Alphonse. She had been asked to render homage too, but she would not bend her knee.

Maids had helped her bathe and brushed her hair until it gleamed. Grey hairs were plucked out – only a few, but not to be tolerated. A maid attended to her brows and hairline. All must be smooth, serene, and beautiful. Drops in the corners of her eyes to make them bright. She had buffed her nails with a chamois cloth, had rubbed olive oil and rosewater into her hands so that her fingers showed her rings to their advantage. The jewels shone. She powdered her face with a concoction of lily root; there was no need to look old and tired today. A wonderful pair of new hose, striped in red and gold, the colours of Angoulême. A chemise with long tight sleeves. Then she slipped on her gown, its close-fitting bodice fastened with a row of tiny pearl buttons. The sleeves, which ended in full loose bands, almost brushing the ground; their red and gold flashed as if to signal danger. And wound around her waist she wore a massive belt of woven gold. She was ready and anticipating the looks of approval, perhaps envy, when she walked into the Great Hall to take her place, to lend even more magnificence to the two queens who sat there, Blanche and Marguerite.

The doors opened and she stood just inside with a small group of ladies. She looked left and right; these were wives of local mayors, the wives of minor knights and castellans. No one of importance.

'The Countess of La Marche,' said a herald's voice near the dais.

At last she was received, but not announced as a queen, not ushered to the king's side, not invited to sit by Marguerite or Blanche, and no one standing for her as she swept in.

Louis and Marguerite sat like unblinking statues. Alphonse stared straight ahead as if there was nothing to notice. Jeanne of Toulouse, the Countess of Poitou, unmoving, indifference on her face; a woman brought up in the court in Paris, no longer devoted to her southern roots; as icy as her insolent *belle-mère*. Blanche poised, calm with her hands clasped in her lap, her mouth set in a straight line. Isabella looked at each and every one. She had not been greeted as a queen; she had not been welcomed as a queen. This was too much to bear, so she would not. Another defiant look at the seated group and Isabella turned to leave. Still no one stood; no one stopped her; no one put out a hand or said a word. She would not cry; they were not worth her tears. It was a very long walk back to the doors. The Great Hall, the *Salle des Pas Perdus*, the vast hall of lost footsteps, where her footfall was now silenced.

'Wretch! You wretch! They were full of delight as they kept me waiting. For three days.' Isabella was beating at Hugh, her fists landing blows on his arms and chest. He tried to hold her off, then to hold her to him, but she spun away.

'The king did not ask me to sit with him. He ignored me. How can he do that to a queen and the mother of a king? And no one called me Queen of England. No one bowed or curtsied. Such spite, all done to disgrace me in front of our people, Hugh: our knights and stewards, our townspeople. He scorned me, that son of the Spanish woman, as if I were lower than a kitchen wench.'

Hugh gestured and looked helpless. Isabella's eyes were hard and her face contorted.

'Did you see their scorn? No, you did not. I cannot say more. The shame is stifling me; I cannot breathe for the despair this brings. And you have sworn homage, given up lands to them with no recompense, no compensation. No, not given – had it stolen; my lands stolen.'

'Isabella, you are making yourself ill with this rage.'

'I am ill with rage? Ill? I tell you, I will die of this rage. I will make them suffer for this, if God does not.' Another gesture from Hugh as he stepped forward to hold her. She lifted her arms and warded him off. One last angry sentence.

'They will lose these lands and more, or else I will lose all I have and die of it.'

She stalked from the house and ordered servants and squires to escort her back to Angoulême. She wanted and needed to be away from here. Let those who would swear allegiances stay. Her place was in her castle high on the promontory, where she could stand and remember the Taillefers and their proud history.

When I was at last received by them, in the chamber where the King sat, he did not call me to his side, did not bid me sit next to him. They rose for me neither when I entered or when I departed...they shall lose their lands...

Blanche rolled up the parchment, the letter from Estienne Savy, and put it into the chest with the others. So

Isabella was provoked by her treatment, but her husband had sworn fealty and even now was entertaining Louis and Alphonse in Lusignan, to give hospitality to his new overlord.

Hugh was expansive and lavish as he showed the castle and its grounds with the fine new buildings to Louis and Alphonse. Marguerite and Jeanne admired the tapestries, the silver and pewter plate, nibbled on the sweetmeats and strawberries, slept comfortably in well-appointed chambers. Hugh re-affirmed his fealty, both for himself and his sons, and reminded them all that Lusignan had been kept as a secure place for Louis's father, when that king had taken the Poitou so successfully. He promised that his shield would be at Alphonse's side. Alphonse agreed that the charter and privileges for La Rochelle would be renewed. Hugh would continue to benefit. Louis attended mass in the chapel and pronounced it a good simple place to worship and left alms for the priest. He frowned though at the carvings of Melusine glimpsed high in the church eves as they rode away to Poitiers. Here Alphonse and Jeanne would take up residence and receive delegations of people intent on showing loyalty. Louis and Marguerite were anxious to make speed and return to Paris. They had two baby daughters to cherish now. No son, but Marguerite was fertile and glowed with triumph.

News filtered through to Angoulême. Hugh had been hospitable, the food was excellent, the castle praised, the beds pronounced most fitting for two high-born ladies. Louis had worshipped in the chapel. Hugh had made promises.

Agnes sat with Isabella as she heard the news, dribs and drabs brought by a messenger on his way to Périgeuex, a pilgrim who had been in Poitiers, a merchant from Flanders hurrying to Bordeaux. Isabella's orders rang out. Horses were saddled, carts readied. Agnes and Geoffroy agreed to accompany Isabella. They spoke in low voices as they started out for Lusignan.

'She needs gentling like a wild animal.'

'She needs to find some calm. Perhaps Hugh will be able to soothe her.'

Beds, curtains, tapestries, blankets, chests, cauldrons, ladles, silver dishes, even the altar cloths and ornaments of the chapel were all being hurled into carts. Isabella shouted at the servants, her commands rough, strong, furious.

'Everything, everything. I am not leaving behind a single item, not a three-legged stool or a pewter spoon must remain.'

The servants scurried around the courtyard loading things at speed. When the Countess of Angoulême, Countess of La Marche and Lady of Lusignan, the Queen of England, lost her temper there was no hiding place from her anger. She reached out and boxed a kitchen boy's ears. 'Be careful with that. Everything must be taken and nothing broken.'

Agnes had been asked to fetch the statue of the Blessed Virgin Mary from the chapel, and the figure with its pious downcast face and the meekly praying folded hands was being wrapped in cloth and placed in the small iron-bound chest that held Isabella's letters and jewellery. Agnes thought it was a pity Mary's composure had not rubbed off on Isabella, who was now roaring at three terrified dairy maids. They were packing away churns and butter moulds, but were awkward and clumsy.

Slap! A hand at a startled red cheek, a hush, a whirring of pigeon's wings as birds flew up, a dog barked. A small short silence and then the chaos erupted again. Hugh stood watching. Did he dare to speak to Isabella? She felt his gaze on her back and whirled around, nearly hysterical.

'Was it not enough that the King of France should insult me when we were in Poitiers? That Blanche,' she spat this name, 'should treat me as some inferior, some servant. I suffered many humiliations during the three days we spent there, in front of everyone, as if I were not of high regard in this, *my* territory. And if I were not, like her, a queen.'

'At Saumur we had one of the high places,' Hugh muttered, as he realised how hopeless it was to begin to reason with his wife.

'A high place at Saumur! You may have had, but little regard at all in Poitiers, in this our fief. I return to Lusignan to find the king and his brother, both have been in this castle, being fêted. You paid homage and more, when I refused.'

Hugh stood embarrassed, ashamed. He looked towards Geoffroy who looked awkwardly back. What could be done?

'Stay far away from me now. You are not welcome in my presence.'

Hugh reached out an arm. She slapped it away. 'You are the most vile and the most abject of all men. You are a laughing stock to our people and to me. Well, I wish you much happiness and honour with your new allegiances. Never again, never do you hear, do I want to see you again. My place is in Angoulême, not here with a man who cannot fight for what is his.'

The journey from Lusignan to Angoulême was grim and joyless. Isabella sulked or raged for the two days it took. Agnes wondered if she was remembering that other journey over forty years ago, when Isabella was twelve. They had ridden fast then, hardly any baggage to slow them down, and Isabella's father full of secrets as he hurried them away. And in Angoulême, six weeks later, Isabella had been married to King John; kidnapped from the Lusignans with her father's connivance. Agnes shook her head as if ridding herself of unwanted memories and set her face towards the hilltop town that was home.

In the splendid castle with its two towers the unpacking began, and Agnes helped settle Isabella into her rooms overlooking the Charente. Here she brooded on injustice, restless in her chambers, endlessly pacing or looking down at the river, which swirled muddy and brown.

A week went by and then Agnes reported that Hugh had arrived. He was at the castle gate, seeking his wife. Isabella refused. Hugh was turned away, camped out in the Templars' house, under the high walls of the Angoulême stronghold. He pleaded with his wife, like some low vassal, to be allowed into the castle. Three days passed. The message was always the same; he was not to enter the castle; her chamber and her bed were forbidden to him.

Agnes observed the sorrow that engulfed Isabella and which seemed to overcome her natural pride.

'Isabella, this cannot continue. You are grey with fatigue and Hugh waits for you, most humbly. He is contrite.'

Finally, Isabella listened to her. Hugh was summoned, and found her leaning against the wall on the far side of the room.

'My pain and my honour are of equal weight,' she wept. 'I am full of despair at the way I have been treated.'

Hugh was alarmed at these tears, Isabella so seldom cried; she was always resolute, treating all with disdain if they showed weakness. He spoke carefully.

'Madame, command me. I will do anything I can to make you recover yourself, to make life happy for you again.'

She turned towards him.

'If you do not do what I ask, you will never be allowed into my bed. I will never be united with you again.'

Hugh stepped closer, eager to do whatever she asked. In truth he did not need much persuasion. He reached out a hand and when she took it he pulled her towards him. He knew what it was to be consumed by a devastating passion for Isabella; he had always desired her. That she aroused a powerful mix of envy, fear and admiration in all who came into her presence was also true, but no one had seen her with a face wet with tears, so tragic and lost. Since she was a child she had been proud and wilful. Now she crumpled against him and he soothed her. His wife, his strong spouse, whom he loved and respected, would bring folly to them both. Somehow he knew this, but now she was in his arms and he held her.

'You only have to command me, my lady, and I will do all in my power. You know it well.'

Rumours began, tittle-tattle travelled around the towns, angry voices and sobbing had been heard, maids all agog reported breathlessly. Everyone knew that Isabella had taken back her husband and that Hugh had promised to obey her every command.

When I recently left you in Paris, coming to Lusignan, I heard many true things there, which I send to you written by my own hand. Do not be upset that it is a long letter since I cannot otherwise tell you everything in its entirety.

For those things that I know to be good for you and the King, by my oath, I do not wish to keep silent...

She had everything carried with her to Angoulême. When the Count saw it, he was very upset; he asked her humbly and devotedly why she despoiled the castle so shamefully; she might buy as many ornaments at Angoulême, and he would willingly pay for them. 'Flee,' she said then. 'Do not remain in my sight...' Then the Count, benevolent as you know him to be, seeing her weeping and hearing these things, was quite moved. He said: Lady, instruct me; whatever I can do, I shall do; you may be sure.' 'If not,' she said, 'you will never lie with me again, nor shall I see you.' And he then swore even more strongly that he would do her will.

Blanche smiled as she folded the letter: she thought Isabella was sad, absurd, a woman full of folly. But she had power. Then she thought, Hugh will betray any oath of fealty to the king and the Count of Poitou. Isabella wanted her lands back and she would plot and plan to achieve this. She placed the letter in the heavy walnut chest where she hid all her spies' correspondence. There would be more to come from this situation, much more, and not all of it good.

XVII

France and England, 1241

Parthenay stirred in the early morning, doors opening onto the streets and the fortified town gate of Saint Jacques creaking as the watchmen heaved at it. The castle stood behind its two sets of walls and the flags set high above the turret blew in the river breeze: the azure and argent of Lusignan with the red band of Parthenay. The hilly wooded slopes fell to the river, to the bridge and the priory of Saint Paul. Pilgrims were already walking south having spent a night there en route to Gascony and Spain. The cattle were being led into the meadows, good strong beasts with horns like lyres; special to this county and much admired, for they were draught animals, as well as providing milk, they supplied meat, and hides for the local tannery.

'Another town created by Melusine. She only had to wave her wand to make this place.' Hugh waved his hand at the town, mimicking his legendary ancestor. Lusignan cousins rode with him, proud of their strong castles of Vouvant, with its keep, and Melusine tower. In the courtyard William the Archevêque greeted them and the others. The Viscount of Thouars, barons and castellans of the Poitou – all had so eagerly assembled. Archvêque's steward and servants found places for the dozen at the table, and the friendly wine merchant from La Rochelle was asked to broach the barrels of red he had brought the day before. Much talk, much indignation, much pounding of fists on the table. Some shouted and unsheathed their swords. Raoul Lusignan called for quiet.

'I am convinced that you, cousin Hugh, Count of La

Marche will be stripped of all you possess. You will not keep that oath of fealty. You will not bind yourself. We know that. And the Capets, the French, will turn on us all. And if my castles here and in Normandy, a gift from the English king, are taken from me, I will fight, as will my brother of Vouvant.'

More voices. One after another, speaking of their fears now that the king and his family thought to absorb all the lands into a French kingdom.

'It will not stop with you, we can be sure of that.'

'And especially since those in Paris have always hated the Poitevins,' someone said. 'They want to subject everything and take control of it by conquest, and they will treat us most vilely. We will be run into the ground like those in Albi.'

The Viscount of Thouars looked at Hugh and raised his eyebrows; their families had been enemies and friends over and over again, now they were united against anyone who threatened the Poitou. He wanted more than Hugh on his side today though.

'We should ask the Gascons and the men of Bordeaux to join us. For a single powerful mercenary of the king can do what he wants, enforce his will in every parcel of land. We will not dare to attempt anything unless we all join together.'

A voice chimed in before he finished.

'We are like serfs! I would indeed prefer to be dead along with the rest of you than to be like this. Even the townsmen fear their overlords because of those hard, violent men they hire to do the dirty work against everyone.'

'Yes! And we are far from the court in Paris and cannot go there to plead, and so are destroyed.'

More brave words, more men standing and declaring for rebellion.

'Let us therefore prepare to resist strongly, lest we all perish together.'

'Submit or resist, which is it to be?'

'For we must be united or one faction will burn with its neighbour.'

*Then they all swore an oath and conspired evil; but I do not know the mode, though I know this well...*wrote Estienne Savy.

Isabella welcomed them all to Angoulême. She was respectful, not high-handed. Many of these men were ones she had quarrelled with and quelled in the past, whose tithes and taxes she had made sure came her way to fill the chests and coffers. Now she provided a lavish feast, smiled and bowed her head to every man sitting in her hall and raised her beaker.

'Worthy among friends, I drink to you all. Our country is the Poitou. Each man in his own land.'

They banged on the table and the wine from La Rochelle was pronounced the very best in Poitou. The entertainment began. Jugglers, heroic tales sung by the minstrels, and love songs from travelling troubadours. Isabella asked for an old song she had heard when staying in the castle in Ribérac, built there by men when they defended the Dronne against the Vikings. The Taillefers were fierce in defence – she must always remember that.

Who weeping and singing go,
Contrite I see the folly of the past,
And, happy, I foresee the joy I hope for one day.

The reconciliation with Hugh had been gradual, but slowly, very slowly, they trusted again. He could hardly remember her hot words and anger. She was so sweet and loving and their nights were long and lingering, full of quiet delight as she turned in his arms and whispered, 'Let us take comfort in each other.'

*Then they all came to Angoulême to speak with the Queen who, against her custom, honoured them very much, even those she did not like, and they repeated their pacts before her...*wrote Estienne Savy.

October in Pons, the barons from Gascony, the mayors and clerks from Bordeaux, Bayonne, La Réole, Saint-Emillion, joined by the seneschal of Gascony; the man who guarded it for the English. All feared that the wish to dominate by Louis and Blanche would spread far beyond the Poitou. And the Gascons looked to their east border, to Toulouse and made careful noises about a league against the French. Raymond VII did not hesitate: twenty years of seething had made him ready, for he had been defeated by them, forced to sign a treaty and his daughter Jeanne taken from him and married to Alphonse. He would go to war against his new in-laws – his daughter on the opposing side. No matter. And as for his part, he would send the information to the Emperor Frederick, who was bound to approve.

*At the end, they swore and formed the conspiracy. I sent my messenger there, who was present in the town, and I would have sent him to you long before, but I was awaiting the end of the conference...*wrote Estienne Savy.

Isabella sat at the table in her chamber and weighed over the work being done to fortify the châteaux. Plans were being made, strategy discussed. Toulouse would attack the Capets in the centre and Raymond had called on an old ally, the King of Aragon, to help him with that thrust. Hugh and his allies would take La Rochelle.

'I believe we must write to my son in England.'

This was not a letter about a dowry but it did make demands. This was a letter telling Henry: *The Poitou is ready to rise against the King of France and to return most loyally to England.*

And another letter made its way to Paris.

Beware, lady, if you should send to the Count and Queen with prayers, for that would make them more proud. They believe in vain that you can be dissuaded from making war, and all they want is some profit from it...

Yet, my lady, the greatest good is of peace. If you can in some way hold them in peace, since your Poitevin land is in a better state now, by the grace of God, than it ever was in the times of the English kings. This you know, truly, whatever your Poitevins say, who always want war. But death will come upon them and their bow will be broken and the sword will enter their hearts for if they make war...they will lose, unwilling and ungrateful...since they are not loved by their own people and the land will, by itself, return to your son Louis and his brother Alphonse... although those of Bordeaux and the communes of Gascony promised that, if it were necessary, they would send 500 paid knights and 500 mounted crossbowmen in service, and 1,000 foot soldiers, But I do not fear this. It is not worth an egg, since I know the Count and the land, and they will not dare to move. If they did, they would be harmed, and all will be yours.

Postscriptum... However, the Count of La Marche and others are having their castles and gates fortified and guarded...wrote Estienne Savy.

Isabella and Hugh made decisions as they gathered speed and force, working towards their goal.

'In December Alphonse will call all his nobles to his Christmas court. In Poiters.'

'And we will declare ourselves his enemies then.'

An impatient, almost feverish, Isabella. She wanted her revenge. And she wanted Hugh to take that revenge with her. No more fealties, no more feasting with people she loathed. He might be apprehensive, cautious even, feeling kindly. She was not. They rode into town and took up their usual lodgings, but this time they had a mass of knights waiting at the town gates.

'We will resist Alphonse with all the force we can command.' And she dressed as she had done before, in her defiant red and gold.

An approach to the Great Hall, the *Salle des Pas Perdus*, Hugh leading, Isabella in his wake. Both entered, crashing open the doors, a noisy disturbance, a ringing clangour.

'My footsteps are not going to be lost in here today.'

Alphonse sat stunned, his welcoming face stupefied. Jeanne of Toulouse went white and still. Knights stood up, alarmed.

Hugh gestured around the space before speaking. His voice was vehement, passionate. 'I declare most strongly to this Alphonse, who sits here as a false man in Poitiers, that I withdraw my homage. I will never observe any bond of allegiance to you. For you have stolen these lands from Richard of Cornwall, my stepson, who even now fights against the enemies of Christ in the Holy Land. I have no duty of fealty to you or to any son of Blanche.'

The shocked silence was broken by a woman's voice, which rang out, clear and strong.

'You are a usurper. My loyalty is with Henry, King of England.'

And with these words Isabella, who had stared with forbidding anger at Alphonse throughout, turned her back and walked, head held high. Hugh followed her, and the tumult followed them. Followed them back to the narrow street and there the escort. Their Poitevin troops drew their crossbows, threatening.

'Now take that flare, take it,' Isabella urged Hugh and he burst through the middle of the troops, a flaming torch thrust at the wooden timbers of the house where they had stayed. Set on fire. No longer needed, for they were no longer vassals of France; no longer visiting the city to make dutiful performances.

'They are escaping!' went up cries of indignation and calls to come back. But their horses galloped hard and at the gates more men, more knights, and the Lusignans disappeared into the night.

It was agreed that as soon as possible those men of Bordeaux and Bayonne, who are the best mariners and lords of the sea, those who have ships and galleys...would come to La Rochelle, preventing the grain and other merchandise from coming into the city, and wine from going out. And at night they burned homes with wine presses and cellars and vines around La Rochelle, which are of great value. And for this, the Count and the Queen secretly pay the wages. The barons incite wars through the land in different places through different people, and the Count and many others say they do not know about it. Meanwhile, the Count buys all grain of every kind and puts it in his castles, preventing any from his land being delivered at La Rochelle or elsewhere. The Lord King and his brother the Count of Poitou should, if it please you, lady, order him to desist, since neighbouring lands should share and deliver foods from one to another. The Count is having his castle Frontignac on the road from Niort to La Rochelle wondrously fortified so he can prevent entry *and exit of all things at La Rochelle...Thus our city would be besieged only because the grain is withheld. And it is already expensive because of that and will become very expensive...*wrote Estienne Savy.

Westminster

...We seek no army from you, but coin to furnish the campaign... Henry was moved to tears as he read. Nothing could be sweeter to his ears than this. 'It has been a constant in my life, the thought of the lands my father lost, always there.' Angevin lands: Normandy, the Poitou.

'And see, my dear little queen, my mother has asked for my help, money yes, but to help those who would be loyal to me and to England.'

And Henry, who so craved affection, the close warmth of a family, who now had a wife and a son, cuddled Eleanor kissing her over and over again.

He sat in the abbey in Reading and sealed an alliance between the Lusignans, his mother and his stepfather.

At the request of my very dear mother Isabella Queen of England, Countess of La Marche and Angoulême, I give in perpetuity in my name and that of my heirs to Hugh, Isabella and their children, all the rights and jurisdictions to the Count of Angoulême; the chateaux of Jarnac, Cognac, and Merpins, Saintes, Aunis, the I'lle d'Oleron, to the Count of La Marche, the archbishopric of Bourges and the bishopric of Limoges, Périgueux, Angoulême, Saintes and Poitiers. Hugh and Isabella will engage and faithfully help Henry III recover his possessions.

Sealed this eighth day of December in the twenty-sixth year of my reign.

He would need to raise money, scutage, taxes, but he would

also need to ask the Great Council, so he would wait for when Richard of Cornwall arrived back from his crusade. His mother, their mother, had asked for his help. The two sons of Isabella united in their quest.

December in Westminster was usually when the court readied itself for Christmas, but first Henry wanted a Great Council meeting to be planned for the New Year. So he ordered the barons to be called for the end of January. Richard was expected back soon. He had visited Frederick and his exotic court of silken tents and Arab dancing girls, as he threaded his way home. Richard wrote back to his brother, choosing his words as he remembered the entertainment of jugglers and dancers that the emperor considered a fitting spectacle for a man of the world. *I enjoyed the scene but how I treasured more the time I spent with Isabelle in the last weeks of her second confinement. She lives such a secluded life, sheltered in the quarters provided for her as empress. We were delighted to talk and she craves news of us all. She is constrained as much as any of her husband's trained birds of prey.*

And then another letter. Henry dashed away his tears and bowed his head. He walked in sorrow to the abbey to hear mass again and pray for the sister he had lavished with gifts and sent south to the emperor who wanted a third wife. She had given Frederick a son, Henry Otto, and a daughter Margaret, born two weeks earlier on the first day of December. But Isabelle had died of the bleeding and the fever, and now lay in her tomb in the Andria cathedral in Apulia: twenty-seven and married for only six years. He knelt on the stone floor and remembered her stepping onto her ship, her wave to all on the shore who watched and waved back. Godspeed.

Surely the New Year would be happier with Richard returned from the Crusades.

'I wish to honour him. He has been successful in the Holy

Land.' Henry both admired and envied Richard, but there was no doubting his exploits. 'Did I tell you? He rescued the brother of Simon de Montfort and many French knights who languished in the jails. And the Knights Templars are the force there once more. That is to be praised.' Henry sat with Eleanor in the Painted Chamber. She was with child again and he put a protective arm around her and fussed about arranging a fur blanket over her knees.

'We could put lanterns in the streets to glow in the twilight, a candle in each. Every house that has a front onto the street can hang one and the candles will be sent from the king.'

She beamed at him. 'He is important to us and we wish to please him, with feasts and a most loving welcome.'

And so when he arrived at Dover, Richard was met by his brother and his sister-in-law, who were full of news about the Poitou, about France, about Hugh and Isabella.

'A council meeting tomorrow, most necessary.' Henry was fidgety and impatient.

A travel-stained Richard was hastened to his rooms, to a bath, to fresh clothes, to the king and queen where they sat side-by-side, holding hands, a chair nearby ready for him.

But first a delicate matter: the possibility of Richard and a new wife. Eleanor leant forward.

'My father spoke well of you when you made your way through his lands to Marseilles.'

'And I of him. He promised me much kindness. Your mother also. A most captivating woman of great charm.'

Eleanor and Henry looked at each other. They had heard from Savoy that Richard had been captivated by another woman in the household. They hoped he was, in fact, talking about Sanchia, Eleanor's younger sister.

'And my sister? Did you find her to your liking?' Eleanor thought that there was no time to lose. Richard gazed down the length of the chamber and could see again the thirteen year old: beautiful, yes; soft and gentle, yes; a little timid, yes – but very pleasing.

'I did.' He looked at Henry, who coughed and said rather gruffly, 'There will be a dowry of course. Some manor houses for you to have extra places to live, perhaps a bequest or a castle when they become unencumbered.'

Eleanor gently pinched the back of her husband's hand. 'I think you have forgotten the royal accounts.'

'Well, I have not forgotten that she is wed by proxy to Raymond of Toulouse!' Henry was beginning to get angry. He hated parting with money when he needed it for the impending campaign.

Richard stood up. He had not been expecting such a brisk outline of marriage plans so soon on his arrival. But if everyone wanted to move swiftly he could not see any reason to stop them. Especially as Henry seemed to be thinking of money, gifts and alliances.

'I think we can manage that man. He has no annulment from his first wife in place and is so busy scheming with the Poitevins he has not yet met Sanchia.'

Henry looked at his wife and then at Richard. 'Our mother has four daughters by Lusignan; the expectation of wedding with the Capets has soured. It could be that Raymond would marry one of those – an alliance that suits us all. We have family connections with Toulouse and these would be made even stronger.' His tone was self-satisfied as he thought through the plan.

Richard agreed.

'We all know the count is fierce; he has excellent knights and fighting men. He stirs up Aragon for our cause. He makes constant threats to the King of France. He seems to enjoy the trouble he produces there! And he would be glad to see England with him if he is to join this league against Louis.'

He walked about the chamber, admiring the tapestries and statues, before he turned back to his extravagant brother. 'And, Henry, not just promises of manor houses and castles.' Richard sounded casual, even careless, but Henry knew that he wanted money and it would be found as always to bind him close. He knew Eleanor wanted that too. She wanted her sister married to Richard: another tie between Provence and England to keep everyone sweet. His little wife was proving clever, and proving it all the time.

For he had to admit his brother was important, seen by those across the Channel as a statesman of some standing; a person who understood all the family wrangles, the ways of the pope and the emperor, and someone whose goodwill he wanted to keep. He waited for Richard to say the necessary words of approval.

'And,' said Richard, 'I will fully support your efforts tomorrow at the Great Council.' A long silence and again Eleanor pinched Henry.

'I will find money for you,' said Henry, at the same time thinking you do well out of me, my brother, for I need you to be at my side and not against me.

He reached out to his own boy, his son Edward, nearly three and walking steadily towards him followed by an anxious flurry of maids and servants.

'He asks for you all morning,' said his nurse as he hauled himself onto Henry's knee and sat there very straight and tall for his age. Henry beamed and hugged him. But Edward was down, impatient and walking around the room. 'He is trying to march,' said Eleanor, 'look at him, such a little warrior,' and both parents smiled indulgently.

Richard rolled his eyes. He thought Henry enjoyed these scenes of happy parents and beloved son too much; he wanted to make a tableau of his life, to show the world a perfect king with a perfect family. But he had already begun to count up his treasure and his castles and rewards; it was a long list. 'I am a rich man' was a good thought to have.

The next day the Great Council, the parliament, took a very strong, stern line against Henry.

'This is believed a bold venture? I think not! You are sent a summons by the Count of La Marche and want money for this? Even worse if it comes from his wife!'

Incredulous voices. Worried voices. Weary voices.

'We have a truce with France. To break this is the utmost foolishness, and our counsel is to negotiate if there is a need.'

'Your demands are great and yet no advantage comes from our helping you. Look at the undertaking to restore Normandy and the Poitou: a failure, a miserable failure.'

Henry seethed. Why did they thwart him?

'I will raise the money on my own if you refuse to assist. I must make war to help my mother and to force the French out of our lands.'

'Your mother and her husband, and all their friends and allies, are not to be trusted.'

'Too much faith placed there in those who raise their heels against their lord, the French king. Treachery is what they know more than any other.'

Henry sulked and kicked the ground. Richard stood by. He had spoken in favour as he had said he would. He looked forward to his marriage and to his increased revenues.

'I will sail to France at Easter. I will make haste to help. I will command knights and lead.'

Almost a collective sigh from the assembly. It was well known that their king was no warrior. His efforts at making a battle plan, at forming strategy and sticking to it were weak and he lacked confidence. If Richard went with him there might be a chance, but their advice was firm: negotiate and do not trust the Poitevins.

The English sailed from Portsmouth in May, a month

later than planned, and urged on by Hugh Lusignan who wrote that he had forces ready, *but make sure you bring chests of coin; there is much to be paid for.*

Richard on one ship with knights and horses. Another Channel crossing. He was seasoned now and stood in the shelter of his cog, bracing himself. Henry and Eleanor on the king's vessel, her body wrapped well under the thick Flanders wool mantle, the baby due in June. She set her face to the wind as the ships left the port. Henry put an arm around her, his wife, his queen. He was so happy that she was always by his side, so determined to be with him, never to leave him. He kissed her cheek and she nestled into his shoulder.

The fleet sailed towards Brittany and landed at St Mathew de Finisterre, to shelter for one night in the abbey there. Eleanor clung to Henry as they watched the storm-battered cliffs and the captain said, 'This is the first and last spur of land any mariner sees when sailing in or out of the Bay of Brest. The wind whistles for us. I will say this: may God help me cross the straits for my boat is so little and the sea is so great.'

'We will be in Royan soon. Royan is calm and safe. We can rest there and prepare.' Henry comforted his wife and they turned away from the rough sea and breakers to pray in the abbey.

And in Royan they did land safely. The English relief force of several hundred knights and half a dozen earls disembarked, a bit groggy on their feet, the horses in need of pasture and water, but they were secure. The troops would allow Henry to flex his muscles and show his prowess as a fighter. He strode ashore smiling at the world. He liked this place. Royan might only be a small port but it was an important staging post facing the Gironde estuary, with strong walls and a solid keep. Cries of gulls, the salty smell of weed and fish; the Abbey of St Nicolas on a rocky plateau by the sea; ships waiting for favourable winds or the tide. He gazed about him, feeling majestic and ready for what lay ahead.

And there sitting near the small castle with her knights was his mother, Isabella.

XVIII

The Battle of Taillebourg, 1242

Recriminations, anger, bitterness. Forgotten. Forgiven. Isabella stretched out her arms to Henry and he came forward and knelt to her. She laughed and said, 'Stand, my son, that I might kiss you.' And he stood, awkward now and conscious of his sea-battered appearance. She reached up and kissed him very sweetly.

'You see, I am not so sharp-tongued that I cannot kiss my beloved son, who has such a good nature that he comes to help me, his mother.'

She tucked her arm in his and they walked to the castle gates.

'Not only me, but also your half-brothers: Hugh, Aymer and Guy. They are ready. Geoffrey and William stand by. You have not met them, but you will this year as we fight the sons of Blanche of Spain. Preparing for battle.' She paused and looked him full in the face. 'And here is my fair son, my first son, the King of England.'

Henry's emotions were in turmoil as he listened to Isabella. She was a woman of some pride, some vanity, full of arrogance. He knew that, for he had been told so all his life. And she had not been with him when he campaigned in France before. Her hostility then had been costly to him. But she was his mother. And she was praising him.

'I have made a stand against the Capets that would crush us; have stirred your stepfather against the wickedness that came our way. He would allow them to take everything, but I say no! Blanche wants to tread on your lands, on your Lusignan brothers, and on the county, which is for Richard.

Did you not make him Count of Poitou?'

Henry nodded. 'He is here too, to fight for what is ours. And we will fight.' He thought of the treasure chests and reassured his mother. 'There are mercenaries from the north who come with us. We can rebuild the realm from the coast to the Pyrenees.'

'We will not be trampled on! But now, please God, it shall never be as they intend, those sons of the Spanish queen.' She hugged him to her side. 'You have a great heart, Henry.'

Inside the castle Isabella swiftly took charge of the arrangements, her orders ringing out, as chests were unpacked and beds made ready. She spoke to Richard and wept over the death of Isabelle, glad that the young empress had seen her brother before she died.

'The last person to see her: someone who knew her from her early life. I know how bitter-sweet that must have been.'

She comforted an exhausted Eleanor, swaying and wretched after the sea crossing and asked for green herb soup to restore her, 'And after that only some simple poached chicken with no salt. Tisanes are to be made from chamomile and dried ginger. They will help you.' And she shooed her away to the comfort of a bed.

Richard had knelt briefly to his mother and then ignored the domestic bustle and paced the room. He wanted to clear his head, to think his way into the strategies and tactics that had to be decided. Isabella stopped his pacing with a frown.

'I ride back to Lusignan in two days. You must prepare as you have never prepared before.' Richard returned the frown. He knew better than anyone here how to prepare for battle.

'For your young queen, Bordeaux might be a better, safer place for her,' she said to Henry, 'away from the fighting that will rage about these lands. We know that Louis has a great army and we are most thankful for your support. Gascons, Poitevins, the Count of Toulouse, and the King of

Aragon, all have rallied. We will shatter the Capets.'

'When I move to engage with Louis, then she will move to the city.' Henry wanted his wife with him for as long as possible. He would rest with her here. After the voyage, some days of soft beds and fine food.

The army flowed like a river into the sea, knights, horses, crossbowmen, archers. All advanced without fear, followed by carts holding weapons, barrels of stone, tents, trebuchets. The roads groaned and cracked under the pounding of hooves and heavy wheels. Louis had wasted no time and the end of April saw an assembly of 30,000 men. And then a methodical prising of control along the Charente, one small town and castle after another. Everything north of the river was his. West of Poitiers he had Fontenay. Fontenay was not difficult to take; a small force defended it, but Vouvant would need the siege engines. The army rode on, confident in the bright sunshine.

By early June the centre of the Poitou was in Capetian hands. And then the advance began towards the Saintonge.

Henry rode from Royan to Pons. More mercenaries joined them, the coin always an allure. Envoys were supposed to arrive to try and stitch together some sort of treaty, but no one came.

But Louis did send a peace offer. A most generous offer considering that he was poised with a huge army on the other side of the Charente.

'Peace! He offers peace to us.' Henry pretended to consider the proposal, delighted to be seen as a commander and a king. 'There will be no acceptance, of that you can be sure.' He turned to his earls and his brother.

'Richard, we will turn away this offer. Why should we do otherwise?'

His confident bluster keyed him up enough to formally

declare war on Louis. 'We are no longer bound to observe the truce.'

Then he walked about the town with ease, in the midst of the men who had rallied around Hugh Lusignan. But no Count of Toulouse arrived. The King of Aragon was not to be seen.

The declaration was read out to Louis. 'You have failed twice in arrangements to meet…'

'I am minded to repent my humility in trying to seek some peace with the King of England.' Louis called for the constable who guarded the sacred *oriflamme*, and the long red and gold banner was fixed to the top of a gilded lance.

'I am resolved to settle this matter. Too often we have bought the Lusignans only for them to sell themselves back to the English when the wind changes.'

He looked around his tent at the assembly of men. Here were those others who also changed sides, but they were with him today: Peter Dreux, Count of Brittany, the Viscount of Thouars, his brother and nephew. The northern Poitou had made up its mind and was fighting alongside the *oriflamme*. Treaties made that Louis was determined would hold. They did not support the Lusignans today. And their strongholds fell. All except the great fortress built by Melusine with one mouthful of water and three handfuls of stone.

Isabella sat in the herb garden in the very early dawn. This was where she had worked so many times, always busy picking the herbs for tisanes to cure headaches, morning sickness, the cramps that came with the monthly flux; the herbs that, pounded into ointment, healed wounds or smoothed lines from hands and faces. Today she was gathering a different basket. Dark blue and purple flowers that grew among stems of deep green glossy leaves, the plants full of bumblebees. She had to wait for them to leave the cowl-shaped blossom.

'All dusted with pollen,' she observed, 'but it is not the pollen I need.' She already had roots dug up from the autumn. First rinsed and washed in cold water, next trimmed and dried, and carefully sliced into strips. Now in June the flowers and leaves were fresh and at their strongest.

'Hecate found your power when she saw Cerebos foam at the mouth, and in that foam you were born.' And in a dream, a feverish dream, she walked back to her chamber carrying the basket to the table where the brown slivers of root waited.

In the middle of July at Taillebourg on the Charente, Louis rode out from the chateau on its outcrop of stone. Three sides protected by sheer rock, it commanded the bridge: a bottleneck. The north of the Poitou was his. Now to strike south across the bridge. He faced Henry who was camped in a field the other side of the river. Henry, who had arrived and joined with Hugh Lusignan at last. Together they stood in battle order. The royal standard flying red with three gold lions: England, Normandy and the Aquitaine. On the other bank, the *oriflamme*: defiant. There were three bridges that allowed an army to cross: one at Saintes, which Lusignan controlled, one at Cognac, too far away – and one here in Taillebourg. Rançon of Taillebourg was the Count who owned this crossing, an old enemy of Hugh, Count of La Marche. He had thrown open the gates of the town to Louis. Rançon wore a ferocious grin and strange long hair parted down the middle and tied with a band like a woman.

'For I swore never to cut my hair until I could take vengeance on that man. He lied to me, a deep rotten lie. I am hopeful that the day is come and I will be shorn soon.'

Henry stared at the river, at the great numbers of French, and the tented camp like some great city, and his own troops not as many as promised. Could he fight? He wanted to force his men onto the bridge, but there were not enough for a rout.

Richard rode up and spoke in measured cold tones. 'You cannot hope to win here today. They clearly have an advantage.'

'I would send you as an ambassador for us?' Henry's confidence ebbed away. This was not the glorious victory he had promised himself.

'Indeed I can cross and talk to Louis, for I see many French knights there I know from the crusades. Some I have even ransomed, after they were captured having suffered a disastrous defeat, such as we might face today.' He looked about him at the paltry army and thought again of his crusade. 'So recently we were together, fighting together!'

Richard rode to the bridge and drew his sword, handing it to his squire who retreated holding it. A neutrality displayed for all to see, so that he could pass and talk, and ask for clemency.

And Louis granted Richard a few hours' truce.

'I have asked. The Capet is polite, courteous, but steely.' Richard was back with Henry, speaking privately and urgently. 'We must break camp and leave quickly or we will be taken. You are in great personal danger. Be hasty for they will cross the bridge. I have been warned.'

But already there was a massive charge of the French knights, who poured from the castle and onto the bridge, harrying the English who were forced to flee. They left in confusion and disorder, leaving behind equipment, supplies and carts, the army racing behind the king, no one stopping until they reached Saintes.

'Not only the stone bridge, you see,' said Richard. 'They had one of wood that they threw across and foot soldiers and bowmen were flooding onto that. We would have been taken on both sides.' They both lay exhausted on their beds, knowing that tomorrow Louis was bound to cross the Charente.

*

In the French camp-kitchens a meal was being prepared, sawhorse tables, roasting racks, tripods and large earthenware pots, baskets of food, all under a canvas awning. Two men had hooked meat onto a large spit where it dripped fat and blood into the fire. The smell of pork and onions was everywhere. Others added more wood to the fire under the cauldron. The cooks were stirring and slicing and tasting. The chief cook tested the pottage for salt and then walked over to the royal tent and called out, 'This tastes well enough. One of you valets, stir yourselves and fetch a dish or two for the king and his brother.'

They all heard the noise where there should be none and whirled around, cleavers, knives, choppers at the ready. Two men standing by the cauldron, caught as they tried to throw a muddy dark brown and blue powder into the food.

'They were throwing venom, poison, into the king's meat and soup.' The cook, brawny and stout, had tackled one to the ground, and sat on him, cracking his ribs. A man with a chopper had thrown it at the other, which caught him in the shoulder. He fell, yelling out in pain.

The wretches were on their knees before the captain of the guard and the king, crying and confessing.

'Yes, it was poison,' they babbled, abject. 'Poison. Not our idea. Oh no. Given to us by the Countess of Angoulême, the once Queen Isabella. She promised us great riches if we could get this into the food. It would numb the senses and death would be agony. She said try for the dish or the cup of the sons of the Spanish woman.'

Louis inspected them briefly. 'I am not sure to believe you or not. But I have been long suffering enough with the troublesome Lusignans, overlooked their arrogance and defiance. No more!'

To his captain: 'Hang them both and get word back to the

227

woman whom they say hired them that her plot has failed. And God have mercy on them and on her.'

Isabella fell to the ground and clutched her head; she began to rock back and forth. The king was not dead. He was not suffering the torture of his skin feeling as if it crawled with ants, of his mouth and throat so burning and numb that swallowing and breathing became impossible; was impossible. That death was the only end to it all.

Agnes watched in horror. The messenger had come and left so quickly she had no understanding of what had happened. She moved to help Isabella to her feet, to wash her face and soothe her. Isabella cried out, 'Leave me be. Let me be, I want none of you around me, I am... Where am I?'

She stumbled to her feet, pulling at her head, pulling off her silky jewelled cap, throwing it to the ground, grabbing at the linen bands that held her hair, shaking and crying and moaning.

Agnes caught her before she fell to the stone floor again, and Isabella looked at her with unfocussed eyes.

'There was a messenger, one who tells me that the king lives, the monkshood venom wasted, all wasted. I did not succeed. The men are hanged. I should die too.' And she snatched up a knife from the table and held the point to her throat. 'I should die too. I should die. Let me die.' The point pressed harder and tiny pearls of blood appeared. Agnes held her and made soothing noises. Isabella drooped, still clutching the carved bone hilt.

The knife clattered hard on the floor and Agnes beckoned to two maids standing by with open mouths.

'Quick help me carry her to bed. Fetch warm water, fresh linen. She has a wound. She has torn her clothes.'

Isabella lay for days in her bed, asleep but restless, her hands plucking at the covers, starting up with wild open eyes that saw nothing, or that saw ghosts and demons. She raged at these and then making strange signs sank down again. Agnes watched over her, worried, for there was no way of comforting her.

The English army rallied at Saintes. The men cheered as Henry rode out on his destrier, with Richard at his side, and cheered even more when de Montfort rode in, summoned from his crusade in the Holy Land to help his brother-in-law – a soldier who would put heart into the battle that was to come. At the gates of the town all charged with great valour, Hugh and his sons and allies in the first clash against the French. Lusignan flags streaming blue and silver like the summer sky. Then the trumpets sounded as the English troops galloped in, and the battle cries from both sides added to the noise. *Royaux, the King, Royaux, Montjoi Saint Denis, Montjoi Montjoi.* The fighting was all among the vineyards and in the sunken lanes around the town walls. Henry rode breathlessly. His heart felt tight and his arms heavy. Battle glory was not as he expected it to be. Richard and Simon were fierce and strong; they called orders to their men and regrouped. He felt afraid and pointless beside them.

The standard-bearer for Hugh charged into the midst of the French, the Lusignan knights following, but far fewer than wanted, for Louis's army grew and grew. A crossbow arrow flew high, swift, sharp and accurate. The bearer was pinned though to his horse, which rode on, bucking and swerving. The man's face contorted, his mouth skewed. His hand still held the banner which slowly and gradually dipped and dipped, until it trailed in the dust, was caught by the vines, and the horse buckled and toppled over.

The campaign was proving a disastrous failure. Henry now realised that Louis had taken the Poitou before he had even arrived. And in the campaign ten years earlier, Louis had politely left him alone to make a fool of himself. Not so this time. He was going to drive Henry out of France in the most ruthless way possible, hostile troops on three sides. Henry turned and fell back to the gates of Saintes, pursued by a French knight who rode behind him so closely that he too was inside the city as the rear-guard pushed in. An unlikely prisoner, who was roughly forced to dismount. He sat on the ground listening to the great discord all around him.

Henry slid from his horse and grooms rushed to lead it away, its flanks heaving. He pulled off his gloves and helmet and gulped down a great beaker of wine, angry and looking for someone to blame. A messenger was sent to find Hugh, and others brought word that Hugh was thinking of negotiating with the French. Henry spluttered angrily and called out as La Marche approached, 'What of your promise? Were you not to bring us as many soldiers as we could wish for? Was I not asked to bring coin to pay for them, which I have done? All eager to face the King of France were they? I see them not.'

Hugh kicked at the ground and spurts of dust flew up. He spoke very softly.

'I did not say that. Never promised that.'

'What treachery is this? I have your writing to that effect. See here. I have my records kept, they show you beseeching me to return.'

'I neither wrote nor sealed that.'

Henry looked at him as if he were mad.

'What is this? Did you not send messengers and letters till I was weary of them, asking for me to come hither and chiding me for my delay? Where are the men you promised?'

'It was not I. God's body! I have made no treaty with you. If you want to blame a person, blame your mother, my wife, not me! She it was who contrived all. Myself privy to none of it.'

Hugh turned away, evasive. He looked to the hills in the

distance where clouds of dust were raised by approaching cavalry. He watched as they trotted to a bend in the road. Peter of Brittany was leading them. He turned back to Henry. 'I repeat we have no treaty obligations and I will take whatever steps are necessary in these unhappy times. We had no promise between us that one could not make peace except with the consent of the other. And I will make peace now for myself and my family.'

And, Hugh thought, I must soon send my son as hostage to Louis to show my loyalty. Henry will sail back to England and I will still be here. My proud castles fell so quickly. First they picked off all those places in La Marche, then everything closer to me and mine. I must claw back something. He knew that in his place Isabella would be implacable, but he would yield.

Henry clenched his fists and snarled. He wanted to strike the man who had conspired and formed the rebellion that had helped to bring about this failure. A campaign that had begun with scraps and patches and was now just tatters in the limestone dust and trampled vines.

'If any promise has been exchanged, it was the work of my wife, your mother, and I was not party to it. I know nothing about this,' Hugh repeated, shrugging his shoulders and gathering his men together. One had rescued the Lusignan banner and held it low and submissive as they rode out of Saintes to meet Peter Dreux.

Richard and de Montfort walked over to where the king stood, dejected, humiliated. Richard spoke heavily, 'There goes a man who knows only betrayal. He never kept faith with any overlord. He is surely to blame for this. He did not believe in the fight; a pretend rebellion.'

'Any who trusted him were rash and foolish.' A pointed remark from de Montfort. 'He nearly delivered our army into the hands of the French.'

Henry spoke in a dull monotone. His anger turning to despair: 'I fought for my mother's honour; it seems her husband does not care about that.'

'We must retreat before the way to Pons is cut off.' De Montfort said.

He began mustering the soldiers; he would do what had to be done. Henry had promised to pay off that debt, the debt that had caused all the trouble at the queen's churching.

2 July. Saintes. For Simon de Montfort. To the barons of the Exchequer. The King has pardoned to Simon de Montfort 600 marks from the first terms of the debt, which he owes him at the Exchequer.

Now he was safer again after the flight into exile, his third child born in Italy while he fought in the Crusades. Not seeing his family for a year, his wife given sanctuary by Frederick. True, it was worth fighting here for all that to be lifted, but he was not going to go easy on this king who, it seemed, lacked all common sense.

As they left Saintes, de Montfort was brutally honest. 'You fought here like Charles the Simple, Charles the Stupid; a king who owned much but lost it. He was locked up by his barons. You should be too, I think.' Cutting, insulting and scathing. Henry flushed and his eye twitched but he was silent, he had to swallow de Montfort's contempt and ride away from this defeat.

The retreat began, the army laying waste to defy any French who might pursue them. Wells were poisoned, crops burnt. A vindictive Henry who felt uneasy when he reached Pons. It was no longer welcoming, so the English rode to the east to Archiac and Barbezieux and then changed their minds and left for Blaye and the Gironde estuary. A forced march of a day and a night, and none ate or slept for nearly forty-eight hours. A good part of the baggage train was lost. At each town, allies slunk away and the army began to suffer fevers from the low swampy marshlands. Henry and Richard fell ill too and everyone dragged to Bordeaux, where Eleanor had been delivered of a daughter a month before.

The English camps were looted and the pickings were rich: barrels of beer, the royal tent, silver candlesticks and even the wine and water cruets and the chalice that served mass.

They did not stop to spin a tale,
The English with their barley ale;
But all of France did dance and dine
For barley ale is not worth wine.

XIX

Hugh stood with Agnes and looked at Isabella who was sitting on the edge of her bed. She was haggard and unkempt. Agnes had prepared a bath for her and Hugh said, not unkindly, 'Isabella, you must wash. There is a bath ready. Get dressed and be ready to leave, for we must ride to Saintes. The king is waiting.'

'A bath? I should take a bath? Will someone help me? I need to dress. You say I must dress.' Agnes helped her stand and walked her to the wooden tub filled with warm water. She carefully took off her chemise and, holding her hands, indicated that Isabella should step into the bath.

Hugh saw his wife, her body the body of a woman in her fifties, not a young girl, not a woman on the brink of motherhood, but a woman who had given birth to fourteen children. Her belly criss-crossed with silver lines, her breasts once so firm and rounded, drooping, her hair turning grey, her throat wrinkled and her eyes no longer bright and challenging, but dull and full of doubt and anxiety. He sighed. How could he tell her that all had failed, that he had asked, indeed *had* to ask, for the Count of Brittany to intercede for him? With his daughter married to Young Hugh, family ties could help. Yolande's father likes his son-in-law, thought Hugh, which is good. He probably likes him more than he likes me. For rumours were swirling that Peter Dreux had publically begged the king to be merciful, but in private had urged him to be severe. With a heavy heart Hugh had sent Young Hugh as a hostage to Louis: a hostage to his mercy. Isabella would have had words to say about that. He could hear her voice:

'What spineless act is this?' However, it was going to be the Lusignans who had to kneel and beg – all of them.

Isabella was dried and dressed; Agnes chose a skirt and bodice of dull faded blue brocade, the pattern of flowers edged in tarnished silver thread, a very simple cap of linen, no jewelled crespinette. Penitent. She must look penitent.

Geoffroy waited in the yard, horses ready. 'I will come with you. An escort is needed. And you may need help.' He indicated Isabella who was quietly weeping. Hugh agreed, but said, 'When we walk – for we will walk from the gates of Saintes to Louis – wait there. I cannot be accompanied by any knight.'

Yolande watched them leave, stony-faced, trying not to weep for her husband held by Louis, worrying about her father, horrified at her *belle-mère* and what she had plotted. Isabella smiled and touched her arm. 'Dear child,' she murmured as they walked her through the doors and helped her carefully into the cart. William and Marguerite sat with her, silent, a little frightened, for their mother kept talking to herself and twisting her rings, counting them under her breath.

'One from John. Did he give me this one too? No, Hugh gave me that one. Where is Joan? She was here. And Henry sent her a silver bracelet. I hope she has not lost it. And where is Henry? He came to Royan to fight the French. I wrote and begged, and he came.'

Aymer, Guy and Geoffrey were waiting in Saintes and when they saw their father leading their family they walked to meet them and watched as Isabella climbed out of the cart with her youngest son and daughter. No one spoke. And together they all walked from the gate to where Louis sat with Alphonse, and with Blanche.

Hugh knelt. His children knelt. Isabella knelt. All were weeping. Hugh, a supplicant for clemency.

'Most gentle king, most gracious king, forgive us this day and have pity on us. We have turned against you through wickedness and arrogance. As is your prerogative and of your great mercy, forgive us our fault. All our faults.'

Hugh bowed his head to the ground. Never before had he been so low, so submissive. Besides him Isabella rocked back and forth, her face wet with tears. Behind him the Lusignans, kneeling, humble and contrite.

Louis stood up and said, 'I pity you Hugh, Count of La Marche. I cannot hold your treachery against you. Stand up for I both pity you and forgive you.'

Hugh stood. Isabella remained kneeling. Hugh looked at Louis, at Blanche, at Alphonse, Count of Poitou. He had knelt to him before, brought him in friendship to Lusignan. He would bow to him always.

'We have made war, I admit, and my wife, Countess of Angoulême and La Marche, admits this too. Isabella, Queen of England, admits this.'

Isabella struggled to her feet as she heard her name, her titles. 'Unsuccessful war,' she whispered. 'The King of France has defeated us. Over and over again he has defeated us.'

'We can do nothing but submit,' continued Hugh.

'Very true.' Cold words from Blanche. And she smiled, as she knew that even as this doleful scene was being played out, the scribes were busy writing the documents, the joint charter that would strip away all power from the house of Lusignan, and not only from them, but all their allies. Her son would be in charge in the Poitou – Alphonse, this precise, conscientious man; a frugal man who kept his financial ledgers with the utmost care. He would be a welcome change in the Poitou, she had no doubt.

Blanche to the assembled crowd: 'There will be no more disorder, no more high-stepping over the rule of the king and his brother, who is your lord. My sons are the rulers here.'

Isabella heard her dully, thinking, 'I can expect nothing from my own son Henry. He is no military leader, no rallying centre for my cause. And Hugh. What happened to Hugh? We always knew which side to go to; to turn from one to the other was easy, profitable, and so we have lands for all our sons.' And then a grip on her heart. Lands now lost. She felt bile rise in her throat. She must not think about that.

Laughter and men calling out, for de Rançon had arrived, strutting and doffing his hat from side to side, shaking his long hair.

'A table. Some scissors. The shears!' he called as he unwound his headbands. His valet came and cut his hair, with the king smiling to see his friend carrying out his vow. Rançon grinned in triumph at Hugh.

'You are humbled. I am avenged. It was worth waiting for.'

There were jeers as the Count of La Marche, his wife and family walked back to the gate, where Geoffroy guarded the horses. Now they had to ride home, to wait for the summons to come to the king and seal his charter. They both must seal. They both must wait.

Pons was the meeting place and here Louis presented the treaty that signalled peace between the Poitou and the Île de France. Hugh and Isabella sat on a bench below the king's table. Isabella was a little calmer, her spirit a little lighter. She had hopes. She ignored the crowd watching with gleeful malice the haughty, proud Isabella. She was being humiliated, and they were mocking her husband who had been so foolishly led. Influenced by this woman who sat here today, looking just a little too defiant for their liking.

'You have three great castles, Merpins, Château Larcher, and Crozant. These will be garrisoned and you will bear the costs.'

A girdle of castles around Angoulême and Lusignan, and the road that led between them and to La Rochelle, all would be watched at all times, from all points. A blow: an expensive blow.

'You will give up your claims to Saintes. Any pensions, taxes or rents paid to you will cease. All lands and chateaux won and occupied by us will remain with the crown through Alphonse. Also the grand fief of the Saintonge, and other places. The list is here.' Louis unrolled the scroll a little further.

To pay for three garrisons, and no rents, no taxes as revenue, how could that be? Isabella stirred, but Hugh put a hand on her shoulder and she sat quiet again.

'The treaties of Bourges, of Vendôme, of Clisson are annulled.'

Louis was determined to break the power of this man and his family, who for too long had dominated the lands below the Loire.

'Hugh, Count of Angoulême, will make homage to the king for that county. As Count of La Marche he will make homage to Alphonse, Count of Poitiers, for that county. As Lord of Lusignan he will make homage to the Count of Poitiers for the chateaux and castellans of Cognac, Jarnac, Merpins and Aubeterre. All the men of the Poitou and the Saintonge will be loyal to Louis, the King of France.'

So much territory lost; all that was conquered by the king would remain his forever. So much disgrace, all those concessions wrung from the French crown over the years to be relinquished in perpetuity.

The treaty was unrolled to show the edge where seals must be fixed. Hugh stepped forward and took his seal from the pouch at his belt: the Lusignan seal with the huntsman and his horn, the small hunting dog behind the croup of the saddle. He pressed it into the green wax: *Sigillum Hugonis de Lenziniaco Comitis Engolism.* And then the obverse side: *Comitis Marchie.* The seal of Hugh of Lusignan, Count of

Angoulême and Count of La Marche, threaded through with blue and silver cords.

Isabella walked a few hesitant steps. Her hands fumbled with the silk tassels of the red wool pouch, stitched with scrolling foliage, the appliqued tendrils of vines. It was among the vines that they had lost the battle. She drew out her Great Seal and held the gold oval matrix carefully – her hands steady now – to be pressed into the wax. There she was standing front, robed and crowned, her hair floating around her face. In her right hand a flower, to show fertility, above that a bird. What had someone written? Women were better at hawking than men because the worst people were the most predatory. *Dei Gratia*, by the grace of God, Queen of England, Lady of Ireland, Duchess of the Normans, of the Men of Aquitaine. Isabella took a deep breath and very firmly pressed her queen's seal into the wax. She gazed steadily at Louis: a queen sealing his treaty.

Louis next: *Dei Gratia, Franconum Rex*. It was done. Three wax seals hanging from the parchment. A clerk was already carrying it away to be stored in a document chest. Hugh took a step back. Young Hugh was brought forward now from the side of the hall, released from hostage as the treaty ceremony was finished. He joined his parents and then the Lusignans began the walk to the gate. Hugh gripped Isabella by the arm and the children formed a protective circle. Nearly there. They could see Geoffroy and grooms holding the horses.

A man broke from the crowd, pointing at Isabella.

'She tried to poison the king! She tried to poison our Count of Poitou, the brother of the king! And her husband and son, they were fighting against the king, against the rightful count, thick in the plot to deny the king his lands. Drag them to prison. They are all guilty. She should hang like the men she paid to throw the venom into the food.'

Isabella faltered. Hugh tried to hurry her on. They must get away. Would the king's knights rescue them? Allies again, surely they would.

Geoffroy had come forward and took Isabella's other arm. Tears were running down her face and her mouth was working. She was trying to say 'I beseech you, leave me be', but all he could hear was 'Leave me, leave me'.

He turned and spoke directly to the scornful crowd. 'The Countess of La Marche and Angoulême was much troubled by the war and allowed the worst sides of her nature, the darkest side, to take possession of her mind. Nothing else was in her but a fog of despair and bitterness. She has repented deeply. And Louis stands without a pain or a blemish.'

'Trial. We need a trial; a trial for treachery.' Voices were calling out and men were elbowing through to the front. Disturbances and scuffles. The guards were alerted now and moving after them. Hugh looked like someone trapped in a nightmare. No way to turn. He had lost all his territory, he had no money and now he was being threatened with a trial, with prison.

Another man shouted, 'Challenge him to a trial by combat. That would settle it and by the look of him he would not win.'

Young Hugh shouted back. 'I would fight any one who calls us out.'

The captain of the royal guard arrived and raised his arms, called for quiet. 'A treaty of peace was made here. One by one the lords of the west have been surrendering their arms and making honest submissions. Today William Archevêque the Sire of Parthenay has given his word and bent his knee. Let us preserve the peace.'

Another call from the taunting mass of people. 'I do not think any champion of France would be ready to meet the Lusignans on the field of honour.'

'Tainted with treason.'
And the crowd satisfied their scorn by singing after Hugh.

> *There was La Marche's folly the most rife,*
> *Who madly dashed his forces 'gainst the King.*
> *Thus did he so he might beguile his wife,*
> *Whose rashness never willed a more ruinous thing.*

XX

Paris and Bordeaux

Louis wanted more than anything to drive Henry out of France. He rode hard from Pons towards Gascony, towards Bordeaux. But it was not easy. There was no clean water and the villages had no food. He stopped to pray in one of the small churches, the sculptured stone doorway showing the Emperor Constantine trampling on the fallen pagans. As he knelt and asked for help and strength he thought of Henry, a young king like him; a father, devout, married to his wife's sister. There must be some way to bring about a truce. He staggered as he rose from his knees, a sudden gripping cramp about the bowels. Two knights caught him and half-carried him to his tent, and the word flew about the camp: the king was ill; he was sick, as his father had been thirteen years before. Not only Louis, others too: sweating fevers and the bloody flux; nobles dying from poisoned well water; foot soldiers falling in the dust and crawling into the ditches to die. A panic set up. This land south of the Loire, south of the Charente, was tainted, not only with treason but with disease.

Louis ordered that the army return north, a better climate, and where he could find doctors he trusted. He sent word to Henry that he was offering a five-year truce and Henry content to be in Bordeaux with his wife and baby daughter agreed immediately. Although it would mean the loss of all those Poitevin lands, he still held Gascony, and he was in no hurry to leave the city and return home. His barons, earls and knights had lost patience though and had gone, asking Louis for a safe conduct through France so they could sail home from La Rochelle or Royan.

'Let them go. Better for me that they go. Better for my country that they go. Let us hope these enemies leave without thought of return.'

And Louis too made his way home back to Paris in time for a celebration of his victory and the feast day for the Archangel Gabriel.

'God is my strength,' said Louis as he celebrated mass. 'Did I not pray for strength in that village church and was granted healing?'

Blanche prayed at his side. She had welcomed Louis home, a proud mother. Serenity and confidence was written all over her face. They had stood together and stared down difficult people. Two of those would be anxious to show their firm and abiding loyalty. The proof would be tested, as plans were drawn up to send an army against Raymond of Toulouse – who had so foolishly begun to fight against the Capets again – to be led by Peter, Count of Brittany, and Hugh, Count of La Marche.

Marguerite rejoiced to see her husband recover so quickly. Louis looked pale still, but he was always pale.

'I was full of fear. It was difficult to think of you lying so weak.' She stroked his head and kissed him softly.

'I am fortunate and praise God for keeping me here.' He kissed her back and she wrapped him in her arms.

'My sister writes that she was ill before the baby came into the world – named Beatrice for our mother. And she was frightened for her life, as the Gascon lords would not protect her in La Réole. They feared for you to invade them.'

Louis looked at her, worried. 'We are rich and safe. No one rivals our power. I would not prosecute war on Gascony and frighten your kin who shelter there.'

She continued stroking his face gently, beguilingly. 'Louis, the truce you will make with the English, you will remember that my sister is wife to the King of England? I do not wish her to be made scared and ashamed.'

Louis promised he would be gracious. 'In truth, I am not a man who enjoys using violence. My mother says we must to keep control, we have so much more now, but…' he shuddered.

Marguerite soothed him and then said with some sharpness, 'You can make some decisions, you are the king.'

Louis lent on his elbow and looked down at his wife.

'Henry can keep Gascony. But now, now the English king will do homage for that land. And pay money; a thousand or so for every year of the truce.'

Henry sat with Eleanor and they rocked the baby in her cradle: Beatrice, three months old, swaddled and smiling in her sleep. Born on the day of St John the Baptist, the 24th of June. He adored these babies that were a family for him; he welcomed the fact that he was now a husband and a father. Glad they were safe in Bordeaux, although it seemed some in Gascony could be as treacherous as those in the Poitou. His little queen fleeing from them to be delivered here, but all well and the baby healthy, with a strong wet nurse to feed her all through the day and night. Henry glanced up as Richard came in. He had been out riding along the estuary, hawking and hunting. Good waterfowl in these marshy lands. He threw his gloves and cloak to a servant.

Henry was anxious to share with him his way of accounting to the world.

'I wrote to Frederick, to tell him of the Battle of Taillebourg. Read the copy there.' He indicated a scroll on a table by the window. Richard unrolled it and read.

You must know that I was winning and would have taken back the Poitou if it had not been for the kiss of Judas, Hugh Lusignan being the main traitor. We were compelled

to retreat after some sharp action. Thouars, De Pons and
Lusignan deserted us. The French King did not press on
after Blaye. Rumours of disaster are irresponsible.

'You did not write of my successful venture to gain time so that we could escape from Taillebourg, and how to thank me for that, you have granted me the whole of Gascony?' Richard was sardonic.

Eleanor drew in a sharp breath. She said very softly, 'I think that Gascony is for the crown. Our son Edward will have this land. A promise made in the heat of battle cannot be considered valid.'

'In the heat of battle? Madame, your husband was lying on a bed in the royal tent when he promised this. And the battle was but a skirmish.'

'I do think I was hasty in making this grant.' Henry stood by Eleanor and put a hand on her shoulder. She continued to rock the baby, humming a lullaby. *Lullay, lullow.*

Richard, furious, gathered his gloves and cloak from the valet and said, 'This is more treachery. You have learnt well to promise one thing and then to take it away. How much has this foolish expedition cost? With barrels of silver for Lusignan and the Poitou, men, horses, ships and armour, upwards of £40,000, and for what? A ghost of some homage and useless service.'

An undertow of violence filled the room. He turned to Eleanor. 'You, madame, are careful of your place in the English court. And clever too, that I can see. I will be careful and clever when I marry your sister.' He strode across to the cradle. 'Another fine niece I have there. I look forward to giving her a cousin.'

Then, his face dark and baleful, he stood very close to Henry speaking at him with some force. 'For now I am determined to leave the king's service and to take a ship back to England. As faithful service to you is not met with gratitude.' They glared at each other, tense. 'Do not stop me! As to be here in Gascony, which I have fought for twice now and am still defending – for it not to be mine is bitter.'

And he slammed out of the chamber and down the steps angrier than he had ever been.

Eleanor regarded her husband who was looking strained and unhappy. 'He will forget all this when he is married. Such rebellion must be tamed though. I would not want our friendship hurt by these hot words.'

'He cannot leave my service without my permission!' Henry was working himself into one of his rages. 'I will have him followed. I will find some rough men who will seize him and he will be thrown into some dungeon to rot and think about what is means to swear oaths of loyalty. I fear he might strike me and not care that I am king. By the throne of God, he goes too far.'

'Hush hush,' Eleanor held his hands. 'We have our family and my family. Your mother proved not to be as loving and faithful as you wanted. Your brother threatens and storms about the place. My Savoy uncles will advise and help us. You have us now.'

And Henry clung to her. He hated to admit defeat, but he was isolated this time. All his allies turned away from him. And he was running out of money: giving it away to the Gascons and men like William Archevêque had proved a disaster; they simply took the silver and vanished. Debts were piling up again. No matter. He would stay in Bordeaux for some months yet. He did not care for the news from London. The Thames had burst its banks and Westminster was knee-deep in water with everyone wading about on horseback. And the barons would be angry with him about this failed campaign. And the Count of Brittany was making trouble out of St Malo, encouraging piracy against the Cinque Ports. And there were problems with Church appointments.

No, he would remain here, seal that truce with Louis, wait for his mother-in-law and Sanchia to arrive, plan Richard's wedding.

The long stay in Bordeaux took them through the winter and into the spring. A truce confirmed with Louis, who had managed to get towns to pledge peace too. So now it was safe for Beatrice of Savoy, Sanchia, and yet another young Savoy uncle to travel to Bordeaux.

'My dearest Eleanor, you look well and happy. And my granddaughter Beatrice, how beautiful she is.' Beatrice kissed her daughter, not seen for seven years. She swooped on the cradle and held the swaddled baby tight.

She beamed at Henry and agreed with him that the wedding of Richard and Sanchia must be splendid, impressive and as noble as possible. Henry began planning with her: the dishes; who to invite; what would be the entertainment; poets and singers, yes, and music of all kinds. No matter what it would cost. He could borrow, he said, with an indulgent air.

Sanchia sat quietly listening, reserved and happy that they would wait here until all the preparations in England for her marriage were ready. Her sister told her stories of that country.

'Colder and wetter than Provence,' said Eleanor, 'but the landscape is beautiful and green, and there are many fine palaces. We have one for hunting at Woodstock and I have a very fine herb garden there too.'

She leant forward and said in a confidential gossipy tone, 'I must tell you, Sanchia, we had an intruder there, even though Henry ordered latticework for the windows. Well, for the Queen's Chamber he did. But a man broke in and would have killed Henry. He stabbed at the pillow a dozen times or more.' A horrified gasp from Sanchia. 'One of my ladies heard him. He had lost his wits. They captured him and he was dealt with. Hung, drawn and quartered.'

Sanchia's eyes were round with amazement, 'Were you not terrified?'

'Oh, but Henry was with me. We were in bed together.' Another gasp from Sanchia. Eleanor took her hands and leant forward again, this time to advise. 'That is where you must be clever. That is where you begin to influence your husband. And always remember your family, and what is good for us.'

It was time for Henry to go back to England. Nearly seventeen months he had been away and now he appointed a seneschal for Gascony and ordered debts to be paid to Bordeaux.

> *To the treasurer and chamberlains. They are to pay out of the King's treasure to the messenger of the mayor and commune of Bordeaux the 417 marks of good and legal sterling, which the King received from them as a loan at Bordeaux.*

Ships sailed, taking the king, his wife, and daughter. One ship carried Simon de Montfort and his wife with their children, returning home after three years. And Henry wanted a victory parade; a desperate attempt to prop up his illusion that he had won against Louis.

'He loves a pageant, does our king!'

Some were incredulous.

'And he wants gifts of gold to welcome him home!'

'This is a diversion, a pompous nonsense. He did not win against Louis, I see there is a truce for five years, but we will pay for that.'

Others obeyed more willingly; a spectacle showed Henry was powerful, and that was important. Everyone wanted a powerful king. So processions of clergy, costly candles all lit up, the crowds in their holiday dress, and bells being rung for the joy of his victory over Louis.

But the men who had returned long before him had their own account of what had really happened in France. Blunders and failure.

XXI

Isabella knew they all considered her unstable, watched her for signs of violence or madness, but her mind refused to dwell on the attempts she had made with her poisons. She hugged a promise to herself; she would never acknowledge that she had made the concoction, it was better to lock away that memory forever. Although sometimes she woke in the night thinking she had succeeded, not in killing Louis or Alphonse, but in killing Blanche. This dream made her tremble with a wicked joy, which she dare not admit even to herself. She pushed these thoughts away and forced her attention onto realistic, practical matters. For the Lusignans would have to live on a few fragments of their great domain. They had sworn to be loyal to the French king, and the whole of the Poitou and La Marche were now on the side of the Capets. That oath and that charter had at least given them some lands, the honour and fiefdom of Lusignan. Angoulême was still hers, and it would go to Young Hugh on her death. Henry was lingering in Bordeaux, and was not to be heeded again.

'I have five sons by Hugh.' Agnes listened to her say this over and over as she walked about the cloisters.

'Isabella, you have done what is right. To widen the breach between the king and your family here would make it even more difficult to provide for them all.'

'My daughters, my daughters: two safely married which is good. Your namesake Agnes, and mine, Isabelle. Marguerite to marry Raymond of Toulouse this year; a union that we are all afraid will not bring anything to anyone. And Alice? Alice will need a husband who cares not that she is a Lusignan.'

'A daughter of a Queen of England, that still counts for some useful alliance,' soothed Agnes, and Isabella looked proud for a moment. She clung to that and to her seal, a tangible reminder of what she had been.

Later Agnes and Geoffroy worried away at the changes they saw.

'She was always vain,' said Agnes, 'troublesome too.'

'And capricious,' added Geoffroy. 'We remember her as a young girl, when she was all those things and also frightened and alone, but brave, determined.'

He rubbed his knee and winced. The bone seemed to rasp on bone. 'I could not fight a battle now, as you know, but I would and can still defend her, as would you in your own way.'

'It is comfort I try to give and some steadying of the spirit.' Agnes considered Isabella. 'She has no power, no authority any more, after years of wanting that above all else. For her it is as if she has died.'

Hugh, with the help of servants, unwrapped a long wooden coffer covered in red and brown leather. This gleamed with stippled and gilt *champlevé*, the colours bright and glowing. Here was sky-blue, silver-grey, green, dark red and white. He had commissioned it from Limoges, with copper gilt medallions showing the blazons of the Poitou and Aquitaine counts and lords, who now swore fealty to Louis and Alphonse. Lusignan – La Marche, Lusignan – Counts of d'Eu, Thouars, Parthenay, Pons, Dreux, Toulouse. The gold fleur-de-lis of France on blue for the king, the gold castles on red for Blanche, and for Alphonse, now the ruler of the Poitou, a heraldic medallion that showed both.

Isabella watched as he opened it, very carefully, very gently, sliding the clasp.

'See, Isabella, the lock is shaped as a serpent. The tongue forms the lock and guards the contents.'

'Which are to be...?' Despite herself she moved to look more closely. It was a beautiful coffer; so much gilt and copper, enamel and burnished calf leather.

'Look, I ordered it to have divisions within for each peace agreement, for each charter, but no division outside. The coffer shows unity.'

Isabella put out a hand to the serpent lock, the head with startling blue enamelled eyes.

'I swear I saw the tongue flicker. She is a Melusine I think.'

Hugh had placed their charter inside and was wrapping the coffer again.

'I will offer this to Alphonse in Poitiers. Others will place their charters here too.' The servants carried it away and Hugh clapped his hands, pleased with this token of peace.

Isabella faced him, awkward, her face working. She tried to be polite. 'What news of your cousins? What news of Vouvant?'

'They rebuild, Louis orders greater defences, their tower stands.'

'And Angoulême stands. The building is so strong.' Her voice broke and she whispered, 'I thought our lives chimed always and in all ways.'

Hugh reached out to her.

They stood close together now, heads almost touching, holding hands very lightly, nervous and unsure.

'Isabella, we did chime together. You became everything. You and your bed was my centre.' Gentle kisses on her closed eyes and mouth. She trembled and broke away.

'You were happy to entertain the king and his brother. They were not your enemies then and are not your enemies now. Your rebellion is over. Take the coffer and the charters to Poitiers yourself. Make your peace. Serve them. It will suit you to be at ease. We are all older.' Her words were soft but under them ran a dark current of distress and sorrow, for he had betrayed her.

She knew the dreams of power and prestige were broken forever, but it was hard to bear the vanished supremacy. Their great swathe of lands carved out of the heart of Aquitaine. Everything forged by Lusignan and Taillefer just handed over to the Capets, who would go on to take more and more, of that she was certain. Paris would rule France.

Isabella walked slowly to the stairs and then turned and smiled at Hugh whose lined face was sombre in the half-light of the Great Hall.

'You were a prince here, Hugh. You ruled as a prince.'

'And you were always the queen.'

A week later, Isabella stood tall and gaunt, her face drawn and her hands restless over her skirt, pinching at the fabric. On the table between the windows lay all the papers, documents, manuscripts, land deeds: the mass of words that made up her life, her life with Hugh, their life together. She picked up one and let it drop. Is this what it had all come to? A muddle of papers and ownership?

Hugh joined her, reaching for a document. He had been to Poitiers. The coffer had been well received. Another written pledge handed over; a promise to ride against Raymond of Toulouse.

He always looks tired and defeated these days, but he will recover, Isabella thought dully. His life would continue in the world of men. And now she must turn away from intrigue. The French king knew the stories of how she had tried to poison him; those two stupid men had not failed to put the blame on her, an easy confession from them. Louis had simply warned her that he knew and let her live with the implications. She was found guilty everywhere, in all eyes the accusing looks, and on all lips the malicious whispering. She could not stare them down as she used to. And after the defeat at Saintes, there was always that sense of panic, her resolution faded.

Henry had written to her. Her son. He was irritated and cross. Before the disaster of Saintes he had wanted so much from her. Written asking for castles, offering to pay for a castle, to pay 500 marks. *But do not fail to hand over said castle, because we do not send you said money right now.* Isabella grimaced. It was always the same: we cannot send you money now. And where were any of the castles she could give him? All gone. She read on. He also wrote that he had not expected to lose that battle. He had passionately wanted to win. She and Hugh had encouraged him to take up arms as yet again the Lusignans attacked the king. He could see now what a turncoat his stepfather was.

I tried to help you, but you always want more from me, he wrote. *It is impossible. And everywhere there are hardships of all kind with no honour attached.*

Isabella knew, as she knew nothing else, that after he was crowned, when that knot of advisers guarded him from her, making it very clear she was not wanted and was in the way, that he had been lost and troubled. That when she had abandoned him with such apparent ease he had always hoped she would come back. She crumpled his letter and then smoothed it out. If only life could be smoothed out so easily. For a moment she was nineteen again, softly singing the old lullaby. *What is it you command me little one, little son, why do you ask me to sing a sweet song, though far, far away I have been an exile, oh why do you command me to sing?* And she had cared, cared deeply about the eternal fact that he was Henry, King of England, and she was mother of a king, and had been a queen. She had clung on to that for years.

Now the panic grew and took hold and sweeping the

papers into a pile she indicated to the scribe who sat under the far window, fidgeting with his writing materials, that all should be put in order. That the lands, castles, farms and monasteries should be made over to the children: to the Lusignan children. How strong she and Hugh had been to conceive and raise nine children, all living, all healthy. She hoped Henry would take them into his court and favour them; he could be a powerful half-brother to have in these times, if they were to be neglected by the French king. And she was sure they would be neglected and spurned: children of rebels and treacherous allies.

'It is better I have nothing. Wanting so much has brought me to this. I will give it all away. Look, even coins with my name, silver coins with Isabella of Angoulême, Hugh of Lusignan and Louis of France. My name stamped on coins.'

She gripped Hugh's hand. 'Make sure you seal too, my husband, seal it too.' And to the scribe who was now gathering the papers into order, 'Hugh Lusignan must affix his seal. Isabella of Angoulême must affix her seal. We are better to give it all away.'

It was an easy task to allocate the fiefdoms, such as they were, to three of their sons. Young Hugh would have Lusignan, of course, Angoulême and La Marche; Guy was to have Merpins, Cognac and Archiac; and Geoffrey would be Seigneur of Jarnac.

'Aymer so very tough, full of anger and violence and not yet able to read his letters.' Isabella had found him a difficult child and he was even worse as a young man. 'He will be endowed with what else we can find, which is not a great deal.'

'And William is so energetic, generous and steadfast. He will make a good knight and find his way in the world. I can give him three fiefs in La Marche, and one more, Montignac on the Charente. From the Abbey at Valence nothing but his name.' Hugh made a helpless gesture. 'Except I have hopes the crown will return some chateaux to us if we prove loyal.'

He thought about how their two families had held all those castles and lands. Poitiers, Saintes and La Rochelle and more, controlling and commanding the roads that linked them, even making sure that the way to Bordeaux came under their aegis. And always the Lusignans were the storm centre of rebellion. But that was over. He sealed one more land deed and reached for another.

Isabella sat with Agnes and Geoffroy in their house. She had walked quickly and secretly through the narrow cobbled lanes of Angoulême, her cloak pulled tight around her and the dark hood over her bowed head. Two servants had carried a chest between them. This was by her feet now as she explained. Some of her old forcefulness returned, some of her nervousness dampened down. She felt safe here sitting with Geoffroy and Agnes.

'I am making sure that all is tidy and straight. We are all getting older, and you, Geoffroy, have become a man who needs an easier life. Agnes, do you not think so? You have sold over half your business to Guillaume, and he will no doubt work even harder now he has a share, while you can take your ease.'

Agnes agreed and patted Isabella's hand. 'You are tired these days. Why did you come to us? We can still manage the hill to the chateau. Geoffroy has his stick and my arm is strong.'

'I know, but I wanted to give you things privately and there are so many people now rushing about from room to room. I am at a loss to say who they are. The old servants, well, they get old and leave, and others vanished after our defeat. Some I think are tempted away by new mayors and these men from north of the Loire, that the Count brings in to manage his affairs.'

She sighed. 'New castellans. I do not know any of them, *prévôts* serjeants. Everywhere you look there is some man to tell you what you should be doing, most zealously. But that is not why I came, to moan about the lost life.'

She opened the chest and lifted out two cloaks: one a deep, reddish brown and richly lined in sable; the other plum coloured wool and trimmed with ermine.

'Agnes, these are for you. You will know how special they are and you will also know how to keep them at their best. They will keep you warm for many winters to come.'

Agnes shook them out and said, 'I will not deny they are beautiful and made of the finest material. You were extravagant always, Isabella, and these showed you in luxury. But they are too grand for me.'

'Nonsense, Agnes, they are right for you. It is time you wore such splendour. Do you not agree, Geoffroy?'

'I do, and, Agnes, you can wear them when we visit Bouteville. It is full of draughts and not comfortable at all. Wrap yourself up in one of these and the wind that sneaks in at every crack in the stonework will not worry you.'

Agnes beamed, carefully folded them onto a table and kissed Isabella on both cheeks and hugged her.

'Thank you, my lady.' Isabella stood still for a moment and then reached into the chest to take out a small coffer.

'Hugh made a splendid coffer for the peace charters – Limoges enamel – and I thought I will do that too. Here is something, which is simpler. The carpenter made it for me. It is walnut wood from the tree that blew down in a storm some years past and he has carved your initials Geoffroy. See? And your coat of arms.'

She handed it to Geoffroy who rubbed his finger over the G and the B, and Isabella handed him the iron key. 'Open it.' Isabella laughed at his surprised face for it was not empty.

He took out the rolled parchment and read a land deed.

The chateau at La Mothe, near Cognac, was given to him by Queen Isabella of England, for all the services he had rendered to her as a paramount knight. For being trustworthy at all times. Isabella had always promised this to him and he had not forgotten, but with everything that had crumbled away he thought it only a dream.

He knelt and bowed his head.

Isabella said, 'I have very little, and this will thank you for everything: for carrying messages from me to Henry in England and back again; for carrying our pleas of surrender to the Capet king; for riding with us when we had to submit; and standing in front of that crowd and speaking for me. I know you would follow always, but you must guard Agnes now.'

He turned away to hide his tears and closed the box on this precious document.

'And, Agnes, one more thing for you. I cannot take this with me, nor would I want to. Use it how you like. I mind not if it is turned into coin or a clasp for those cloaks.'

And Isabella took the small gold collar with its slightly beaten surface – the circlet she had worn on her wedding night to John, that had been used to crown Henry in Gloucester when there was no crown of England to use – and gave it to Agnes.

No one tried to arrest Isabella. There were no charges against her. She made it known she would always deny the accusations. Louis had judged the evidence weak and to bring a former Queen of England to trial would make the difficulties with that country turn to yet more war. And he wanted to go on a crusade, not call an army together against the English.

'If there were damning evidence of the clearest kind, if I wanted to bring her before a court, I could,' he explained to his mother. 'I do not want a trial for her, and I am not sure you do.'

The question hung in the air, but Blanche was prudent and discreet and getting tired of plots and threats, although her spies were still useful. Isabella had once had all she wanted; now she could learn to live with very little.

But a clamour grew about the countryside and towns, voices whispering louder and louder.

'She was always a base influence.'

'Remember all those men she scorned? Remember how she took those DuPuy boys hostage?'

'And thought nothing of keeping her own daughter a hostage too, until the pope told her to return Joan to England!'

'And they say she used witchery to entrance John Sansterre. He could not get out of bed for her wiles.'

'The Count of Marche was *thrown* out of her bed, but he soon came crawling for her. What magic and spell does she use?'

'I say she is more Jezebel than Isabel. She wants control of men and she gets her way by making them crazy.'

And now outside the walls the knots of men stood looking for trouble, looking for Isabella.

She packed with speed, everything that had meant something already given away. Hugh ordered an escort and one servant was found who would travel with her for the journey.

'I will send a cart later with some more of your goods and clothes, but now you must flee as fast as you can. There is one spare horse.'

Isabella's voice was low and broken, 'I am ever grateful for your help.' And for the first time she felt humble before him, her head bowed. He acknowledged her humility with a half-smile and pulled her to him. They embraced, holding each other close, remembering all the years before, but neither lingered or looked back.

Isabella rode out of the west Angoulême gate, the double

tower of the chateau so proud and the cathedral close by. Where she had been betrothed to Hugh IX Lusignan when she was nine. Where she had been married to John Lackland, John Soft Sword, when she was twelve. Where she had married Hugh le Brun, Hugh Lusignan, when she was thirty-four. And that had been a choice she had made, by God! A man she had loved as she had never loved John. But her ambitions had run through both marriages. Thwarted by John and his friends and advisors, she had made sure that here in France she lived her life the way she wanted. Her dignity, her royal status and her determination to be seen as Queen of England, these thoughts troubled her now. Pride and ambition had become tangled into a restless panic and it was time to ride hard for sanctuary, for Fontevraud.

XXII

The Abbey lay in a slight valley, near the Loire, surrounded by woods. As they approached they could hear the chanting of the *Kyrie eleision*: the last service of the day before the silence, the great silence that would last until the morning. It was Compline, where mutual forgiveness is offered to all. Isabella was relieved to have arrived before nightfall and before the abbess had retired. She was weak and waves of fatigue washed over her. The ride had been long and two nights of sheltering in mean little towns had been uncomfortable. Her dreams were so troubled, she had woken with tears on her face and could not remember who she was crying for or why, but sadness stared back at her in the dark, black nights.

'Come, we must look after you and care for you. We offer sanctuary here for many; the poor, those beaten hard by life and made low by ill-fortune.'

Such a tall, strong woman in her white tunic and surplice with a black girdle, a big white collar covering her shoulders and then the black veil; her cowl was the black of the Benedictines. Adele de Bretagne, a formidable abbess, as they all had been since the Abbey's foundation: 300 nuns, 200 monks, and all under the rule of the abbess; an abbess who had seen her humiliation and would offer some refuge without a murmur of distaste, who walked with her now, guiding her through the cloisters. She had welcomed Isabella and Hugh on their way to Saumur when Isabella had thought to humble the royal family. Now she was to be her protector.

Isabella stumbled on the flagstones. Adele steadied her and led her on to the refectory where she was given hot soup and bread. Then Adele led her to the choir of the church. Isabella stood at the row of stately tombs, close to the altar. Eleanor of Aquitaine side by side with her husband Henry. Their children, Joan of Toulouse and Richard Coeur de Lion lay nearby. Isabella swayed. But Adele held her arm and together they knelt and called for mercy. She was turned gently away from the huge church and taken back to the refectory. Her escort had gone to the stables and the one Angoumois servant with them. Adele gripped her hand.

'We have prepared a special and secret room for you so you will be safe from harm. And the nature of the stories that follow you mean that some *will* seek to harm you. The room is small, dark. But it can be entered from this room, through the hearth. It is secret to outsiders, who see the thick stone and do not see the hidden door. The vaults are below and that is an escape if necessary. Come.'

They ducked through a concealed door and down steps to a dismal room, a narrow bed with a thin horsehair mattress hardly covering the rope base. One roughly woven linen sheet, and over this a quilt stuffed with lumpy wool. A small table only big enough to hold a candlestick and a metal cup. A prie-dieu made of battered, scarred wood: oak, ages old. The cushions where she would kneel or rest her arms were worn away, just a hint of burgundy red cloth. It would hold her missal; the brown leather cover disappearing into the gloom, the gold illumination vanished and swallowed up.

A hook on the wall, where a black cloak hung, ready to make her anonymous and to be as one with the hundreds of nuns. It was almost to the ground and had a deep hood. The black dye had missed one small corner of the hem and the dirty white streak drew her eye. A small painting hung on the wall above the bed: a crucifixion scene with a ladder leaning against the cross.

'This you must climb,' said Adele, 'with patience,

humility and obedience so that you too can be united with God. Perhaps one day you will be able to offer your heart.'

Isabella lay on the bed in her shift and thought that when the cart arrived with her clothes, her plates, her statue of the Virgin Mary, she would have to give them all away, for there was no room here in this uncomfortable cramped sanctuary. She was safe, she knew that, but already waves of unhappiness flooded through her. Was she guilty? She must be, for all said she was – guilty and without honour. She wept, 'But I am not evil'. A girl brought up with pride and a belief in her place as a countess. She was related to kings and emperors, she had been important. A girl who had been Queen of England. She thought of her royal seal, still to be used if needed. Now they said she was only to be called the wife of the Count of La Marche.

She climbed off the bed. Prayers were needed and she opened her missal, small and square. A fleeting thought of Mathilde who lived by hers, happy in her convent, content to visit outside when invited, but far happier to return.

But she had been a queen, and three times each year she had worn and shown the people her crown. Isabella touched her head: no crown, and all that long chestnut hair, once so beautiful, now greying and thin, all the lustre gone, just bundled into a coif. She must forget. Was that not why she was here? To forget and be forgotten?

She turned the leather-bound embossed cover and the several pages of velum. There were beautiful, large illuminated initials burnished with gold, and then a miniature of two queens, one showing the other a monster. She cried out, recoiling in horror, her hand over her eyes.

In the night she wept again, and was glad that her costly and precious rings, her jewels, her gifts from John and Hugh, had been packed away to be given to her daughters. She had kept one, only one: a circle of gold with garnets and rock crystal; the simple ring she would wear now. She turned it on her finger and took comfort from its familiar band and the feel of the rough stones embedded in the gold lattice. When she woke in the early hours she looked at the ring and at her hands, and said to the room, 'I do not know these hands. They are mine, but are changed. The woman who owned them has gone.' She remembered a morning prayer to say every dawn from now on.

In great disease and deadly sin,
Many a one this night fallen has,
That I myself should have fallen in,
Hadst thou not kept me with thy grace.

Life became slow and quiet and her time in the secret room was dull. There was nothing to fight for as she had fought for power, for independence all her life. She marked the hours with the prayers and the several daily masses of the Abbey. She was roused once to old ways when asked to use her Great Seal, as Marguerite divorced Raymond of Toulouse and married Aimery of Thouars. Then all those symbols, her seal and a chancery clerk sent from her Angoulême, were no more. The little ring she had with her was so loose now she gave it to the clerk with a letter for Marguerite. Better she have it for this second marriage.

'I have no pride. It is subdued by grief,' she said to Adele. 'And what have I done to my family? I have deprived them of their lands and nearly ruined them.'

'You clung for too long to the state of queen. And still you think of earthly treasures, land, possessions. Reconcile with your sins. Redemption can be yours.'

'I have tried with your help, and with the help of all who live here. I have made my testament: money for Fontevraud so that masses may be sung for departed souls. I had a daughter who sang a carol once at Christmas. I can hear it still. But these songs will be sadder.'

A flash of her old self as she added, 'And money to pay for the repairs of the nun's clothing.'

Something gnawed at Isabella's spirit and at her body. Her meals were meagre, but they were all she could eat. The black cloak enveloped her and she bowed under its weight. She felt shrunk in on herself. The winter had been cold that year and spring a long time coming. April still bitter with late frosts, but in May some warmth arrived and the cowslips and daisies spangled the grass in the middle of the cloister. Isabella walked very slowly over the great stone paths to the scriptorium. She wanted a fair hand to write a letter for her – an important letter. Her sight was failing and a novice guided her, touching her shoulders, left, right, so she knew which way to turn.

Divina permissione *Dowager Queen of England implores the illustrious and excellent King of France, Louis, to look upon her children by Hugh, Count of La Marche, with favour and to receive their homage. She also begs the King to make good and safe their inheritance as set out in the testament sealed by Hugh, Count of La Marche, and his wife Isabella. She asks this with all humility.*

They brought the letter to her as she lay propped up in her narrow bed, and guided her hand to seal it: her little seal for private matters; a coat of arms showing the three lions of England and the red and gold lozenges of the shield of Angoulême.

She sank back and whispered, 'Bury me in the churchyard as someone who has nothing. As simple and plain as all who are buried there.'

The priest administered the Viaticum. 'May the Lord Jesus Christ protect you and lead you to eternal life.'

Her hands scrabbled over the quilt and she was almost

breathless now, but her lips moved as she prayed for her sons; all her sons; all her children.

They carried her body from the dark enclosed space in the gloom of the thick walls. It had always had the air of a tomb, the priest thought, but kept this to himself. The nuns washed the body and wrapped it in a white winding sheet. The shroud now prepared Isabella for burial, nothing to remind anyone of the great beauty she had once been; her face was sunk and her body so wasted away; small and humbled in death. No bells to announce her funeral. Silence except for the prayers read aloud as the small procession walked to the nun's chapel and churchyard outside the Abbey. The casket covered in a rough white linen pall and a wreath of rosemary.

Then I shall pass
From bed to floor,
From floor to shroud,
From shroud to bier,
From bier to grave,
And the grave will be closed up.

The Lusignan children anxiously confirmed the peace treaty with Louis, writing: *Our dearly beloved mother Isabella, of good memory who was Queen of England.* They held onto the hopes that Louis would give them back some power, some revenue, some prestige.

Henry heard of his mother's death after a morning walk back from Westminster Abbey with his three master masons. They had returned from France, from Reims, from Chartres, and they were full of the new style; plans had been drawn and the excitement about pointed arches, ribbed vaulting, and rose windows consumed him.

'We will have a long single aisle and the highest vault we can engineer,' he exclaimed and justified the expense to himself over and over again.

'I laid the foundation stone for the Lady Chapel twenty-six years ago. It is time to build for Edward the Confessor an Abbey of the most brilliant aspect.'

Messengers crowded into his chamber and he read the obituary letter from Fontevraud with a frown and then slumped in his chair.

Lady Isabella, much respected Queen of England, Countess of Angoulême and La Marche, and mother of the illustrious Lord Henry King of England died here on the fourth day of June and was interred in our burial ground. She lived a life full of adversity and difficulty. She stayed with us only a short time but she was our benefactress of many thousand pounds for her keep, for the maintenance of the Abbey, clothing for all and for other numerous expenses.

Some mourning must be arranged at once. He called two scribes and set about a flurry of instructions. *Payment for the friars and students of Oxford and Cambridge. To the treasurer etc. To an annual feast. In memory of the soul of Isabella, Queen of England. They are to pay out of the King's treasure. They are also to pay 50s. for each year at the Exchequer for the sustenance of a chaplain at Westminster, celebrating divine service for the soul of Queen Isabella, the King's mother.*

Alms for the poor all over England. He sent word to Mont St Michel Abbey in Normandy that her obituary must be inscribed there, and a daily mass at Marlborough where John had taken her directly after her coronation, and where she had sheltered during a time of chaos.

An English scribe wrote; *The Countess of La Marche, mother of the King of England and of Earl Richard of Cornwall, formerly Queen of the English, Isabella by name, went to her fate about this time very much in need of the intercession of endowed prayers for her soul.* And in the margin of his manuscript he sketched a crown, upside down.

Young Hugh and Yolande had been anxious, but it seemed that life was slowly becoming normal again. Alphonse was scrupulous about restoring the exhausted countryside, villages and towns. Roads were mended, trade returned and the steady seasons with their rhythms of sowing and reaping settled everybody down. There were good harvests and patient administration with no fickle seigneurs interrupting everyone's efforts with demands.

'We will be steady and tranquil, I think.' Young Hugh was reading the letter sent from Poitiers to explain the new systems that were being put in place. 'He is a man who wants justice and fair taxes for us all.'

'I am glad for this.' Yolande was with child again and more than anything wanted some peace for the confinement. 'We will be content to be here and manage the Lusignan lands.' And she looked at herself in the box mirror that Hugh had given her when another son was born. Once Isabella's. Such a precious piece of beautiful *champlevé*. Translucent green enamel with silver gilt scrolls making young shoots, small squares showing the three gold lions on red, the arms of England, and then the blue and white bars and four lions of Lusignan. Yolande thought it the most beautiful of gifts and closed it with a contented sigh.

And this year would be the year when Hugh would inherit Angoulême and she could not help think that to own both chateaux would be very fine. Hugh grinned at her, seized her about the waist and danced her around the chamber.

Epilogue

A year after Isabella's death it was obvious that for Guy de Lusignan, Geoffrey de Lusignan, William de Valence, Aymer de Lusignan and Alice de Lusignan, there was nothing to hold them in the Poitou. They appealed to Henry and joined his court in England. Henry favoured them as much as he favoured his queen's Savoyard relatives and the native English barons seethed with resentment.

Aymer was made a prebend in the church and later became the Bishop of Winchester. William married a wealthy heiress, a granddaughter of William Marshal. There were no surviving male heirs of the 'Greatest Knight', so this Lusignan became the Earl of Pembroke. Alice was promptly married to John de Warenne, 6th Earl of Surrey. Guy and Geoffrey fought fiercely alongside Henry in the future and were paid pensions. Guy was rumoured to have left England with paniers stuffed with gold. Henry also paid pensions to his married half-sisters who were in France. In this way he supported his mother's memory.

Henry also continued to remember his mother with references to her as a spiritual beneficiary of a hospital and a financial award to a lepers' home in Windsor. He joined her name with that of his father John in the benefactions, and was proud of the sculptures depicting them together in Worcester Cathedral. He considered that he had a claim to Angoulême, but renounced it finally in 1258. Richard of Cornwall and Eleanor Montfort still clung on to the idea that it was theirs.

Richard of Cornwall became very rich indeed, partly due to Henry forever staving off trouble by rewarding him, and partly due to his inheritance in England from Isabella. He was a good warrior, a competent man of business, and knew how to drive a hard bargain. When England needed new coinage in 1247, he provided the initial capital and shared half the profits of the mint with the Crown. He always had ready money. He became King of the Romans, but like his title of the Count of Poitou he never realised the position.

Eleanor and Simon de Montfort were forgiven and prospered under Henry until the 1260s. Theirs is a long and complex story, which had a huge effect on English history and their own families.

In 1249 Louis demanded that Isabella's widower, Hugh Lusignan X, accompany him on a crusade. He was at the triumphant capture of Damietta but died there too, slain by scimitar.

Young Hugh, Hugh of Lusignan XI, and Yolande had a happy marriage and seven children. He was killed in 1250 in the Battle of Fariskur, Egypt, which was the last major battle of the Seventh Crusade. Yolande never remarried and Henry paid her a pension of £50 a year. She died in the chateau Bouteville.

Louis continued to be extremely devout and built Sainte-Chappelle to house relics such as the Crown of Thorns and a fragment of the True Cross. This reliquary of great bejewelled beauty amazed and delighted him. He died of dysentery in 1270 on the Eighth Crusade and was canonized in 1297.

Blanche lived to be sixty-four and was a powerful regent for Louis when he was young and later when he was away for years on crusades. She dealt energetically with great problems in the newly expanded France and its ambitious lords.

The Lusignan and Counts of Angoulême line died out in 1308, as the two brothers, Hugh and Guy, were childless. Two sisters, Isabelle and Jeanne, who inherited Angoulême, sold it to the French King.

Peter of Brittany also went on a crusade in 1258, where his advice was ignored by Louis, who followed that of his reckless brother Robert of Artois and the army was led on hopeless march to Cairo. Peter fought more bravely than most, was captured, but when released died from his wounds on the voyage home. His grandson, another John of Brittany, married Beatrice the daughter born to Henry and Eleanor in Bordeaux.

In 1254 after yet again more serious trouble in Gascony, Henry was in France. He made a detour on the way home to visit Fontevraud.

Here he prayed at the tombs of his ancestors: Henry II, Richard I and Eleanor of Aquitaine. He asked where his mother was buried and when he found her grave in the simple churchyard he had it transferred to the abbey church, helping to carry the bier. He made offerings of precious silk cloth to the church and ordered a carved wooden effigy of her to be placed above the stone coffin, showing her robed and crowned as the Queen of England. She now had a resting place like other kings and queens. Although Henry had decreed he should be buried in Westminster Abbey, he also willed that his heart should be buried at Fontevraud. And in 1291 it was.

Bibliography

Some of the books and sources that helped in the writing of The Tangled Queen trilogy:

Baker, Darren, *Henry III: The Great King England Never Knew It Had*. The History Press, 2018

Benton, Janetta Rebold, *Art of the Middle Ages*. Thames and Hudson, 2002

Carpenter, D. A., *The Minority of Henry III*. Methuen, 1990

Carpenter, D. A., *The Reign of Henry III*. A&C Black, 1996

Davis, J. P., *The Gothic King*. Peter Own, 2013

Fougere, Sophie, *Isabelle d'Angoulême, reine d'Angleterre*. Edit-France, Payr, 1998

Gillingham, J., *The Angevin Empire*. Arnold, 2001

Goldstone, N., *Four Queens: The Provencal Sisters Who Ruled Europe*. Phoenix, 2009

Hanley, Catherine, *Louis: The French Prince who Invaded England*. Yale University Press, 2016

Harwood, Brian, *Fixer and Fighter: The Life of Hubert de Burgh*. Pen and Sword Military, 2016

Jordan, W. C., *Isabelle d'Angoulême, by the Grace of God, Queen*,.Revue belge de philologie et d'histoire, 1991, 69

Lewis, Mathew, *The Son of Magna Carta*. Amberley, 2016

Leyser, Henrietta, *Medieval Women*. Phoenix Press, 1996

Morris, Marc, *King John*. Hutchinson, 2015

Oram, Richard, *Alexander II: King of Scots 1214-1249*. Birlinn Ltd, 2012

Painter, Sidney, *The Scourge of the Clergy: Peter Dreux Duke of Brittany*. Octagon Books, 1969

Painter, Sidney, *The Lords of Lusignan in the Eleventh and Twelfth Centuries*. Medieval Academy of America, 1957

Pernoud, Régine, *Blanche of Castile*. Collins, 1975

Soulard, Isabelle, *Femmes de l'ouest au Moyen Age*. Geste, 2009

Vincent, Nicholas, 'Isabella of Angoulême: John's Jezebel'. In: *King John: New Interpretations*, edited by S.D. Church, Boydell and Brewer, 1999

Vincent, Nicholas, *Peter des Roches: An Alien in English Politics 1205–1238*. Cambridge University Press, 2002

Wilkinson, Louise. J., *Eleanor de Montfort, A Rebel Countess in Medieval England*. Continuum, 2012

Warren, W. L., *King John*. University of California Press, 1978

Online Resources

Too many to list but the following were important:

www.magnacarta.cmp.uea.ac.uk The Magna Carta Project

www.finerollshenry3.org.uk/home.html The Fine Rolls of Henry III

www.finerollshenry3.org.uk/content/month/fine_of_the_ month.html.

Wilkinson, Louise J., Fine of the Month: May 2006: *The Dower of Isabella of Angoulême*

Jessica Nelson, Fine of the Month: May 2011: *A Queen and Sister: Joan, the Wife of Alexander II of Scotland, and Sister of Henry III of England*

https://gallica.bnf.fr/. Savary de Mauléon et le Poitou à son époque par Bélisaire Ledain

http://fmg.ac/Projects/MedLands/ANGOULEME.htm.

Epistolae: Isabella of Angoulême. Available at: https://epistolae. ctl.columbia.edu/

https://www.persee.fr/doc/bec – Les préparatifs d'une invasion anglaise et la descente de Henri III en Bretagne (1229-1230). Élie Berger Bibliothèque de l'École des chartes Année 1893 54 pp. 5-44

For more information about the Coffret that Hugh Lusignan had made to hold the treaties between him, other Poitevin lords and the Capets go to this link, which describes the Coffret in detail, with wonderful images of both it and the 13th century medallions: https://digital.kenyon.edu/ archives/

The gold matrix on the cover of Part 2, which was pressed into wax to make Isabella's seal, is in the archives in Angoulême.

This is the seal which she treasured all her life and a tangible 800 year old link.

The arms of Isabella of Angoulême as Queen of England are the red and gold lozenges of Angoulême and the three lions of England impaled or joined together. This can be seen on her tomb in Fontevraud and is used on the cover of Part 3.

Author's Note

In the years between 1217 and 1246, England and France squabbled over the previous Anglo-Angevin possessions in France. In truth, the problems began much earlier, in 1159, and the rivalry refused to go away. Phillippe Augustus, Louis VIII and his son Louis IX were determined to drive the English out of south-west France, and equally determined to take the Languedoc and crush the Cathars. In all of this the various popes played their parts, supporting or reprimanding as it suited them. Loyalties at that time were to families, dynasties, overlords; there was no nation state.

In Part 3 of *Isabella of Angoulême: The Tangled Queen* I have traced Isabella's life for the almost thirty years of her time in the Poitou. She struggled hard against the powerful men who would stop her claiming her inheritance, but she managed to forge a large new domain, almost a princedom, across the centre of France, with the formidable help of her second husband Hugh of Lusignan. This was a threat to the Capets, the French ruling family. Indeed it was this alliance that John had stopped in 1200 when he took Isabella away from Hugh Lusignan's father and married her himself. But the tangle of politics, passion and pride did not stop. As Henry III sought to regain the lands John had lost, Isabella turned every way to try to keep control of what she had won. In the end it was not a baron or a lord who brought her down but another queen, Blanche of Castile. Their lives had many echoes, both widowed with a young son who became king. In both cases very devout royal sons who built beautiful monuments in their capital cities for the glory of God. Westminster Cathedral and La Sainte Chappelle.

But Isabella was not given the chance to be regent in England. She was not named in John's will. The circle closed around Henry, cut her off, and she returned to Angoulême. Blanche on the other hand was endorsed by her dying husband as the best person to lead France. And as she encroached on Isabella's territory, scorning her place there, the manoeuvring began.

I have written about Henry III and Isabella's other children by King John, where their lives entangled with hers and where events in their lives affected what would happen in France or underpinned their character. I have written about their dynastic marriages, which help to explain the web of alliances that existed. I have written about the council of men who influenced Henry III, all of whom Isabella knew from when she was Queen of England. Obviously a great deal else went on at that time in England and its problems with Wales, Scotland and Ireland.

Since Louis IX wanted more than anything to be at peace and go on a crusade in 1243, he let Henry III keep Gascony. This led to further troubles in future years, with English kings assuming they had control of parts of France. 1337 saw the start of the 100 Years War.

The chroniclers were harsh to Isabella; she was seen as a Jezebel, a woman whose words were quick and cutting. But she was a woman living in a time when to succeed and to make your dreams a reality you had to be tough. Her life was never quiet and easy. One writer says she chose power over parenthood, but in France she had both. Altogether she gave birth to fourteen children, all of whom lived to adulthood. So she must have had great physical strength as well as mental fortitude. Emotionally she was probably full of conflict, the Tangled Queen indeed.

Nicholas Vincent writes that it can be argued that without Isabella and her treatment by King John there would have been no Plantagenet collapse in 1204, no Barons' war and civil war in England and no Magna Carta. No humiliation for Henry III in Poitou, no Lusignans at his court to cause more in-fighting. The French sometimes refer to the Battle of Taillebourg as the precursor of the 100 Years War. Isabella cast a long and influential shadow.

The Abbey at Fontevraud has now been restored, but the tombs and effigies were badly vandalised, especially during the French Revolution. There are no human remains within the church. In 1816 suggestions were made to bring the damaged, painted wooden gissants back to Westminster Abbey, but this was refused. However, the tombs were better preserved for the future. A nineteenth-century account of how Isabella's effigy was made show that it was well and finely chiselled. She was dressed in a loose flowing, purple silk gown, thickly sown with small gold crescents, and at her waist, a richly ornamented belt of crimson leather. A fine linen chemise showed at the neck, which was fastened with a plain circle of gold. An ample yellow silk mantle decorated with cinq foils and dark grey fur was secured across the shoulders with a gold band. On her head a coverchief and a low crown of the mural form inlaid with large rubies. Every inch a Queen.

Acknowledgements

This trilogy would never have been written if it had not been for *An Aquitaine Historical Society*, which has provided others and I with many years of interest, education, information and entertainment. As a result of a winter study group I discovered Isabella of Angoulême and over seven years she has been my constant companion. Now her story is finished and I hope the books have brought her to the attention of far more people.

I must also thank Michael Hicken, who is a longstanding member of *AAHS*, for translating some tricky Latin pieces.

And thank you Biggles and Plume who have spent seven years sitting, sleeping and scratching in my study as I wrote.

The chroniclers are ambiguous about whether Henry III stopped in Jersey or Guernsey on his way to St Malo in 1230. As a person with long deep connections with Guernsey, I, of course, chose Guernsey. This brings me to John and, as always, heartfelt thanks to him for his unstinting support. He hand-drew all the maps and family trees before they were digitised and in truth, his drawings are rather wonderful.

You can follow me and all sorts of news and views about things historical, Isabella, and much more, by going to the following links.

www.ericalainewriter.com
www.facebook.com/ericalaineauthor

Lightning Source UK Ltd.
Milton Keynes UK
UKHW041621080123
414979UK00002B/12

9 781781 327340